The Thousand Days of Disbelief

- Book Two of 'The Thrice-Cursed Godly Glories' Trilogy -

Jim McPherson

I0684408

A *PHANTACEA* **Mythos** Mosaic Novel
published by James H McPherson

ISBN 978-0-9781342-1-1

This is a work of fiction. All the characters portrayed in this book are either fictitious or used fictitiously.

THE DEATH'S HEAD HELLION

Copyright © James H McPherson

A *PHANTACEA* MYTHOS PRINT PUBLICATION

www.phantacea.com

Conceived, written and produced by Jim McPherson
Cover and interior collages prepared by Jim McPherson

James H McPherson, Publisher
74689 Kitsilano RPO
2768 West Broadway
Vancouver BC
V6K 4P4 Canada

CHAOS COMES CALLING

Her groom of not so long ago lay on the up-chucked ground in front of her ungodly uncle. There'd be no faerie-oven for Tomcat *'Squirrelly'* Tattletail this time. Not unless the voracious, seemingly still semi-mercurial fiends left enough, for them, indigestible but salvageable piles of gnawed bones and slit sinews, moderately solid puke and non-diarrheic crap, behind after they finished devouring him.

The bringer of this destruction, Unholy Abaddon, the Unity of Chaos, had assumed close to what must be his most fiercely formidable guise. Commonly long-bearded, darkly hairy, and broad-shouldered, he had additionally rendered himself a giant maybe eight feet, maybe nine feet tall, scarlet-skinned and absolutely massive.

Not yet registering her, he folded his arms in front of his chest. Almost casually, even dispassionately, he surveyed the havoc his arrival and the release of his protean, apparently kept-starved or never-fed demons were causing.

At least eight arrow-like sparklers, their tips lit and blistering, poked out of the tangled mane of muddily woven and matted hair ringing his head. To both compliment and compound his apparent but weirdly aloof ferocity, he looked to be dressed in bearskin minutes removed from a grizzly he'd out-wrestled in a bear pit and skinned alive with his bare hands.

He wasn't holding his trident or *'trishula'*. It was behind him; its three prongs and lower curvature framed him. It was as if he'd rammed the whole thing upwards, out of the ground instead of into it, which would account for the temblors. Its fork-ends, on its only partially emerged shaft or *'danda'*, protruded at a ratio of maybe three times his already impressive size.

Morgan Abyss, the Melusine Master of the Weirdom of Cabalarkon, was almost pleased to see him. "I was hoping for Harmony but you'll do fine – for starters."

"Good, because with an attitude like that I no longer feel inclined to ask you to move all your ringots to one hand."

"Huh?"

"Dad sent me here to disarm you, Master. Guess I'll take them both now."

The black bolt smote her harder than its whitish kin did Squirrelly last night.

Print publications featuring

Jim McPherson's

PHANTACEA Mythos

include:

- *PHANTACEA* **One to Six**
(A series of comic books featuring various artists)

- **Forever & 40 Days – The Genesis of** *PHANTACEA*
(A graphic novel with artwork by Ian Fry as well as
background material and a short story featuring the
Damnation Brigade, the Death Dodgers & Signal System)

- **Feeling Theocidal**
(Book One of *'The Thrice-Cursed Godly Glories'* Trilogy)

- **The War of the Apocalyptics**
(The first entry in the *'Launch 1980'* story cycle)

- **The Death's Head Hellion**
(A mini-novel derived from *'The 1000 Days of Disbelief'*)

In one form or another, all are available for ordering through:
www.phantacea.com

Send inquiries, certified cheques and/or money orders care of:

James H McPherson, Publisher
74689 Kitsilano RPO
2768 West Broadway
Vancouver BC
V6K 4P4 Canada

Auctorial Preamble

"The Thousand Days of Disbelief", Book Two of *'The Thrice-Cursed Godly Glories'* trilogy, consists of three distinct mini-novels. Although comprising a whole, each segment is complete unto itself. At some point in time they may come out in one volume. That point is, for now, in the future.

Many of the characters featured in the mini-novels are immortal or seemingly immortal. Their influence is thus felt throughout the ages covered by the overall trilogy. Indeed, some of those listed on the reference pages counted with Roman numerals hardly ever appear in the mini-novel at hand, whereas a few others are only mentioned in it.

"The Death's Head Hellion" commences on page 1. The first chapter of the next mini-novel chronologically, "Contagion Collectors", is provided as a bonus. It begins on page 127.

========

SEDONPLAY 4824/25
– "THE DEATH'S HEAD HELLION" –

(Extracted from a capsulated character companion for *'The Thrice-Cursed Godly Glories'* Trilogy)

Index

1. Myrionymous Devils – An Ease-of-Identification Key

2. Shining Ones: First, Second and Third Generation Devils

- The Moloch Sedon
- The Six Great Gods and Goddesses (Thrygragos Lazareme, Thrygragos Byron, Thrygragos Varuna Mithras, and the often three-in-one Trigregos Sisters: Demeter the Body, Devaura the Soul or Spirit & Sapiendev the Mind)
- Master Devas
  - The Firstborn Unities of Lazareme (Balance, Chaos & Order)
  - The Thanatoids of Lathakra (Tantal, Methandra & Klannit)
  - Significant Additional Lazaremists (Tvasitar, Chance)
  - Significant Additional Mithradites (Belialma, Pyrame)
  - Significant Byronics (Rudra & Umashakti Silvercloud)
  - More Lazaremists (Rumour, Librarian, Krepusyl, Metisophia, Ghoster, Bar-

dol, Irisiel, Skinless, & Fangfingers)
- More Byronics (Djerrid Ruin & Sedona Spellbinder)
- More Mithradites (Gravedigger, King Harvest, Vetala, Geld Neargon, Djinn
Domitian, Tammuz, Osiraq & Novadev)

3. Deviants, Demons, Faeries and Mandroids

• Deviants (Legendarian, Morgan Abyss & Pusan Wanderlust, plus the Q-names
of the 10 members of Q-Troupe, including Tomcat *'Squirrelly'* Tattletail)
• Definite Demons (Primeval Lilith, Daemonicus)
• Mandroids (All of Incain, Magnus Minus)

4. Mortal Descendants of Original Extraterrestrials

• Cabalarkon, the Undying Utopian, Cabby the Daddy
• Utopians of Weir on Earth
• Illuminaries
• Scientocrats
• Trinondevs
• Imbeciles
• The Sarpedon Underclass

========

1. Myrionymous Devils

Devils (meaning big and little gods) within the ***PHANTACEA*** **Mythos** have
a variety of talents, titles and given names. With the exception of the first and
second generations of devazurkind as well as, perhaps strangely, Pyrame Silverstar
(qv), devils did not start receiving individual names until roughly a thousand years
after they became individually solid deities circa 2000 Year of the Dome (YD).

Even then, the names they received came from their sworn as well as mortal
enemies, the Utopians of Weir on Earth. Before that they were mostly known by
their attributes. Indeed, in the Years of the Dome 4824/5 devils still tend to call each
other by their titles or attributes.

What follows is an ease-of-identification key to the more common terms used
during "The Death's Head Hellion" to refer to some of the most prominent devils
appearing in the mini-novel:

• Balance – see Harmony

• Bodiless Byron – see Byron

• Crimson Queen – see Methandra

• Datong Harmonia – see Harmony

• Pauper Priestess – see Pyrame

• Perpetual Presence (adult, female)
– see Pyrame

• Perpetual Presence (adult, male) –
see Sedon

• Perpetual Presence (child, female) –
Tralalorn (not in mini-novel)

- Eye-Mouth in the Sky – see Sedon

- Hot Stuff – see Methandra

- King Cold – see Tantal

- Lightning Lord Yajur – see Order

- Lunar Uma – see Umashakti

- Mirrors, the Mirror Mentalist – see Klannit

- Miss Myth – see Methandra

- Mithras's Virgin – see Methandra

- Providence – see Pyrame

- Scarlet Empress, Seeress or Sorceress – see Methandra

- Sed-mom or half-mom – see Pyrame

- Sparky – see Order

- Uncle Abe, Uncle Abe Chaos – see Chaos

- Undying One – see Lazareme

- Unmoving One – see Byron

- Yajur – see Order

========

2. Shining Ones: First, Second and Third Generation Devils

- The Moloch Sedon
  - the All-Father of Devazurkind; the Mighty Eye-Mouth in the Sky; the Devil Himself, capitalized;
  - also known as Dark Sedon on account of his star shining darkly (i.e., as invisibly as most stars do) during the day; at night it, his mighty eye-mouth, is by far the brightest star in the heavens above the Hidden Continent of Sedon's Head;
  - solitary member of the first generation of devazurkind; acknowledged king of chthonic or earthborn daemons or demons since Ragnarok, circa 234 PD (Pre-Dome);
  - grown or developed, more so than engendered let alone created, by the Male and Female Entities on the Trigon Asteroid, part of the First Weir System, in the dim recesses of the time-space continuum; somewhat later on in terms of the linear passage of time, the same time-tumbling Dual Entities nuked Weir Star;
  - the appearance of Supernova 1987A provided photographic testimony to their success at obliterating its solar system, which included the first Weir-world, if not everyone then alive within it;
  - the Entities started the process that resulted in the seemingly immortal, but nowhere-near-almighty, Moloch by using the right eye of Cabalarkon, a then wholly alive Utopian biogeneticist, for raw material; consequently Sedon still

regards the now undying Utopian as his father, hence Cabby the Daddy;

- Sedon's essence made up the Sedonshem, which transported surviving devils throughout the cosmos until reaching the then Whole Earth in 669 PD;
- Sedon later used his essence to form the Cathonic Zone or Dome (consequently also the Sedon Sphere) in order to separate the consequential Outer Earth from the thereafter Inner Earth of Sedon's Head;
- that occurred in the Year of the Dome (YD) Zero (4000 BCE); the Death's Head Hellion mini-novel takes place in YD 4824/5 (A.D. 824-825).

- **The Six Great Gods and Goddesses**
  - the Thrygragos Brothers and Trigregos Sisters comprise the entirety of the second generation of devakind;
  - the Three Great Gods are Thrygragos **Lazareme** (aka sometimes the Lackland Libertine, but most commonly Thrygragos Everyman), Thrygragos **Byron** (aka both Bodiless Byron and the Unmoving One due to that fact that he's all head, with his facial features frozen in the same expression, not because he can't transport himself wherever he wants on the Inner Earth), and Thrygragos Varuna **Mithras** (who does not appear in "The Death's Head Hellion" mini-novel for reasons noted in passing therein);
  - the Great Gods are obliged to share the worship they receive from their devotional adherents, including their azuras and devic children, plus the adherents of their offspring, with the Moloch Sedon; similarly, they can no more disobey him than their offspring can disobey them;
  - because they must have worshippers in order to flourish, Great Gods, like their offspring, are not allowed to kill lesser beings;
  - if they do, Sedon will cathonitize, catasterize, or ill-star them (i.e., fuse their spirit selves or essences, often along with their power foci, with his such that they thereafter shine out of the night's sky above the Hidden Headworld);
  - the Three Great Goddesses are Trigregos **Devaura** (the Spirit or Soul), Trigregos **Demeter** (the Body), and Trigregos **Sapiendev** (the Mind); they do not appear in "The Death's Head Hellion" mini-novel due to the fact that the Moloch Sedon abandoned them on the Second Weirworld comparatively shortly after the ignition of the First Weir Star;
  - their terrible talismans do, however; hence why "The Death's Head Hellion" mini-novel is an integral part of *'The Thrice-Cursed Godly Glories'* Trilogy;
  - the Six Great Gods and Goddesses, possibly with spermatic contributions from the Moloch Sedon, are the lone parents of the third generation of devazurkind;
  - like their solitary father Sedon, and the majority of their third generational offspring (the so-called Master Devas), they generally sport three visible eyes;
  - the Trigregos Sisters are sometimes referred to as the three-in-one goddesses because, except to give birth to Master Devas, they rarely separate; hence why the third generation are always triplets.

- **Master Devas**
  - dictionaries often define *'devas'* or *'daevas'* as *'the shining ones'*; hence also the

English word *'devils'*, meaning *'little gods'*;
- collectively occasionally called Sedonites or Sedonists, the Outer Earth Bible's Sheddim (meaning *'demons'* in Hebrew, always plural, and sometimes spelled *'shedim'*) may refer to Master Devas;
- so might the Assyrian *'Shedu'*, defined as a protective or beneficent deity, since it too looks and sounds a little like Sedon; (museums such as the Louvre and the British Museum preserve effigies or simulacra of the Shedu as such, under that name);
- Master Devas compose the third generation of devazurkind; the Trigregos Sisters always bore them simultaneously, in threesomes;
- they believe their fathers are one or another of the Thrygragos Brothers; hence why it's accepted that there are only three devic tribes: the Lazaremists, the Byronics and the Mithradites;
- Mithradites, however, originally were much more abundant, by a factor of two to one, than either Lazaremists or Byronics;
- some point to this as proof the Moloch Sedon couldn't resist making spermatic contributions of his own to their totality; (suchlike wise guys, and gals, therefore suspect there's a fourth tribe of Master Devas, namely the Sedon Spawn);
- like their fathers, if not their solitary grandfather, Master Devas are incapable of telling lies or violating their sworn oaths; they also generally sport three visible eyes and cannot disobey their fathers;
- in addition to wiping out thousands, if not millions, of Master Devas when they nuked the first Weir Star, the Dual Entities rendered surviving members of all three generations of devakind infertile;
- it was not until Master Devas gained demonic bodies, starting a number of decades prior to 2000 YD, that they were able to have children of their own; these were the equally immortal or near-immortal azura spirit beings, hence devazurkind;
- when Sedon himself, Great Gods and/or Master Devas possess sentient beings for procreative purposes, their resultant offspring are often long-lived and, once in a while, unnaturally gifted mortals known as deviants; the titular Death's Head Hellion, for example, is believed to be a deviant.

- The Firstborn Unities of Lazareme
   — **Harmony**, called Datong Harmonia by bygone Illuminaries of Weir on Earth; the Unity of Balance as well as Panharmonium (her pet project, a planetary panacea for beneficial devils and their worshipful multitudes alike);
   - reputedly, by a matter of a few seconds, the first Master Deva ever born; beauty incarnate as well as loveliness personified, conceivably the most popular devil on the entire Inner Earth in 4824/5;
   - her power focus or Tvasitar talisman is a golden torc, the so-called Necklace of, as you might expect, Harmony; from it she conjures her golden, chainmail gowns and the broken chains often seen manacled to her wrists; from them she sometimes shoots, what else?, chain lightning;
   - her fortunately rarely manifested alter ego is the nihilistic Nemesis, a relent-

less avenger along the lines of the Classical Furies.

— **Chaos**, called Unholy Abaddon by bygone Illuminaries of Weir (after the Biblical Angel of Apollyon, the Bottomless Pit); the Unity of just that, Chaos;

- his power focus or Tvasitar talisman is the Chaos Blade, which he keeps forever-sheathed out of fear of causing a chain reaction that would bring irreversible carnage to the world, if not the cosmos;

- its sheathe is the shaft or *'danda'* of a trident or *'trishula'*; the trident's prongs are the black blade's hilt and side-guards; from it he shoots black bolts of lightning;

- boasts that he never possesses anyone; considered something of a scatterbrain in that he changes his outward appearance frequently, sometimes without even realizing he's done so.

— **Order**, called Thunder and Lightning Lord Yajur by bygone Illuminaries of Weir; the Unity of just that, Order; his brood brother sometimes refers to him as Odour or Ordure;

- from his power focus or Tvasitar talisman he shoots vajra bolts – white lightning of the non-alcoholic variety;

- goes by Sparky when he's in altogether human form;

- some consider him the inventor of the caste system, whereby devotees don't have to be told what to do because they are born into their occupations;

- like virtually all Lazaremists, including their Great God of a father, Thrygragos Everyman, the Unities are at heart anarchists in that they consider rules, and those who enforce them, demonstrably wrong-headed and hence worthy only of scorn;

- Chaos and Order hate each other passionately; they'd seek to annihilate each other, and all that stands between them, if Harmony didn't always do just that, stand mollifyingly between them.

- The Thanatoids of Lathakra

— **Methandra** Thanatos, a firstborn Mithradite known variously as Mithras's Virgin, the Scarlet Empress, Seeress or Sorceress, the Crimson Queen to Tantal's King Cold, and Miss Myth, after Mythland (the Jewel in Sedon's Crown, on a map of the Hidden Continent of Sedon's Head), her official, but evidently not-so-inviolable protectorate (in the western third of the Mystic Mountain range), beginning as a result of Thrygragon in 4376 YD;

- also known, accurately, if perhaps somewhat disrespectfully, as Hot Stuff; the red-skinned, almost always masked and thoroughly covered (in fabrics invariably coloured different shades of red) giantess whose power focus is a firebrand or matchstick (cane);

- a self-proclaimed death goddess, that of heat and fire, forever-lusted-after by the Moloch Sedon and her brood brother Tantal (King Cold); consequential other major mover behind the expansion of the Empire of Lathakra;

- mother, while being subsumed by a be-brained daemon or demon pre-Genesea (the Great Flood of Genesis) of Klannit, the world's first azura.

— **Tantal** Thanatos, firstborn Mithradite most commonly known as King

Cold;
- the Frozen Isle of Lathakra (off the Cattail Peninsula, on a map of the Hidden Headworld), once Sedon's Horn then Sedon's Lens, Monocle or Cataract (off Sedon's Human Eye, the Gulf of Corona), is his devic protectorate;
- a gigantic, blue-skinned, icicle-bearded, archetypal-Viking whose power focus or Tvasitar talisman is a labrys (a double-headed war axe);
- self-proclaimed death god, that of cold and ice, he's the major mover behind the expansion of the Empire of Lathakra, which began circa 4730 YD;
- pre-Dome father, while being subsumed by a be-brained daemon or demon pre-Genesea (the Great Flood of Genesis) of Klannit, the world's first azura;
- besides his thought-father, Thrygragos Varuna Mithras, probably the most prolific male Master Deva in terms of having azura offspring.

— **Klannit** Thanatos, something of an anomaly in that she isn't a Master Deva but is, instead, the world's first known azura;
- as a possessive azura she is a spirit being incapable of gaining solidity by possessing debrained demons;
- conceived and given birth while be-brained daemons or demons subsumed her devic parents, Tantal and Methandra Thanatos, also otherwise just spirit beings at the time, prior to Xuthros Hor, the 10th patriarch of Golden Age Humankind, causing the Genesea or Great Flood of Genesis in Year Zero of the Dome;
- has no power focus or Tvasitar talisman as such, though she does have a very non-azura-like affinity for mirrors, which she can use for remote viewing and travelling between-space (the same as in-the-know witches use ensorcelled stones);
- unbeknownst to just about everyone, perhaps even including her parents, she and a highborn Lazaremist known as Tvasitar Smithmonger have been lovers – her via a succession of willing host-shells – seemingly forever.

- Significant Additional Lazaremists
— **Tvasitar** Smithmonger, a third-born called Vulcanian, Anvil or Anvil the Artificer by his fellow devils; resides on Sedon's Peak, in the centre of the Cattail Peninsula (Sedon's Ponytail on a map of the Hidden Headworld);
- since sometime a few decades before 2000 YD, he has been using molten Brainrock or Gypsium, the miraculous Godstuff bubbling out of the Peak's lava lake, to forge devils their power foci or talismans, hence Tvasitar talismans and why he's often thought of as the devic Prometheus;
- the cliffheads or cliff-faces overlooking the Peak's lava lake, filled as it is with molten Brainrock or Gypsium, are said to resemble the Trigregos Sisters;
- his magnificent megalithic domicile, which he constructed atop the middle cliffhead, is known as the Prometheum;
- along with demons debrained by exposure to Brainrock, power foci or Tvasitar talismans allow Master Devas to become solid entities, which they never were until he discovered how to make them;
- his talisman is an anvil, hence Anvil the Artificer.
— **Chance**, called Wintry Moira by bygone Illuminaries of Weir; a fifth-

born also known variously as Lazareme's Luck, Fata Fortuna and, most commonly among devils, Dame Chance;
- because of her dangerously unpredictable attribute, coupled with her nevertheless undeniable attractiveness, some refer to her as the luscious Lady Luck;
- the devic half-mother of many eventual Legendarians (Jordan *'Q for Quill'* Tethys, a recurring deviant sometimes recalled as the legendary 30-Year Man or Woman, as well as 30-Beers);
- she's the half-mother of the various members of Q-Troupe excluding, just perhaps, Squirrely (Tomcat Tattletail);
- the half-mother of Master Morgan Abyss, aka the Death's Head Hellion;
- her azuras are called Fatazurs;
- her power focus or Tvasitar talisman is the 3-spoke wheel of fortune traditionally known as the Triskelion.

- Significant Additional Mithradites
— **Belialma**, Sinistral Lust of Satanwyck (Hell on Earth, Pandemonium, Sedon's Temple on a map of the Hidden Headworld); Hell's Belle, also sometimes called the luscious or lascivious Lady Lust as well as Bouncing, Beguiling or Bedazzling Belialma and variations thereof;
- a second-born Mithradite whose power focus or Tvasitar talisman is the Ruby Red Apple of Concupiscence; like her fellow Apple Goddesses, Concord and Discord, she carries it as the pupil of her third eye;
- always an object of desire, her reciprocal interests cross tribal boundaries to include not just Unholy Abaddon, the Unity of Chaos, and his brood brother, Lord Order, but their father, Thrygragos Lazareme;
- Bouncing Belle resides in her bastion of bliss overlooking Pandemonium, the capital of Satanwyck, where she entertains her paramours, who also include Zuvem *'Gravedigger'* Nergalis.
— **Pyrame** Silverstar, the Pauper Priestess, the fabulously female (adult) Perpetual Presence; sometimes called Providence, among many another name or title; though only a ninth-born, possibly the most important female Master Deva around in 4824/5 YD;
- devic half-mother of all the Sed-sons (or sedons, small case); for mystical reasons, two or three of the mortal boys have to be born, on both sides of the Dome, every generation in order to maintain it;
- with neither a protectorate to call her home or a power focus to call her own, the secret to her success is generally thought to be the demon (presumably Primeval Lilith, the Demon Queen of the Night) she occupies;
- unless programmed otherwise, All of Incain obeys her; hence why she can often be found occupying the She-Sphinx on the Prison Beach of Incain, at the bottom of the Cattail Peninsula (Sedon's Ponytail on a map of the Hidden Headworld), about as far south as one can go on the Head without having to swim or ride in a boat;
- because of her complicated and never fully explained connection to the Female Entity, All of Incain and its inspiration if not probable creatrix, First Weir's Mother Machine, as well as, arguably, the demon she generally con-

trols, Pyrame's the only Master Deva immune to Trinondev eyeorbs or prison pods;

- consequently, at least in terms of devils, though not azuras, only her and her seemingly forever-mate, the Moloch Sedon, can operate in the Weirdom of Cabalarkon (Sedon's Devic Eye-Land on a map of the Hidden Headworld) with impunity.

- Significant Byronics
— Rufous **Rudra** Silvercloud, Bodiless Byron's firstborn son, his Beast Master, also his Storm Lord;
- brother-husband to sister-wife Umashakti;
- joint devic over-ruler of the former Weirdom of Kanin City when the ever-expanding Empire of Lathakra reached its walls;
- rather than either surrendering or fighting the Thanatoids and their allies, including the Unity of Chaos, he joined them.
— **Umashakti** Silvercloud, Unmoving Byron's only remaining firstborn daughter;
- a Moon Goddess consequently sometimes called Lunar Uma, her attribute is gravity; hence why devils usually address her as just that, Gravity;
- sister-wife to brother-husband Rudra; joint devic over-ruler of the former Weirdom of Kanin City when the ever-expanding Empire of Lathakra reached its walls;
- rather than either surrendering or fighting the Thanatoids and their allies, including the Unity of Chaos, she joined them.

- More Lazaremists
— **Rumour** of Lazareme: devic half-father of the first Legendarian;
- probably does not appear in "The Death's Head Hellion", but is mentioned in it fairly frequently because his power focus or Tvasitar talisman, a multipurpose Brainrock quill, transfers to the Legendarian, a recurring deviant who, whenever he returns to life, does so in his dying son or daughter, grandson or granddaughter;
- Rumour was supposedly eaten by faeries circa 4000 YD in the Land of Daybreak;
— **Librarian**, Biblio Drek, Lazaremist ambassador to the former Weirdom of Kanin City until his disappearance during the expansion of the Empire of Lathakra;
— **Krepusyl** Evenstar, second-born sister of Metisophia; sometimes called Miss Mist and the Grey Lady;
- primary devic over-ruler of faeries-friendly Crepuscule, the Land of Twilight (Sedon's Outer Nose on a map of the Hidden Headworld) until her disappearance during the expansion of the Empire of Lathakra;
- formerly Mariamne Dawnstar, she once of the Land of Daybreak on the other side of the Hidden Headworld;
— **Metisophia**, aka Titanic Metis and Wisdom of Lazareme;
- second-born brood sister of the Grey Lady (Krepusyl Evenstar) and the de-

vic Anthea, who vanished not long after becoming a solid entity circa 2000 YD;
- devic half-mother of the first Legendarian by younger brother Rumour;
- power focus or Tvasitar talisman is an all-seeing cauldron that she wore à la the Olympian Athena as a breast plate;
- Methandra Thanatos confiscated her cauldron during the expansion of the Empire of Lathakra; as a result of this, Metis lost her demonic body and promptly vanished from sight.

— Djinn **Ghoster**, one of Lazareme's heliodromuses, sun-runners or messengers until his disappearance during the expansion of the Empire of Lathakra.

— Ursine **Bardol**, a highborn companion of Chaos (Unholy Abaddon) on the Cattail Peninsula;
- fell out with Chaos over the expansion of the Empire of Lathakra, which Bardol opposed, and subsequently disappeared.

— **Irisiel** Mercherm, Lazareme's preferred Heliodromus or sun-runner until her disappearance during the expansion of the Empire of Lathakra.

— **Skinless**, the Skinless Rasp or variations thereof; a comparatively lowborn Lazaremist called by bygone Illuminaries Rastha Aragon;
- a White Godling flagellant with a flail for a power focus;
- an obvious masochist with a strange, even loving relationship with Fangfingers (Faustus Vladuca);
- beginning around 4730 YD, an early, but comparatively inconsequential ally of the Thanatoids of Lathakra during the expansion of their empire.

— **Fangfingers**, a comparatively lowborn Lazaremist called by bygone Illuminaries Faustus Vladuca after a combination of Dacian, Carpathian, Gothic and/or Slavonic deities, folk legends or heroes;
- devils tend to refer to him as the Fop because he fancies himself something of a fashion plate, one with a penchant for wearing a black opera cape with red lining;
- has, for a power focus, a Brainrock glove with fangs rather than claws on its fingertips;
- a Black Godling with an unsavoury reputation for sadism in that he welcomes animal sacrifice;
- along with the Skinless Rasp (Rastha Aragon), with whom he seems to have a strangely loving relationship, he became a comparatively inconsequential ally of the Thanatoids of Lathakra in the early days of the expansion of their empire.

- More Byronics
— **Djerrid Ruin**, Byron's Bowman, one of Byron's autumnal Zodiacals, as such associated with Sagittarius the Archer;
- called his Green Man due to his proclivity for assuming the form of a 3-eyed, vegetative human somewhat reminiscent of the work of the famous Milanese painter Giuseppe Arcimboldo (1527-1593);
- in Goatwood (Sedon's Beard on a map of the Hidden Headworld), where he's worshipped by hollow-boned avian-humans and garudas, sometimes ap-

pears as a be-winged, feather-robed and eagle-headed angelic sort.
— **Sedona Spellbinder**, a second-born Nucleoid who acts as Byron's mouth-piece when the Great God chooses not to communicate directly (albeit by telepathy since neither his lips nor tongue moves);
- considered something of a sorceress or enchantress in that her body is composed entirely of particulate matter akin to faeriedust, hence Smoky Sedona;
- despises Thrygragos Lazareme and his Unities because they did nothing to stop the expansion of the Empire of Lathakra, which cost her her traditional territory in and around Lake Sedona (named after her), in the midst of Iraxas (the Penile Peninsula, Sedon's Mutton Chop on a map of the Hidden Headworld).

- More Mithradites
- The Three Nergalids, Mithradite fertility gods individually thought of as the Planter (Zuvem Nergalis, better known to devils as Gravedigger), the Grower (Nergal Vetala), and the Reaper (Underlord Yama Nergal, King Harvest);
— **Gravedigger**, a fourth-born called Zuvem Nergalis by bygone Illuminaries of Weir; generally manifests himself black-skinned;
- name in part derives from his power focus or Tvasitar talisman, which is a Brainrock spade with a razor edge, and in part because he's sometimes called the Nergalids' Planter even though he alternates planting duties (of Vetala-Fecundity) with King Harvest;
- among his other love interests include bedazzling Belialma (Hell's Belle, once again Sinistral Lust of Satanwyck in 4824/5);
- an early-on-ally of the Thanatoids of Lathakra.
— **King Harvest**, Underlord Yama Nergal, a fifth-born who started to manifest himself as a skeletal Death God, complete with dark robe and hood, only a few decades prior to 4824/5 YD;
- also one of the three so-called Earthlings (his brood sister, Shal Ereshkigal, and his brood brother, Gibran Nimiki, being the other two); as such he often appeared robust and muscular as befits a God of Miners;
- along with his triplet-siblings and the two other Nergalids (Zuvem-Gravedigger and Vetala-Fecundity), another early-on-ally of the Thanatoids of Lathakra;
- originally, as befitting an Underlord, his power focus or Tvasitar talisman was a miner's pickaxe;
- when the Lathakran Empire conquered the Penile Peninsula (formerly Iraxas, Sedon's Mutton Chop on a map of the Hidden Headworld), he helped cathonitize Vanthysces, the Byronics' Grim Reaper;
- he thereafter fused the latter's power focus, a scythe, with his own, thereby cementing his position as the Nergalids' Reaper even though he shares fecundating duties of Vetala with Gravedigger;
- more so than the Thanatoids of Lathakra, he's considered the devils' primary Death God.
— **Vetala**, Nergal Vetala, more commonly addressed as Fecundity by her fel-

low Master Devas;

- though only a twelfth-born Mithradite, she's a Moon Goddess like Lunar Uma, a Byronic firstborn; her power focus or Tvasitar talisman is considered a moon-sickle in that its blade is shaped like a crescent moon;

- Vetala becomes pregnant by one or the other male Nergalid come the New Moon and gives birth every Full Moon;

- her azuras, who number in the thousands – more like tens of thousands – by 4824/5, are called Vetalazurs or Nergalazurs, albeit only if their fathers were either Zuvem or Yama;

- Vetalazurs seem to be only good for animating Dead Things, thus in effect rendering them zombies;

- an early-on-ally of the Thanatoids of Lathakra; when the Lathakran Empire conquered the Penile Peninsula (formerly Iraxas, Sedon's Mutton Chop on a map of the Hidden Headworld), thus displacing the Byronics who'd ruled it for millennia previously, she stayed behind to oversee its affairs on their behalf;

- Vetala resides in the former Weirdom of Manoa, called the Gleaming City due to its golden walls, at the time of "The Death's Head Hellion" mini-novel;

- most of the husks animated by her azuras cannot function in pouring rain; that said, husks that were amphibious when alive can still swim now that they're dead;

- despite this unusual drawback, the native Iraches worship her much more fervidly than they ever did her Byronic predecessors;

- this is because her azuras animate Irache Dead Things and the Iraches, who resemble North American aboriginals in almost every respect, always practised ancestor-worship; thanks to her they can now invite their deceased relatives over for tea and buttered scones.

— **Geld Neargon**, often called Toad (sometimes to his face), due to the fact he commonly appears as a hermaphroditic batrachian (toad), albeit one wearing a crown;

- said crown, his power focus or Tvasitar talisman, is properly known of the alchemical or elemental mitre (after his father, Thrygragos Varuna Mithras); it consists of four layers: one rectangular, one triangular, one circular, and one conical; he sometimes calls it his noggin neutralizer; disrespectful devils often disparage it as his dunce cap;

- the Deva Dand or Lady-Lord of Androgynia, the Land of Neutrality, below Sedon's Temple (Satanwyck) and cheek-side of Sedon's Ear (the Aural Sea) on maps of the Hidden Headworld;

- dislikes being called the Neuter because both sets of reproductive organs are fully functional; he thus bears his own azuras;

- faithful to his beliefs, he refused to take sides during the Era of Empires, which was why the Thanatoids of Lathakra and their devic allies had to dispose of him prior to conquering (instead of just absorbing) Androgynia, his nominal protectorate;

- Harmony, the Unity of Balance, admired Neargon's unflagging support for her dream of the planetary panacea she referred to as Panharmonium so much so that concern over his disappearance, amongst many other Master Devas, during Lathakra's expansion finally led her to a key discovery – the existence of ringots.

— **Djinn Domitian**, Mithras's lion-headed (leontocephalic) herald and primary Heliodromus or sun-runner until Thrygragon in 4376 YD;

- power focus or Tvasitar talisman was a fanfare trumpet, hence Mithras's trumpeter;

- devils often referred to him as the Masochist since he enjoyed being dominated;

- sometimes depicted in Mithraea on the Outer Earth, where he's generally known as Zurvan.

— **Tammuz** and **Osiraq**, Mithras's torchbearers; sometimes depicted in Mithraea on the Outer Earth, where they're commonly referred to as Cautes and Cautopates; devils think of them as Mid or Equinoctial Spring and Mid or Equinoctial Autumn;

- devils addressed their triplet-brother as Midsummer;

- called **Novadev** by latter day Illuminaries, he was responsible for drunkenly destroying Strongyne, the Island of Strong Women, circa 2500 YD on the Outer Earth (1500 BCE), thus abruptly ending the so-called Mad Goddesses' Mediterranean Matriarchate;

- for his troubles Sedon cathonitized him instantly – but the term *'going Novadev-nuclear'* terrifies devils and Illuminaries of Weir alike in 4824/5.

========

3. Deviants, Demons, Faeries and Mandroid Monstrosities

• Deviants

- When Great Gods and/or Master Devas possess sentient beings for procreative purposes, their resultant offspring are often long-lived and occasionally unnaturally gifted mortals known as deviants.

— the **Legendarian**, aka always Jordan *'Q for Quill'* Tethys, the legendary 30-Year Man or Woman, as well as 30-Beers;

- a multitalented musician, painter and recurring tail- as well as taleteller who, whenever he returns to life, does so in his son or daughter, grandson or granddaughter, albeit not until they're irrecoverably dying, whereupon they recover, though now as him, not them despite looking nearly identical;

- all Legendarians develop a telltale scar in the middle of their forehead, about where a devil would have his or her third eye; it's about the only physical difference between what they looked like before he took them over;

- when he comes back he keeps the memories of whomever he was previously but additionally brings with him his own memories, which date back to his first incarnation circa 4000 YD;

- can read tee-tee tails, which only Illuminaries of Weir, some witches and very few other non-devils can;

- even as a woman, he suffers from a procreative imperative (the compulsive need to reproduce such that he can succeed himself or herself, quite literally, lifetime after lifetime); as such, he may be the natural father of Morgan

Abyss, the Death's Head Hellion, as well as many a member of Q-Troupe;

- most crucially, Rumour's Quill, what Tethys sometimes calls his power pen as opposed to power focus, follows him from lifetime to lifetime;

- among many other purposes he uses it to draw himself and others between-space (the Weird, the dark-grey universal substance of Samsara, mundane reality), provided they've previously given him permission to do so;

- he can draw on anything, even the air itself, but generally draws on a pad of paper or parchment that he splotches out of the nib of his quill; he naturally calls it his splotch pad;

- Rumour's quill being Brainrock, its ink is too; as such it never runs out;

- anyone can use his quill while he's dancing the legless limbo between lives but it always comes back to him whenever and wherever he reincarnates;

- it can, however, be stolen; if held or taken far enough away from him, he can't will it back to himself either.

— **Morgan Abyss**, Melusine Master of the Weirdom of Cabalarkon in 4824/5, called the Death's Head Hellion due to the fact that she manifests a death's head atop her Master's Mace as if it's her personal gargoyle;

- the fact that she's not a pureblood Utopian allowed Pyrame Silverstar and her demon (presumably Primeval Lilith) to take her over some years previously, whereupon they manoeuvred her into the Mastery of Weir.

— **Pusan Wanderlust**, a self-psychopomp or Wayfarer in the Wild Weird (between-space, the dark-grey universal substance of Samsara);

- in this respect she's like garudas, mutated ravendeer, pterippi flying horses such as Attis's Pegasus, Kore's hellhounds, All of Incain and virtually any devil who has a power focus, which is why Pyrame, who had to give up all the Tvasitar talismans she'd acquired over the centuries on Thrygragon (Mithramas Day 4376 YD), began to rely on All in order to get around;

- also known as Trailblazer because she can supposedly track anyone between-space (aka the Weird or the Grey); most often called Goat, which she considers complimentary;

- a resolutely female faun or fauna (a female satyr) who's been around perhaps 1,500 to 2,000 years longer than Quill Tethys (the Legendarian); fauns famously have a voracious appetite for sex;

- unlike Quill, Pusan can only recur in her daughters or granddaughters (when they're on the verge of dying);

- deviant father was Taurus Chrysaor Attis whereas her devic half-mother was most likely Amal-Althea, Lazareme's female healer;

- a pedum or shepherd's crook that once belonged Goatfish, one of Byron's female Zodiacals (Capricorn), who vanished during the heyday of the Outer Earth's Goddess Culture circa 2000 to 2500 YD, automatically returns to her whenever she comes back to life.

— **Q-Troupe**, presumed sons, daughters, grandsons and/or granddaughters of Quill Tethys (the Legendarian);

- all claim Dame Chance (the Master Deva bygone Illuminaries named Wintry Moira) is their devic half-mother; all are over 20 in 4825 YD; 20 is the minimum age Legendarians can come back in their descendants (an age that,

perhaps curiously, applies to incarnations of Pusan Wanderlust as well);
- a few have Jordan for a first name, some have Tethys for a last name, but all go by their Q-names: *'Quick'*, *'Quiff'* and *'Quit-It'* are triplets; *'Quail'* and *'Quack'* are twins; three others answer to *'Quaff'* whereas one accepts either *'Quiddity'* or *'Quid'*; the last of them, *'Squirrelly'*, eventually admits that his full name's Tomcat Tattletail;
- all make their living as entertainers travelling in the same group, which is fronted by Dame Chance.
— Tomcat *'Squirrelly'* **Tattletail**, possibly a deviant, a faerie trickster, a be-brained demon, the latest Daemonicus or, just maybe, an ever-smiling devil in disguise;
- a metamorph or shape-shifter; when on the Inner Earth, often affects the guise of Thrygragos Lazareme as Harmony most commonly sees him – as a blue-skinned, golden-haired pretty boy, albeit with only two sea-green eyes, which suggests he's a faerie trickster more so than anything else;
- one theory is he's what became of Rumour of Lazareme after faeries ate him circa 4000 YD; Harmony calls him trillion-timing Tommy, on account of he's loved her and left her many times over the centuries;
- a master musician whose favourite instrument is a syrinx or panpipe.

- Definite Demons
    — Primeval **Lilith**, Demon Queen of the Night; the thought-immortal queen of chthonic or earthborn daemons or demons;
    - imprisoned by the Dual Entities within All of Incain (then better known as Ginny the Gynosphinx) on the then Whole Earth sometime much earlier than 669 PD (pre-Dome), which is when the Sedonshem landed atop Kanin City, or even 725 PD, which is when the Sedonshem arrived on the Moon;
    - fused with Pyrame Silverstar, then unnamed, sometime after All of Incain ate the latter circa 725 PD (the year Thrygragos Lazareme led the devic expeditionary team down from the Moon, where the Sedonshem was then hiding from the dozens of Utopian millennial or generational ships that had been pursuing devakind since time almost immemorial).
    — **Daemonicus**, Dusted Daemonicus, possibly aka Smiler or the Smiling Fiend; possibly also Tomcat *'Squirrelly'* Tattletail; reputedly indestructible, pre-Sedon king of chthonic or earthborn daemons or demons;
    - one probably incorrect theory is that he's born, and reborn, of Mother Nature, as a counterbalance to the Moloch Sedon.

- Mandroids
    — **All** the (self-proclaimed) Invincible She-Sphinx of Incain; once Ginny the Gynosphinx; Mandroid Mother Machine as well as occasional monster maker;
    - ages-old construct of the Dual Entities from their 61st lifetimes (as Alorus Ptah and Trishtar Thrae, the second version of the Biblical Adam and Eve);
    - in all likelihood based on First or Second Weirworld's technology; responsive to Pyrame Silverstar due to the Pauper Priestess's purported duplication

of the Female Entity's brain patterns in the distant recesses of linear time (possibly during the Male Entity's 3rd lifetime, which in part took place on the first Weirworld);

- All's head resembles that of the Female Entity whereas the head of the Egyptian Sphinx (aka Andy the Androsphinx, her long dormant male counterpart) resembles that of the Male Entity;

- more often than not huge and winged; a therefore perhaps surprisingly mobile psychopomp – meaning she can travel at will through the Weird (between-space, the dark-grey universal substance of mundane reality), though always leaves a root of herself behind on the Prison Beach of Incain;

- used by devils, especially Unmoving Byron and Varuna Mithras (prior to Thrygragon), as both a temporary holding cell or as a long-term prison for their transgressing fellows;

- rather, Mithras's firstborn deviant son, Chrysaor Attis, who ceased recurring as of Thrygragon, stuck devils in All on his father's behalf;

- in addition to their fathers, though not the Moloch Sedon, whom she's designed to eat, All tends to be responsive to highborn devils;

- although possessed of a modicum of sentience, if not much in the way of actual intelligence, still a machine; can be turned off and on as well as reprogrammed.

—— **Magnus Minus**, origin unspecified, might be a demon but, just as likely, might be a mandroid; may have been a monster made by All of Incain, the Dual Entities or even Pyrame, through All, since she seems to know a lot about him – including how to revive him after howsoever many centuries of moribundity;

- self-proclaimed as well as self-named mighty Minotaurus of Minius (Absudyl, the Subterranean Realm of the Mandroids);

- regardless of whether he's more mandroid than demon, he's a daemonic demiurge, one who fancies himself a latter day Daemonicus in that he's a demon king lacking subjects but completely capable of fashioning them;

- Minius, which Magnus Minus also named, after himself, is the western terminus of the Upper Head's Hell-Well (which begins in Satanwyck, Sedon's Temple on a map of the Hidden Headworld); as such, it lies directly beneath the Weirdom of Cabalarkon (Sedon's Devic Eye-Land).

========

4. Mortal Descendants of Original Extraterrestrials

• Utopians of Weir on Earth

—— **Cabalarkon**, Cabby the Daddy, the Undying Utopian; a biogeneticist when he lived and worked on, or travelled off of, the First Weirworld;

- when he was a wholly alive Utopian Scientocrat the Dual Entities used his right eye to jumpstart the process that resulted in the Moloch Sedon, hence Cabby the Daddy;

- currently subsists in a tub of life-preserving but animation-suspending Cathonic Fluid beneath the Citadel of the Thinkers in Cabalarkon City;

- it, like the rest of the territory composing the Weirdom of Cabalarkon (Sedon's Devic Eye-Land on a map of the Hidden Continent of Sedon's Head), is named after him.

— **Utopians** living in the Weirdom of Cabalarkon at the time of the Death's Head Hellion are brought up to hate Sedon and his devic progeny;

- oddly, as if to prove their non-Earth heritage, pureblood Utopian men are always black whereas Utopian women are invariably white;

- hybrid or mixed-blood Utopians of either sex living in or around former Weirdoms on the Inner Earth tend to be indistinguishable by skin colour;

- the few pureblood Utopians (U-bloods) who yet live beyond the Dome on the Outer Earth avoid having children by purebloods of the opposite sex because their offspring still look to be of a different race than one or the other of their parents;

- mortal, if usually long-lived by human standards, their equally atheistic ancestors pursued the Sedonshem throughout the cosmos from their bases on the first then second Weirworlds;

- with never-demoralizing, yet only rare successes, their forefathers desired nothing less than to eradicate devakind before they could spread even more of their corruptive immorality;

- the be-all and end-all of Utopians stuck on the Whole Earth (either beneath the Cathonic Dome or due only in part to an absence of functional spacecraft beyond it) remains the destruction of their ancient enemies.

— **Illuminaries** of Weir, Utopian polymaths, supposedly learned in a wide variety of not-necessarily-related matters; the highest educated class in Cabalarkon;

- often act as advisors to the reigning Master, who's usually elevated from their rank; very seldom are they not pure U-bloods;

- Morgan Abyss, the Melusine Master of Weir in 4824/5, is not a fully trained Illuminary, just well-studied;

- an outsider born in the subcontinent of Aka Godbad (Sedon's mouth, lower lip, lower jaw and goatee on maps of the Hidden Headworld), she attained her Mastery mostly because she was secretly possessed of Pyrame Silverstar, a ninth-born Mithradite and Sedon's favourite since long before devils arrived on the Whole Earth en masse in 669 PD.

— **Scientocrats** of Weir, still nominally scientists but, by the time period of "The Death's Head Hellion", long more like functionaries charged with keeping Weir's archaic, First and Second Weirworld machinery operating as well as it can;

- even though they're highly educated, most scientocrats are specialists in their chosen fields; they can't match Illuminaries when it comes to sheer breadth of knowledge.

— **Imbeciles** of Weir, also the idiots of Weir; inbred and therefore very much low functioning Utopians; almost always purebloods, hence the inbreeding;

- they nevertheless live much longer than most non-Utopians, sometimes into their 2nd or 3rd Century, longer in very rare cases; their longevity is due in large measure to the "food" churned out by the Weirdom's replication units, all of which were salvaged from their grounded and thence buried millennial or generational vessels;

- they leach off the Sarpedon underclass's mental emanations; it is the imbeciles of Weir whose own mental emanations empower the Master of Weir and thereby keep everything extraterrestrial that still works still working.

— **Trinondevs** of Weir, Weir's Warrior Elite, almost always purebloods who manage to overcome their inbreeding in order to function as soldiers;

- their main weapons are ever-so-useful eye-staves, the eyeorbs atop of which double as prison pods in that they can suck devic and azura spirit being out of the shells they're occupying and into them, thus incarcerating them;

- once an eyeorb is full it ceases to function as anything except a prison pod; if it's not replaced, the eye-stave becomes useless; Trinondevs, who can be male or female in 4824 YD, tend to wear robes or gowns, hoods and veils when going into action;

- their eyeorbs operate by willpower; among many another thing, they can manufacture near-impenetrable house- or personal-gargoyles about their wielders and project solid bursts or rays via psycho- or telekinesis.

— the **Sarpedon** Underclass; named after the Sarpedon dynasty of Ancient Crete from the time of the Mediterranean Goddess Culture out there (roughly 2000-1500 BCE, 2000-2500 YD);

- Sarpedons were Utopians trapped beyond the Dome thousands of years earlier, Minoans (also called Etocretans) were human whereas the followers of Europa's mythological third son Rhadamanthys were devils;

- Pyrame Silverstar was Queen Tanith throughout that time but there remains considerable debate as to whether the Moloch Sedon was Rhadamanthys;

- Pyrame believes that to be the case but readers of "Feeling Theocidal" know the real identity of this Rhadamanthys;

- NOTE 1: suitably twigged, the myth of Europa, sister of eventual King Cadmus of Thebes, and her abduction from Asia Minor by Zeus, while in the form of a pristine-perfect, white bull, is one of the foundational building blocks of the *PHANTACEA* **Mythos**;

- NOTE 2: the *PHANTACEA* version of the Europa and Cadmus myth has them living at the end of the mad goddesses' Middle Sea matriarchate rather than at the beginning; in other words, circa 1500 BCE (2500 YD) rather than 2000 BCE (2000 YD);

- Sarpedons did not begin returning to the Inner Earth until circa 1000 BCE (3000 YD); their return allowed Utopians throughout the Inner Earth to revitalize their degenerating species;

- by the time of "The Death's Head Hellion", however, their descendants, while still largely pureblood, are treated much like slaves or Hindu Untouchables by the imbeciles of Weir, who also leach off their potent mental emanations like psychic vampires.

========

The Death's Head Hellion

- Years of the Dome 4824/5 -

Jim McPherson

A *PHANTACEA* **Mythos** Mini-Novel
published by James H McPherson

ISBN 978-0-9781342-5-9

1. Prologue: The Empire of Lathakra

<u>**Up to 4824 YD – The Era of Empires**</u>

It had been the Age of Lazareme since Thrygragon.

========

For the most part, Master Devas who had Thrygragos Lazareme, aka Thrygragos Everyman, as their father abhorred rules and the rulers that went with them. Nonetheless, starting shortly after the Year of the Dome 2000, Head-worldwide travellers began realizing that, perchance by coerced bent, but much more likely by individual inclination, the principal nations, tribes or societies that populated the Cattail Peninsula, Sedon's Ponytail, invoked Lazaremist Master Devas in their rituals far more often than they did god-devils from either of the other two devic tribes.

Even though it couldn't be considered a hard and fast rule, let alone a decree, Sedonic or otherwise, that indicated the Cattail effectively belonged to that Great God's offspring. Just as truthfully, for most of the Head's subsequent history as a hidden continent, the Cattail fell within the sphere of influence of that most extremist of Lazaremists: Unholy Abaddon, the Unity of Chaos.

In terms of raw might only his immediate brother and fellow Unity, Lord Order, matched Chaos. Called Yajur by Illuminaries and Sparky by his friends, of whom he had virtually none, Order did, however, have an impressive number of devotional subjects. Fortunately for the advocates of peaceful coexistence, the vast majority of them dwelt north of the Cattail, in the Head's occipital regions.

Just as highly significantly, around the same time period – roughly the equivalent of 2000 years prior to Augustus Caesar's reign as the Outer Earth's first Roman emperor – cannibalistic Angelycs and other devic loyalists or thralls began to build the Gypsium Wall along the relatively narrow isthmus separating the back lands of Sedon's terra-formed, earthly skull from those of his ponytail.

This not particularly broad, coast-to-coast obstruction, as much as construction, quickly came to be called Sedon's Hairband. After rendering it bizarrely repellent, in the literal sense, the Unity of Harmony or Balance, the lone female of the three, just as quickly claimed it as her primary domicile more so than domain.

Arguably in her own way just as powerful as her two triplet brothers, her uncanny control of the synonymous Brainrock or Godstuff that made it up was also what made the Gypsium Wall a physically impassable barrier. She made it thus under and over the isthmus, to a very impressive depth or height, as well as along its surface. Not done yet, she rendered the offshore seas and skies to either side of it so turbulent only the most fearless or foolish of coastal navigators or aeronauts had the guts to even try traversing them.

Almost as outlandishly, her resplendent residence, called her High Seat, appeared and disappeared, here then there, along the length and breadth of the wall, seemingly of its own volition. That it did so on a daily, sometimes even hourly basis, suggested there was something of Faery, capitalized, about it.

While that may be, just as conceivably Harmony brought it with her between-space wherever she went. If that was the case, then she packed it off her power focus, her golden torc – the Necklace of, duh, Harmony, as Jordan *'Quill'* Tethys might put it – in much the same way witch-adepts carried their far less grandiose Shelters, also capitalized, with them off their teleportive stepping-stones.

Non-fans did not disparage Thrygragos Everyman as Lord Lazy because he actively defended his Age. Pretty much irrefutably, they put him properly down because he let his three Unities defend it for him. Dark Sedon, the bordering-on-almighty Eye-Mouth not so much in the sky as making it up, would have been aware of that.

Presumably the All-Father of devazurkind was also incapable of handling the, as of Thrygragon, late Thrygragos Varuna Mithras's two remaining firstborn, King Cold and the Scarlet Empress of Lathakra (most commonly named, albeit at first not by themselves, Tantal and Methandra Thanatos).

The Frozen Isle of Lathakra, the Crete-sized and -shaped domain they came to share, began as Sedon's Horn. The first time he moved it, not long after Thrygragon, it became known as Sedon's Cataract, or Lens, because he placed it off his geographical Human Eye, the Gulf of Corona.

A few more decades passed and, lesson not learned, they still wouldn't tow the line. Or tow it the way he wanted, put more accurately, with the resolutely virginal Hot Stuff – called thus for a variety of very good reasons – more like tugging his linen with him on top of her. So, as additional punishment, he moved the still frozen island to the opposite side of his world: to off the mid, eastern coast of Chaos's Cattail Peninsula.

The Mighty Moloch must have reckoned one firstborn, the Lazaremist, would object vigorously to two firstborn Mithradites, the Thanatoids of Lathakra, taking up residence off his millennia-ceded territory. Equally so, he must have reckoned the Thanatoids wouldn't take him toying with them so cavalierly lying down, especially not – the Virgin being the Virgin – lying down together.

Sure enough, circa 4730 Year of the Dome, Tantal led his Fire King berserkers and Methandra's by now just as belligerent – because they'd been just as forcibly transplanted – Intuit intellectuals in a full-blown military invasion of the Cattail. Sure enough also, Abe Chaos sashayed more so than slashed forth to meet him.

Sure enough penultimately, the Legendarian, who was still an Intuit intellectual of the feminine persuasion, was there to witness what the Moloch Sedon no doubt anticipated would be an epical battle. And sure enough finally, that then-current Quill Tethys invited them round to her place, an igloo on the north-easternmost tip of Lathakra, to crack a few pills before they got to cracking each other's heads as if uncooked eggs.

Remarkably, instead of a battle royal there emerged an alliance cordial; at least there did with respect to the three firstborn. Even more remarkably, throughout the most gruelling of times – through thick and thin gruel dick-dildo, again to quote the Legendarian – it remained a popping-pilsners, as in affably beer-guzzling, association of ambitiously cocksure, not to mention tauntingly rebellious, highborn. The better part of a century later, they could declare a thoroughly disproportionate immensity of the Hidden Headworld theirs for the re-dividing and/or retaining.

There were stacks of setbacks along the way, hence the better part of a century. Most gallingly, most ongoing-incompletely to the Lathakrans, after the Byronics lost their foothold on Sedon's Ponytail, then were driven, much more eventually than inescapably, out of Sedon's Mutton Chop, they dug in their holistic heals. They shielded the Aka-Godbadian subcontinent (Sedon's Mouth, Lower Teeth, Lip, Jaw and Goatee) inexhaustibly. They also did it, the Empire's therefore biggest holdout in terms of area, successfully.

For now!

========

Due to the fact that, for so far immortal devils, Aka-Godbad's indigenous population of sentient, but credulous and resultantly reverential inhabitants approached the invaluable, the Lathakrans vowed they'd be back for another go at it once they conquered the rest of the Inner Earth. They made no such vows when it came to the Upper Head realms of Satanwyck or Subterranean Temporis, however.

While both were vast territories, they thus far remained unconquered. Since, strategically speaking, both realms would be more trouble acquiring than they'd be worth keeping, chances were they'd stay that way. For one, even with its multiple dimensions, some of which reputedly linked with other worlds as well as, just possibly, the Outer Earth, Satanwyck came stocked with chthonic, as in earthborn, demons.

Fundamentally demons were anti-devil. That made them much more prone to despise devil-gods than revere them. The only howsoever-begrudging exceptions to that, to them, sorry state of affairs were Sedon Himself, as the pre-Flood acclaimed-for-eternity King of All Demons, and Sed's designated, hence unchallengeable viceroys. As for Temporis, it remained just as unwanted because its moronic Mantel half-lifers were nearly as next-to-useless when it came to providing nutritious devil-worship as demons.

Counter-intuitively Sedon didn't seem to care, one way or another, what the Thanatoids were up to, they and their cross-tribal allies, prominently Abe Chaos and the two enduring firstborn offspring of Thrygragos Byron, Rudra and Umashakti Silvercloud. Which was, namely, stealing adulation properly due him, and nobody else, for themselves. He'd certainly never – or thus far hadn't ever – opposed them.

More tellingly, neither had he sought to assert his will and simply order them to stop all this conquering-the-Head claptrap. Not quite as inexplicably, throughout the expansion of the Empire of Lathakra, Quill's Uncle Abe's immediate sister, Quill's therefore Auntie Harm, had somehow prevented their ever-so-formidable, immediate brother, a notorious teetotaller, from taking to the field in defence of the status quo.

There wasn't much debate as to the reason for Yajur's forbearance. Harmony being Harmony, she'd have been sleeping with someone throughout most of the century the Lathakran Empire was expanding. And for a change it wouldn't have been his and hers Thrygragos of a Lord Lazy father.

========

Besides Byronics and, later on, Mithradites threatened with humiliating, effective demotion in the estimation of their peoples, not to mention their prayers, there'd been Lazareme-Lands' loads of resistance to the Thanatoids building the mightiest, most far-ranging empire of the Era of Empires. Initially there had even been hostility from the Unities of Harmony and Order, though not from their famously flaccid father, who slept through most of its first year of expansion.

Sometime the next year, 4731, Harmony managed to rouse him. No doubt to her howsoever-unquenchable outrage, the Lord Laziest of Great Gods promptly went binging with King Cold and Abe Chaos. On top of that, they did it most conspicuously in the neutral confines of her very own Dinq Doinq Danq Cavern Tavern in southeast Marutia, Sedon's Cheek.

Traditionally, the north-easternmost slope of the Diluvia mountain range lay within the sphere of influence of Mithradite Master Devas. That its devils, notably Diluvia Ran, a tenth-born, so-called Lesser Apocalyptic, that of Flood, had essentially deeded the Danq to her, as a cross-tribal hangout if nothing else, testified how much devils of every distinction relied upon Harmony to help preserve the convivial spirit of Thrygragon.

While it might be argued that its actuality was far more distressingly conflictive than convivial, devils were bound by their oaths and no Era of Empires could change that. Nonetheless, incidents she found almost as irritating as Thrygragos Lazareme as good as putting his stamp of approval on Headworld turmoil followed.

Within a decade, Lazaremist resistance in the Cattail had vanished. Many of the Master Devas that, therein, had opposed Lathakra had done a dot-ditto. They had disappeared. At first that didn't seem so strange. Displaced from their regular haunts, they could have just gone into hiding.

For a devil the easiest place to hide was inside a non-devic, but necessarily sentient shell. Save for pureblood Utopians and/or witches ensorcelled against it, there was no way to prevent possession. Furthermore, regardless of whether the chosen receptacle was a willing or unwilling shell, so long as the occupying devil kept his or her presence benign, as in made no effort to usurp control of the individual and thereby alter their behaviour, there was no reliable way to test for possession. Nor, due to unawareness of it, could the thus-haunted sentient indicate possession.

No matter where they went in whole wide cosmos, let alone the whole wide world, Master Devas had been doing that sort of thing next door to forever. Yet they were also by nature both undisciplined and gregarious. So it was that, when, after an absence of decades plus, nary a solitary spirit had resurfaced, rumours rampaged. They weren't coming back and it wasn't because they didn't want to; it was because they couldn't.

So, what had become of the missing devils? Could minor immortals be killed the same as Thrygragos Varuna Mithras apparently had on Thrygragon? And if so, how and by whom? And if not, where had they gone? Where could they have gone?

Surely not to the Outer Earth – the only reliable gateway through the Dome to there was All of Incain, Pyrame Silverstar's pet devil-eater.

Questions asked needed answering. Three explanations seemed plausible, if improbable. The lost devils could have been ill-starred or cathonitized; they could have been defeated and imprisoned within All (Incain lay on the southernmost extremity of the peninsula and therefore the Head itself); or they could have been captured and confined inside Trinondev eyeorbs, which appropriately enough were also known as prison pods.

Except …

Ill-starring resulted in previously unseen, yet usually highly visible, new stars suddenly shining down upon the Head from Cathonia (the Cathonic Zone, Dome or Sedon Sphere). Great Gods, their firstborn and even lesser devils, so long as they were inside their protectorates and accordingly empowered by a massive plurality of their resident adherents, could cathonitize Master Devas. They couldn't do it as easily as Sedon but, in any event, no new, Head-worldly internal stars ignited during this period.

If third generational devils fed any other third generational devil to All on Incain then Pyrame Silverstar, who was as resistant to All's digestive tracts as she was to eyeorbs, hence why she could ride the She-Sphinx with impunity, would know it. She didn't. Harmony asked her and Master Deva couldn't lie any more than they could break their oaths or disobey their fathers.

As for getting captured and confined inside prison pods, that implied egregious stupidity more so than circumstantially compounded carelessness on the part of the thus rendered-wretched devil. That said, while devic idiocy was hardly unheard of, since they were designed to work against them devils couldn't wield prison pods.

They had an alarming failsafe built into them by Pyrame's patron, who was actually a matron, the likeness of whose face All generally displayed – a face that, except for the third eye, Datong Harmonia seemed to share, at least she did when she was alone and looking into a mirror. Without countervailing commands from the high-minded Trinondevs to whom they were attuned, eyeorbs went ballistic by themselves whenever devils were in the vicinity.

Which along with the Six Cursed Objects – cursed albeit only as far as Great Gods and Master Devas were concerned – explained why all except two devils avoided the Weirdom of Cabalarkon at all costs. Those devils were the Moloch Sedon, when he came down from the sky in order to visit his thought-father, the Undying Utopian, Cabalarkon himself, and his forever-mate, Pyrame Silverstar, when she was ruling it inside its non-pureblood master.

Such was the situation in late Tantalar 4824.

========

As for the Outer Earth, Dark Sedon maintaining the Cathonic Dome denied the Thanatoids and their allies access to it. Similarly, the Mighty Moloch not altogether always in the sky also denied them any opportunity to conquer Cabalarkon. For them even to make the attempt would invite his eternal wrath.

Or so most of those living and dying on the Hidden Headworld believed.

****

2. Daring Disharmony

Pre-Mithramas 4824 Year of the Dome – Sedon's Peak

Devil-gods were disappearing inexplicably. No more, she vowed.

========

Like the Moloch Sedon, Sedon's Peak regularly blew its top. It did it so often Sedon's Cork would have been a better name for it. One day, circa 2000 YD, it blew so irrevocably it became akin to evermore uncorked. Only three sharply fractured pinnacles, which to this day overhang the massively enlarged caldera, remain of the peak itself. In the right light these cliffs or crags displayed phantom faces of their own; female faces like All of Incain's, only ones with three eyes.

According to many Master Devas, ones boastfully asserting astonishingly good memories of exceptionally bad times, the spectres gazing down from the crags had to be emanations sent across the cosmos by their simultaneous mothers. However, the last time any of them could have seen the second generational Trigregos Sisters was simply too long ago, in the far, far too distant past, to justify any claims of photogenic precision.

Regardless of whom, if anyone, they may or may not represent, atop the central cephalic crag the Anvil Artificer, who was better known as Tvasitar Smithmonger, built his impressively massive domicile. Which, he being justifiably thought of as the devic Prometheus, he naturally called the Prometheum. Tvasitar wasn't there, though. She'd just been through the megalithic masterpiece, senses cranked into highest quest mode.

Beneath the cliff heads a lava lake lapped the correspondingly colossal crater's rim. To call it thus, though, was also somewhat of a misnomer. Lava didn't fill it; molten Brainrock did. The smithy made devic power foci – hence Tvasitar talismans, hence also why he was thought of as the devic Prometheus – out of the same ever-replenishing, some-said-miraculously consequential Godstuff. And that's where she found him.

Not surprisingly, even though hardly anyone lived on its lower slopes, over the course of the many intervening centuries since devils first achieved individual solidity most everybody conceded Sedon's Peak was his devic protectorate. Truth told, while inviolable protectorates didn't technically exist until after Thrygragon – and to this day Lazaremists still hadn't acquired their father's stamp of approval to declare any of what was effectively theirs already his, her, its or their private property – he had lived and loved up here long before its cataclysmic uncorking some three millennia previously.

Right this minute her never little brother, size-wise, was doing the latter as keenly as he was doing it brazenly.

========

Almost universally, for humans as well as sentient non-humans not just on, in, under or above the Inner Earth of Sedon's Head, accidentally happening upon two people making love chalks up as one of life's most embarrassing moments. This holds true for devil-gods too. It also holds when the people one stumbles upon are devils.

Considering whom, at first, second then third look, he appeared to be lying under when she popped out of the Weird, her eyes probably were doing a dot-ditto, lying. Entirely unexpectedly, but moderately delightfully if they were sooth-seeing, she now had yet another mystery to solve. Who the fuck was her brother fucking anyhow?

Puzzles intrigued Datong Harmonia, as wayward Illuminaries of Weir named her once they started returning from the Outer Earth sometime during the previous millennium – the Hidden Headworld's fourth. That didn't mean she liked them. In truth, because it had to do with the disappearance of, for the most part, her younger siblings in Lazareme, she hated this one.

Hated the first one, put better; the one that brought her here riddles to resolve. So many devils, familiar as well as mostly familial, basically content and certainly long-established ones, shouldn't just vanish without a trace. Not for so many years they shouldn't. There had to be a rational, if dreadful, explanation of some sort.

After she reamed him out for bashing so many of their brothers and sisters unto a state of nascent, as in born again, spirituality on behalf of the vindictive Thanatoids of Lathakra, Chaos had to agree with her. At the very least what they should do, once they were defeated in battle, their bodies immolated and their power foci confiscated, was return to Sedon's Peak, where they became solid individuals in the first place.

That's what he would do. Then again, Harmony pointed out, he wasn't so much a glutton for punishment as one for delivering it. Be that as it may, he countered, no new Master Devas had come into being since Weir Star went supernova, uncountable thousands of Earth-years pre-Head.

Its deliberate detonation didn't accomplish everything its instigator intended. It certainly didn't wipe out all the devils caught in the resultant, galaxy-wide splattering of nuclear energy and elemental matter. But, as the Moloch Sedon, the Great Gods, and they themselves could attest, it did sterilize the devic survivors. Save for their azuras – which, he reminded her unnecessarily, didn't start coming into being until after devils started experimenting with their newly animated bodies – that much was undeniable.

Since plenty of debrained demons, leftovers from shortly after the Peak's uncorking, continued to litter its slopes, why should their brother bother hoarding them? Rephrased, even if he had his reasons for doing so, surely Tvasitar could spare the mere dozens it took to replace the daemonic bodies Abe and his comrades in conspicuous cruelty rendered irretrievable.

Plus, he noted, for him sounding a rare, optimistic chord, although the smithy had never managed to fashion a replacement power focus for anyone, who could say for sure he wouldn't someday succeed in doing just that? Summing up, Abe reiterated, also highly unusually for him, going to Sedon's Peak was precisely what he would do.

Given that he virtually never repeated himself, she could take a hint. So that's precisely what she did: came here, conundrum to crack. But – after her long friendship with the Legendarian, punning having become addictive to Harmony – it now seemed she had to get to the bottom of another one first.

That punned suitably silently; that was her younger brother in Lazareme gyrating gymnastically underneath Top-Stuff's bottom. Seemingly composed of mobile stonework he was as hard as he was hard to mistake. Not so, appearances to the contrary, his companion in carnality. Top-Stuff couldn't be Hot Stuff, could she? Yet, if it wasn't, then who was it?

The maybe-mystery devil had her brow furrowed in appreciable concentration. The not unattractive wrinkling thereby obscured her third eye, assuming on fourth look she had one. Since, however many she had, they were as closed as the smithy's, she could probably retreat without being spotted. Except again, no. She had to know.

Inquisitiveness was hardly her most distinguishing trait – loveliness perceived, as well as personified, had that distinction – but it was as within her as crinkly butterscotch hair, golden torc power focus and retracted chains were without her. (Provided as per usual with her, she was looking into a mirror.) She had no way of being 100% sure how either of these two would see her if they opened their eyes and regarded her right this second. But, given their present entwinement, maybe it would be as Top-Stuff.

If, after aeons resolutely a virgin, he was in fact as well as friction her first, why reward Tvasitar Smithmonger with her defloration? Was it the price he demanded she pay for his aid in helping her and her allies dispose of devils without leaving a trace of their whereabouts?

Couldn't be. Or, if it was, then it was incredibly non-Lazaremist-like. Other than their Lord Laziest father, anarchists like most of them were did not have rulers, per se, but they did have rules. Rather, they had one, a sensibly qualified one: ahimsa. Apart from in self-defence, they would do no harm.

Moreover, presuming Miss Myth wanted azuras, she could have seduced her fabulously fertile father back when he was available for procreative duty. That's what Harmony did her first time out with a body entirely her own. Of course she chose Lazareme – who wasn't particularly good for much of anything else, it had to be said – as opposed to Mithras, multitalented but insufferable egoist that he was.

Then again, be it for many multiple millennia, or not much more than the merest of minutes in her case, what was so special about a maidenhead? Zip answered that. Unless it was zilch, nada or, dare she pun again, dick? Mithras no longer being an option, she could almost definitely still have her brood brother Tantal, who was as prolific as either of the two male Nergalids. And, should she so desire it, Grandfather Sedon would undoubtedly drop Pyrame just as cheerfully post-Tvasitar as he would have pre-Tvasitar.

Nonetheless, what madness was upon her? Was she channelling Venus to Vulcan instead of, to slightly mix mythologies, Heady Athena to anyone? Sure, her brother was relatively highborn, but he was no firstborn, and she had always been more of a snooty sort than a sooty sort. Which might be today's best pun yet.

Tvasitar became a smithy only partially because he was in the right spot, here, and at the right time, circa 2000 Year of the Dome, when Sedon's Peak erupted not so much devastatingly as devil-making ultimately. He actually enjoyed working with his hands, albeit by hammering Brainrock malleable, not massaging flesh suppliant.

Because of that, it seemed to many that it was almost as if conspiratorial circumstances chose him to be here then, and to stay here thereafter, which he certainly had. Harmony didn't share that opinion. It seemed to her patently obvious that Brainrock, not circumstances, chose him.

Debrained demons formed devic bodies, yes. However, Tvasitar Talismans allowed devils to maintain their thus individualized independence indefinitely. Vaporized Godstuff could de-brain daemonic bodies anywhere, yes as well. But thus far only the Anvil Artificer had demonstrated the ability, let alone the expertise, required to craft power foci out of its molten state.

Arguably that made him more valuable than even Great Gods. So, might that explain Methandra's choice? Only if she reckoned herself capable of having devic children, Harmony figured. Which she might; which in turn might account for her lofty estimation of her own worth.

Tvasitar had certainly used the remote possibility that, someday, a fourth generation of devils would begin coming into being as his excuse for never wanting to leave Sedon's Peak. Presumably these would be true devils, not azuras, the forever spirit beings whose only real functions were to animate the dead, calm the wildest and most vicious beasts or, less reliably, inspire potential worshippers with respect to the devil-gods they should worship.

As devic fantasies go, it was hardly a malignant figment. It did verge on unhealthy obsession, though: a self-rooting fixation with what wasn't yet and probably couldn't be ever. Indeed, so stagnating was it, in the much more than two and a half millennia since its uncorking, he'd only left *'home'* to attend their nowadays no longer practical, clan get-togethers.

There hadn't been one of those held since Abe, with many more howsoever-sheepishly to follow, went over to the Lathakran side the worst part of a century ago. Even before that, though, he'd only leave here when their mutual father summoned him elsewhere. And he only did that reluctantly, without the slightest hint of enthusiasm, because devils couldn't disobey their sires.

Wherever he was, his contributions to conversations struck Harmony as about as revealing as the cold scraps of metal, the raw material of his trade, that he would jabber on and on about purely because he felt obliged to say something. To judge by responses he muttered more so than uttered when she attempted to engage him otherwise, he seemed to consider grunting chatty.

Evidently, she could hear despite covering her ears, he didn't just grunt while speaking or working. Succumbing yet again to that poor, non-nunnish habit she'd picked up over recent centuries from Quill Tethys, she noted to herself that black-smith bellows were obviously not just for increasing drafts to a fiery forge. Clearly they were equally useful for stoking flames of the passionate assortment.

As for the party of the upper part, she had never come across her so small. With their subtle matter, daemonic bodies devils could be any size they fancied. However, the former Crimson Queen of Mythland invariably appeared in public as a giantess. Furthermore, in the millennia since they both became solid individuals Harmony could never recall seeing her not wearing a facemask and hair-hiding hood before, let alone not wearing any clothes period.

Buxom worked but so did igneous. Of course, they could be applied to the beauteous but voracious Belialma as well. Plus, towards the beginning of the 48th Century of the Dome, that second-born Apple Goddess had reclaimed the throne of Pandemonium – which she'd given up in the aftermath of Thrygragon – and could thus call herself Sinistral Lust of Satanwyck once again.

Despite that, despite them going at it so admirably actively, so inexhaust-ibly sturdily, the Unity of Balance knew she wasn't witnessing Hell's Belle bawdily bouncing her brother's balls. For one thing, Belle generally appeared more so the buxom-former and less so the igneous-latter. For another, although the almost-as-highborn Mithradite had as her power focus the Ruby Red Apple of Concupiscence, Harmony had never seen anyone alive whose skin was that red, unnaturally aurous-reflectively so.

On top of that – no pun attempted this time, though she snickered involun-tarily anyhow – Quill Tethys told her some time after Thrygragon that Ovid, an Outer Earth poet who wrote in Latin, described in his *'Metamorphosis'* a stunningly attractive woman having fiery golden hair, which Top Stuff certainly had. Tethys, though, believed Ovid had inherited a corrupted leftover from the half-millennium-long Goddess Culture of circa 2000 to 2500 YD, albeit beyond the Dome.

With some merit, Tethys argued Ovid, whom he'd never met, was probably writing about Methandra, not the mortal Medusa moments before Heady Athena, Ovid's Minerva, gave her venomous vipers for hair to go along with a stone stare. Harmony had suffered much the same fate in terms of mangled mythologies that were purportedly about her. Most of them were set in the same 500-year period, so she tended to agree with Jordy's assessment of that legend.

Recalling it now, and her reaction to it then, didn't quite pull her out of eyes-deceptive, denial mode. Still, they were making love on what doubled for Anvil's outdoor bed – it looked to be a fully functional, albeit huge and, in all probability, hugely uncomfortable iron anvil. That didn't surprise her overly much. Semi-cor-roboratively, what did was that it was on the shore of a lava lake spitting and sput-tering what must be scorching hot, molten Gypsium not fifty yards behind them.

Godstuff magma melted daemonic bodies the same as vaporized Brainrock dissolved daemonic brains. So, who else could it be?

Eyeballs validated encouragingly, discretion warred with impatience discour-agingly. She should return between-space, wait unnoticed therein until they were done and decent, then come back pretending she'd seen nothing untoward. Where-upon she could hopefully satisfy her genuine curiosity and politely inquire as to what game Miss Myth was playing at in Tvasitar's good-as-protectorate.

The astoundingly gifted, in so many respects, lone firstborn-female Mithradite would speak to her – Harmony was one of the few devils Methandra would deign to converse with directly, let alone civilly – but her temper was predictably volcanic. No matter how innocently she made it sound, there was no way to guarantee the Thanatoid would react rationally to her catching them together.

If Hot Stuff blew, battling-bad big-time, and if Tvasitar took her cause and thereupon sought to assert his authority, here in his own territory, well, two against one might prove marginally tricky. Being her junior, Tvasitar would never dare to challenge her ordinarily but, supposedly being her equal, Miss Myth might feel obliged to flare forth blazingly. The Headworld really didn't need two new stars, did it?

If that truly were make-it-Mistress Myth, whom she'd always admired for her pernickety, no-man-is-my-master individualism if nothing else, then she'd rather not risk having to indulge her with an undignified hullabaloo. Depending on their severity, hullabaloos for Harmony could provoke the emergence of her just as incredibly non-Lazaremist-like alter ego, the nihilistic Nemesis of, most notably, circa 2500 YD.

Not wanting to waste the momentum it would take to go away and come again another day, she took the only other option presenting itself right then and there. Happily, for all three of them, the two who belonged here were going at it as intently as they were obliviously to her presence. Preparatory to probing Miss Myth the way devils usually did, with their eyefire, Harmony opened wide her devic eye.

Unleashing it clandestinely, as if she was dealing with one of her triplet brothers, both of whom were as psychically dense as they were thick-headed, she overcompensated. Immediately regrettably, instead of reading her, as she would easily have any ordinary devil, she scorched her – fatally.

Correction: Not who was that; what was that?

========

"Come again?"

"A homo – as in a homunculus. And you killed her, you bitch!"

========

"That's no way to address your elder, third-born. Besides, if I killed a lesser being, then Sedon would have instantly ill-starred me. And I'm still right here, not shining up there."

Plus, she might have added, but didn't, the non-vaporized vestiges of the Methandra-lookalike she'd inadvertently immolated still lay lifeless, smoked and smoking, on Anvil the Artificer's anvil-shaped bed. Which, not surprisingly, also wasn't moving. It still sat where it had been, on the shoreline betwixt the lava lake and where he now stood infuriating her, heedless of his own continuing good health.

Instead she said, close to tauntingly: "So what's a homunculus – other than being a half-life, a semi-sentient Mandroid or some sort of fleshy eidolon you somehow manufactured yourself in order to jerk off even more perversely than usual? Be precise and see that you do so respectfully. You don't; I'll give you a whipping so severe it'll leave chain marks on even your horny, rock-hard hide."

"Why should I give a flying fuck about your petty threats," he raged back at her, "Let alone pander to your oh so delicate sensitivities? You're no embodiment of Panharmonium. You're daddy's toady, a murderess as unbalanced at the rest of my sickening excuse for a family. By the provisions of the accord you thrust down the throats of the rest of us after Thrygragon, this place passes for my inviolable protectorate. Grandfather won't do it; I will.

"Cathonitize, cunt!"

Crashing together, as if cymbals, the two stony slabs that passed for hands in his concrete case did nothing for the night's sky in terms of illumination. Were there anyone else present besides the highborn Lazaremists it might have in terms of temporary deafness, however.

"Protectorates need populations," Harmony sneered commensurately loudly. Almost in relief, once his melodramatic crass-clash-clapping failed to produce anything personally perilous, she found herself unable to resist fay-saying contemptuously. "And lava louts don't count."

"How about Brainrock gouts? They'll soon turn you into a Disunity."

If she was any other devil, that might have proved correct. Most daemonic bodies burned as if tinder. To call them highly flammable had aspects of the understatement to it. And molten Brainrock was dangerously hot stuff, small case. If Tvasitar were any other devil save a Great God or a firstborn, he wouldn't have been able to conjure fistfuls of the glowing gunk and hurl them at her.

Brainrock liked him but, by comparison, from the top of her glowingly golden, butterscotch curls to the tips of her curled-up, similarly splendid slippers, Harmony was all-Brainrock. Rather, she was when she put her mind to it, which she was doing now. She didn't so much stand there and take it as she stood there and took it into herself.

What doesn't kill you, they say, makes you stronger. Master Devas couldn't be killed that way – though most would have been burnt bodiless Spirit Beings again – but absorbing the Godstuff definitely did make her feel stronger. As for the lava louts, they were next.

Blocky, lumbering lumps only vaguely humanoid in size and shape, they were so borderline-brainless they didn't even qualify as chthonic critters. Tvasitar must have imagined them rearing out of the ground, still bubbling up and blistering over, because that was what they did. That was also when she began extending barbed, but shatter-ended, Brainrock chains out of the lustrous manacles she'd already conjured clamped about her thus luminous wrists.

Too stupid to be petrified, the malformed, largely Gypsium golems advanced upon her robotically. Their fists formed sledgehammers, unless they formed anvils. They had every intention of pulverizing her, precisely and with a maximum degree of disrespect, unto crushed-gooey slurry.

Probably only another cement mixer would perceive her as loveliness personified but, in effect turning the tables on them, that was what Harmony tit-for-tat became. In a brief blur of routing, interlocking links, she did her functional impersonation of a pastry blender. She didn't whisk them into kin of the bricks her brother should be shitting by now. That would have taken more time. But they did transform akin to the diarrhoea most likely already dribbling down his fiery ferric legs.

"Oh please, oh please," he mock-begged her snidely. "Don't smite the smithy."

Since by then he could have passed for a huge, naked, napalm-man – one ignited on the sizzling griddle of his own ground, which explained how he could still move as well as speak – it was difficult to tell if he was dribbling anything except sarcasm. Whereupon, breaking into a nearly face-splitting smirk, he suddenly bellowed, as smithies were wont to do, an additional, deliberately provocative rebuke: "You filthy father-fucker!"

At which point, thus self-emboldened, he really started letting her have it.

========

Devils in their own protectorates – or equivalent, in the Lazaremist land at hand – may only be as potent as the degree their followers' unquestioning faith in them allowed. But he was seriously steamed. Implacable anger doesn't just super-charge humans. Be that as it may, Tvasitar's eyefire blazed but barely fazed her. A succeeding series of megaton earthquakes did, however, shake her butt-backwards onto the smithy's barbecuing patio.

Her humiliating dislodgement achieved, he proceeded to knock her about relentlessly, knockers over knockwurst. After been flipped over and over again, as if a steak on his spatial spatula, she deigned to fret a few hurtful bolts of chain lightning in his direction. She did so only to remind him, as gently as she could, that brotherly love had its limits and they didn't extend to sisterly searing.

Suchlike niggling jolts only served to rile him the more. He no longer wanted her done to a turn, medium-rare. He wanted her overcooked, horribly unpalatably. He wanted her broiled unto inedibility even for the few faerie fireflies, the carrion crows and the daemonic salamanders, who could actually swim in molten Brain-rock, that were his usual companions in this hellscape.

Astrophysically speaking, cometary tails projected in front of their debris-dusted, ice-ball nuclei, not behind them. The substantive, comet-like fireballs that Tvasitar launched out of his lava lake, misnomer that it was, did no such thing. They did stream upward in number to a variety of apogees, whereupon they did arch downward more rocket-like than comet-like. They pile-drove so destructively into Harmony that, in short order, she looked forevermore wretchedly ruined.

The most beautiful cinder he'd ever beheld, her three eyes sparked only briefly before darkening dully. Even her neck-torc, the first power focus he crafted for any Master Deva after his own anvil, glimmered very nearly imperceptibly until at last it too extinguished. As per its legendary namesake, the Necklace of same, albeit hundreds if not quite yet thousands of years belatedly, evidently no good ever came to anyone wearing it.

Overdone mission accomplished, he ceased the barrage of Brainrock and materialized a ring-like object on the, for humans, ring finger of his left hand.

"See this, most wondrous firstborn?" Tvasitar snarled maniacally, as he waved it at the grilled-grotesque remains of her daemonic body. "We devils don't usually marry and this isn't my wedding band. But I know your spirit-self is still hovering around here somewhere. It'll be stunned pretty much paralytic, but that's only for the time being, so I'll make this as quick as I can before activating it."

He wasn't slavering so much as drooling melted metal. He was also as good as gloating long-windedly. "Klannit Thanatos is my one true love. She's the Thana-toids' lone azura-offspring. They had her pre-Flood, when the demons that ate them prior to Ragnarok had sexual congress. As an azura, she can't animate debrained demons like we can; never could, no matter what I did to them. But, a few decades ago, we discovered she could mobilize pre-formed homos; at least she could."

He pointed the ring at her remains, if possible, even more menacingly. "Neither of us knew homos even existed until Grandfather moved Sedon's Tongue over to this side of the Head in place of sister Dawnstar's Land of Daybreak. But there was a trick to it. She has to grow into them as they grow up. Plus, she can only do that one at a time.

"That's number one. But it's neither here nor there in terms of you and me, is it? This is: We both know Utopian prison pods can and do suck in azuras way more easily than they do devils. Indeed, as you'd be able to verify because you were there, whereas I wasn't, Thrygragon proved eyeorbs only had to be open in order to vacuum them up like moths to flames or odours to socks.

"But Thrygragon proved something else. Azuras were nowhere near as useless as devils like father and you believed. What with two Mithrant legions setting up to do battle with thousands of just as heavily-armed fanatics feverishly loyal to we Lazaremists and our Byronic allies, almost everyone feared there'd be across-the-battles-board carnage in Sedon's Mole come that day.

"Thrygragos Varuna Mithras himself, though, had no intention of wasting the lives of so many potential worshippers. To that end, he thought he had all the angles covered; that he could counter anything you in particular, along with your equally treacherous, fellow firstborn, on all three sides, could throw at him. He was also smarter than nearly everyone else in that he knew azuras weren't useless. Unfortunately he did think they were eminently expendable.

"Before Kanin City's Trinondevs, in their cosmicars, even attacked him, Mithras commandeered vast numbers of azuras emboldening soldiers marshalling throughout the Mole. Then, in what Klannit condemns as azura-genocide, he forcibly used them as a kind of cosmic energy to reprise the godhood of Kronos, or Saturn, and turn back the hands of time. In all the intervening hundreds of years, you lot straight-on-fucking each other, like the amoral rats you are, hasn't come anywhere close to replenishing the numbers irretrievably lost that Mithramas minute so long ago.

"But what if the Trinondevs had arrived earlier? The azuras they took out would never have been destroyed; they'd have just been imprisoned until someone released them. Klannit knew that because that's what happened to her. Her mother Methandra found the prison pod she'd been sucked into and took it to Mythland, her by then official protectorate. In its safety, she released her by force of will alone.

"It gave her an idea, though; one she had Klannit bring to me because, hey, who would you come to if you wanted something made? What if devils had doohickeys like Utopian eyeorbs, ones they could use to take out other devils without risking themselves? They had suchlike at the start of Thrygragon then Mithras would never have had the opportunity to wipe out so many thousands of your babies.

"This is the result of our subsequent centuries of experimentation. It isn't all risk free of course. You have to wreck the devil before he or she wrecks you. So it's not for everyone, just firstborns like you and devils in their protectorates like me. We call them ringots. Like it?"

"That wasn't quick."

========

Harmony was – rather, Nemesis was! The wings she gave herself were flexible razor-blades. They could dice anything, even devils in their own territories.

========

"Got any extras?" she, Harmony again, in one basically Brainrock body as well, put to him once she was done putting his instructions into brutal, merciless practice.

Having thereby returned to him the disfavour of wrack and wretched ruin, albeit without any of the ensuing extemporizing, he wasn't in any condition to respond verbally. Nor was he in a mood to do to it any other way. However, his consequential inability to do much of anything anymore trumped his disinclination to do diddle cooperatively.

He resisted her eyefire-reading him about as successfully as he avoided her ringot-implementing what he couldn't help but tell her. Which is to say not at all.

Tvasitar did have many ringots. As it happened most of them were already filled with devils her Abe, the Thanatoids of Mithras, and the Silverclouds of Byron took out during the expansion of the Empire of Lathakra; the very ones she'd come here to inquire about, one mystery to demystify.

Because he never left his protectorate, whereas they were busy conquering the rest of the immediate world, they figured it safest to leave them here on the Peak. And of course that was exactly what Abe had been saying without, having given his word to keep their existence a secret, being able to say it straightforwardly.

As Chaos had also reminded her, necessarily as matters played out, Tvasitar had mounds of debrained daemonic bodies leftover from shortly after the Peak erupted most devastatingly long centuries past. Dead demons being definitely dispensable, there were not quite as many lying around by the time she departed the now devil-free, because one of the extra ringots wasn't empty anymore, ex-good-as-protectorate.

Conundrum cracked.

========

As for the phantom faces in the remnant crags overlooking the lava lake, Harmony reckoned they were grinning when she left Sedon's Peak.

****

3. Heady Moments

Tantalar 25, 4824 Year of the Dome – The Weirdom of Cabalarkon

The Devil in his commonest guise has two stumpy, goatish horns. So does the Moloch Sedon, eponymous as well as literal overlord of the Inner Earth of Sedon's Head. Wags such as 30-Beers sometimes refer to said Head as Sed's Shed for purposes purely alliterative. It only ever had the one horn, though, hence – duh – Sedon's Horn.

The 'duh' comes courtesy of said 30-Beers, also known as Jordan 'Q for Quill' Tethys, aka additionally the legendary 30-Year Man (or Woman), but best remembered as the Legendarian. The professional, hence inveterate, tail- as well as taleteller often features himself as the hero of his own stories.

And that in itself is more than a little odd since, with exceptions few and far between, the Hidden Headworld is close-to-congenitally predisposed to anheroism.

========

Awakening to the sound of a door opening and closing, he scratched his stubble. Manfully ignoring the almighty itching of the, to some, telltale scar in the lower part of his forehead as he did so, he stretched languorously. Propping himself up he looked toward the bathroom doorway tent-pole-expectantly.

He envisioned Morgan *'Q for Aquatic'* Abyss sloshing into their lately shared bedroom atop Cabalarkon City's ages-old Masters Palace. Being partially an amphibious Melusine, an enticing, for humans, form of Piscine, who hailed from Byronic territories in the southern Head, she'd be fresh from her morning immersion. At the hopefully bare minimum, she'd be naked.

He'd looked toward the wrong doorway.

By the time he'd readjusted his sightlines it was too late to conjure his quill, eject its splotch pad, and thence dot-draw himself to safety. This was entirely due to the fact that, much to his terminally abbreviated shock and ever-after-abiding shakes, instead of his maybe daughter (from an earlier incarnation), the Master of the Weirdom of Cabalarkon, he beheld his likely great-grandfather, arguably the Devil Himself, striding towards him third eye already flaring angrily.

At least Dark Sedon, as always male and with blood red-skin, hadn't manifested his preposterous pitchfork. That would have made for a truly holey as well as unholy death. He wasn't altogether naked either; though in a sleeveless, richly embroidered burgundy manteau, one worn overtop of nothing more than an immaculate swath of linen loincloth, he wasn't far off. Clearly, if not yet in terms of obvious erectility, he'd dressed for the anticipated ease of undressing.

Tent-pole morning wood suddenly shrivelling size-wise unto that of a dinky, well-chewed toothpick, Tethys snapped as to the why of that. When you drink upwards to thirty beers per day, you not only tend to sleep deep into the next day, you often lose track of the days themselves. He'd plain forgotten that, so long as Pyrame Silverstar possessed her, what was Morg's bed to share with whomever she pleased on Mithramas Eve became exclusively, for him and for her, Sed's bed on Mithramas Day.

He had just about enough time to give himself a mental whack across the old ear-hole before yet another 30-year lifetime ended as abruptly as it did both momentarily agonizingly and more than two decades prematurely. Devic eyefire can burn anything, including deviant flesh, crackling crispy.

========

In some respects ironically, Mithramas Year of the Dome 4824 marked precisely 448 years since Thrygragon, perhaps the singly most infamous day in Headworld history. Since he was brutally murdered no less than a half-dozen times, probably more, in a matter of one wintry afternoon, it was definitely the singly most tormented day in all his thus far limitless lifetimes.

When Tethys told the his- and her-stories of Thrygragon he often entitled it *'Feeling Theocidal'*. He probably wouldn't call any story he'd eventually tell of today's fatal encounter with the All-Father of devazurkind *'Feeling Homicidal'*, however. If anything, the Moloch had come to the Weirdom of Cabalarkon feeling amorous as well as obligatorily social.

Sed would seek to impregnate Pyrame-Lilith-Morgan with their latest Sedson. Regardless of whether their union was fruitful, he'd tarry awhile to recuperate and then tarry a few more times before getting out of bed. He'd thereupon venture down into the catacombs beneath the Citadel of the Thinkers in order to visit his Daddy Cabby, the undying Utopian who'd essentially sired him, in his sarcophagus full of life preserving, but animation suspending, Cathonic Fluid.

He'd end Mithramas as he'd been ending damn near every midwinter day since he'd released Pyrame-Lilith from All of Incain a few years shy of 4,824 years ago. He'd do so at his earthly home in Grand Elysium's beyond merely palatial pyramid. After holding court and feasting, though not on baked babies as monotheists believed; after, therefore, ever so conspicuously indulging his physicality absolutely shamelessly, to levels unattainable by man nor beast nor most other devils; he'd finally nod off, whereupon he'd wholly return to his starring role in the Sedon Sphere.

So, no, premeditation didn't enter into the killing equation. His was an act of undeniably piqued spontaneity. That Dark Sedon roasted that Legendarian that day of all days could only be considered coincidental. True, it wasn't much of a surprise. They never did like each other much but the crime was his, not Sedon's. Hardly for the first time, Jordy was simply in the wrong place at very much the wrong time.

Besides, even though Sedon forbade them killing lesser beings – for fear of the almost invariably everlasting punishment of instantaneous catasterization (aka cathonitization, but best known as ill-starring amongst their nevertheless often-unkind kind) – devils could get away with killing any Legendarian at any time.

That was because he and, in those days with only one other, non-chthonic exception, he alone kept mindfully coming back in his sons and daughters, or their sons and daughters. On top of that, who would dare even attempt (let alone dare it successfully) to penalize the Moloch Sedon, he who spent most of his time being the mighty Eye-Mouth on top of them all in the night's sky?

Not any day average Tethys, that was for sure.

========

She didn't inherit the Mastery of the Weirdom of Cabalarkon. Neither was there any of the true blue, as in pureblood Utopian, about her. There was a great deal of the true blue, as in aquatic, about her, however. That meant she had to take the non-traditional, but long ago established as honourable route to achieve it.

She had to earn the unswerving, psychical support of the real powers behind its throne, that of the idiots of Weir. Which she did; then she had to keep it.

========

"THERE YOU ARE, WHORE."

"Here I most certainly am, Sed."

"WHAT – NOT MASTER?"

"I'm the Master. At best you're the whoreson."

"WHAT'VE YOU DONE TO SILVERSTAR, PISCINE?"

"First, I'm a Melusine Piscine, and then only maternally. Second, it isn't Pyrame you care about and we both know it. We also know that I've been, um, sharing her company of late. So I shouldn't have to tell you that the tiresome old darling remains something of the intractable, as well as inexplicable, romantic when it comes to you.

"I'm anything but of course; couldn't be anything but or my butt wouldn't be in this throne. Fortunately, as annoying as carrying her around like a satchel of shit was until relatively recently, she proved not as inextricable as I at first feared she would. That said, as for the one you do care about, her I kept.

"Next question you have to ask yourself more than me is how flammable is she?"

Having been rendered a throwaway slab of thoroughly charcoaled meat mere minutes earlier, Jordan *'Q for Quill'* Tethys was dancing the legless limbo, as he commonly postulated his state of being when he was between incarnations. As an utterly unaware soul-self in what might well be Limbo, or some sort of deadhead-oblivion similar to it, he would have had no idea what precisely happened after his latest killer either materialized or, less likely, stomped into Morg's throne room.

Quill Tethys would have been able to describe Morgan Abyss, however. As a Piscine, let alone as a Melusine Piscine, both properly capitalized, the gills behind the ears were a given. So were the slightly scaly skin, the fleshy folds between her fingers and toes, what made them akin to paddles, the excessively sharp teeth and the overlong nails, which verged on fangs and claws respectively.

Were he around, having been sleeping with her for a few days he could and would, for a beer or thirty, delineate the curves, orifices and protuberances of her body in micrometric detail. He would happily say her forehead was a little too broad, even oblong, somewhat flat and oddly depilated, as if she shaved off not only her eyebrows, but her forelocks as well. (Which she did; he'd helped her do it a couple of nights previously. And that wasn't all she shaved, he'd have added with a wink and a gestural nudge, nudge.)

Her wispy hair, which flowed down her strangely pronounced spine like a glistening waterfall, was reddish with streaks of silver highlights that she might have dabbed on herself. The reddishness was one of the reasons he – most recently, in 4824, a he, put better – suspected she might be one of his daughters or granddaughters. Male or female, when white-skinned he or she often had thin, reddish hair. By contrast most Piscines of either sex had white or otherwise colourless hair.

Another reason was that a couple of incarnations earlier, when he just happened to be a white guy with reddish hair, he'd mated with a mermaid. Mermaids (not to be confused with naiads, who were faerie farts) gave birth to Piscines; indeed, dependent on the sub-species, some Piscines morphed into mermaids when they were fertile. Piscines also had human lifetimes, she was about the right age to have been the fruit of that Jordy's loins and, besides, Morgan Abyss did sound a little like Jordan Tethys.

The silver streaks, though, were definitely reminiscent of Pyrame Silverstar, the devil who, self-admittedly, had been occupying her, on and off, for a number of years now. Other than Sedon Himself, the self-determined, fabulously female Perpetual Presence was the only devil that could function in the Weirdom of Cabalarkon.

That Sed, the lone, always male, Perpetual Presence, could was testament to his near-omnipotence beneath the Dome. Which after all was made up mostly of his essence, thus the Sedon Sphere. That she could, alone of all second or third generational devils, had everything to do with a flaw built into Weir's eye-staves by their designers on the de facto first Weir World, which had been obliterated many, many, multiple multi-millennia earlier. They simply didn't affect her.

It was Pyrame whom Quill Tethys drew himself here to see. It wasn't his idea but there were some Master Devas he never said no to and, his devic half-parents being Lazaremists, one of them was his eldest aunt on both sides of the bed. That'd be Datong Harmonia, the Unity of Balance. Moderately intriguingly, even though she was a much lower born Mithradite, Pyrame was another.

Devils possessed others, yes, but they had daemonic, subtle matter bodies of their own. While that made them shape-shifters they tended to retain an outwardly consistent look. With or without three eyes, when she appeared as a standard human, Pyrame presented herself as drop-dead beautiful, which Morg wasn't – at least she wasn't by many men's reckoning. When not going about as a non-human, in disguise or with a tetrahedral head, Pyrame also always sported silver hair, which Morg didn't naturally have.

Over the more than eight centuries of his recurring existence, he and Pyrame had become friends. She'd never deigned to sleep with him before, not as herself anyhow, and in a way she still hadn't. It was 2-eyed Morg who came to him that first night, 2-eyed Morg who spoke to him in her voice, not Pyrame's, and 2-eyed Morg who invited him to stay with her in the Master's bedroom every subsequent night up to and including last night, Mithramas Eve.

A procreative imperative, combined with daily consumption of upwards to thirty beers, might explain how he failed to notice the ring Morg kept on when she didn't have anything else on. As for why he failed to look into the bag of trinkets Harmony asked him to bring up here, and then have Pyrame-Morg deposit in Cabalarkon's Stopstone-lined vault alongside thousands of reputedly full, extraterrestrial eyeorbs, hey, love is far more blinding than binding.

He could no more refuse Auntie Harm than any man, woman or child, human or otherwise, could refuse your mother's nipple when you were a wee, babe-in-arms nipper. Unfortunately for not just that him, Harmony wasn't just even more droppants gorgeous than Pyrame Silverstar, at least she wasn't to almost everyone with the alleged exception of the Moloch Sedon.

Evidently she was burnt-dead duplicitous.

========

Until 4725 Year of the Dome – Mythland, The Jewel of Sedon's Crown

Pyrame loved him, yes, but Sedon didn't love her. He used her. One way or another their deviant, always mortal, but sometimes curiously short-lived half-sons, the sedons (small case), helped maintain the Cathonic Dome. That, to learned speculators, suggested Pyrame wasn't really their half-mom; that Primeval Lilith, the thought-immortal queen of earthborn demons, had that honour.

Probably from his perspective alone, since it was forever unrequited, the mighty Moloch's lone great love was Methandra Thanatos, Mithras's Virgin.

========

The putative Devil could never be accused of being imaginative. Neither, in their interminable efforts to maximize the quantity and concomitant fanaticism of their individual followers, could his descendant devils ever be accused of passivity. Mindful of it being well into the Era of Empires by then, Pyrame Silverstar decided she could do more than he ever would in terms of eliminating she whom Pyrame felt amounted to her only beyond-momentary threat to his lustful attentions.

Devic protectorates had already proved inviolable only insofar as a preponderance of their populace revered their overlords and overladies unconditionally. Methandra's Mythland, once the Jewel of Sedon's Crown, proved stunningly easy to violate at least twice. In 4725 YD the Pauper Priestess, called such because she had neither a people to call her own, nor a place to call her home, stood poised to complete its re-conquering.

She, ostentatiously riding a winged she-sphinx of Headworld notoriety, entered it exultantly. They were at the head of an army numbering in the thousands. Every one of them worshipped her devic allies at the time. Significantly, none of those with her were her devic allies. The reason for that was that the celebrated she-sphinx she rode was none other than All of Incain, who ate devils.

Save for one person, an Intuit hand-talker like most of its Crimson Queen's adherents, Mythland was empty. That person offered her a mug of locally produced pilsner. "Nothing like glacial meltwater for fine pills," she said, signing as she imparted essentially the same meaning mentally.

Pyrame took it, had a sip. She agreed, tentatively but also non-vocally – devils, being bodiless spirits both originally and for most of their largely extraterrestrial existence, were used to employing telepathy in order to communicate. "I've always been more of the white wine aficionado myself. But, hey, who am I dispute a connoisseur like you, Jordy?"

"Who indeed?" replied the Legendarian immodestly, albeit with an acknowledging nod of her head to go along with hand-signs. "I've a message for you by the way. It's from the Thanatoids nowadays exclusively of Lathakra. Rather, I've a message from them for you to pass on to your bubbly boyfriend. You'll appreciate why I'm reluctant to deliver it to him, the joy above us all, personally."

"He'd kill you and, no matter how often that happens, getting killed hurts."

"Except this time he might decide to do it really, really slowly."

========

Tantalar 25, 4824 Year of the Dome – The Weirdom of Cabalarkon

A hundred years earlier, the Legendarian, a female Intuit at the time, gave Pyrame Silverstar a message from the last two remaining Mithradite firstborn. She was to pass it on to the devils' mutual grandfather, the Moloch Sedon.

The message wasn't 'We'll be back to retake Mythland'. It was: "We'll be back once we've taken the rest of Sedon's Head!"

========

"THAT RING ... THAT'S WHERE YOU SUCKED HER!"

Everyone knew Dark Sedon didn't speak so much as boom. Still, not being there to record it any which way, including accurately, the Legendarian would have had to intuit, non-capitalized, if not out and out invent, also not capitalized, the dialogue that transpired between them in the Masters' throne room after the Devil howsoever-entered it, 4-pronged pitchfork in all probability in hand by then.

He wouldn't have had to conjecture that it would be packed with citizen-petitioners; next-to-imperceptibly-aging idiots and their usually similarly well-preserved caregivers alike; Morg's faithful, superbly educated Illuminary advisors, many of whom nevertheless came across as only borderline-competent; and her Trinondev Warriors Elite, the supposedly single-minded cream of a very suspect crop.

It was at that time quotidian, as in every day she publicly attended to affairs of state. However, he would have had to guess, not that it was overly important anymore, as to who and how many. Similarly he couldn't be positive what Morg was wearing at the time. But he'd have no problem making that up either.

Dependant on where you were, and how much beer you were supplying for free, he'd draw her on his splotch pad, the tablecloth if you fancied a memento to take home with you, or in the air itself if he was showing off. Obliging sort that he was, he'd proceed to draw her dressed in whatever you wanted.

(Assuming you wanted her dressed in anything, which not many did. Tethys nudes, even ones he didn't sign, were prized almost as much as his landscapes. Like the latter, the former weren't just breathlessly beautiful; they were so real looking it almost seemed like you could breathe the air they depicted.)

Should he be describing her verbally, and not visually, the word 'brocade' would feature heavily in his vocabulary. Silk, linen, wool, you name it; she loved natural fabrics for their feel as much as she did for their decorative potential. She also hated the crap Utopian replication units produced in terms of clothing as much she did the crud they did for eating – what kept the wing-nuts of Weir thriving long into their second, third and sometimes even fourth or fifth centuries of life. She was fond of primary colours, reds and blues predominantly, so go from there.

He'd drawn her throne a few times. It appeared unique to the airy world, if not necessarily to any of the Headworld's numerous undersea realms. She claimed she'd fabricated it out of coral somehow softened for facility of manipulation. Next, presumably Piscine-proprietarily, she'd hardened it for functionality. She'd undoubtedly fashioned it impressively. If she wanted to present herself as a formidable ruler, one you messed with on pain of dying very nastily indeed, then she'd succeeded.

Identical facsimiles of golden-skinned sea monsters constituted its foot-and-armrests. Two more of the horrors overarched her head. With demonically glowing, burning coal eyeballs, wickedly razor-sharp teeth, thornily extrusive backbones and serrated, saw-toothed fins, they were truly terrible to behold. She'd assured Tethys they were based on the real thing as well. Which almost made him foreswear swimming – in anything except beer, albeit figuratively, it nearly went without saying.

Other than Trinondev eyeorbs, the main reason Master Devas in particular stayed away from the Weirdom was because its Master controlled the so-called – by Utopians – Six Sacred Objects. These were the Male Three: the Mask of Byron, the Cross of Mithras and Lazareme's Cloak of Many Colours; and the Female Three: the Soul of Devaura, the Body of Demeter and the Mind of Sapiendev.

Most Masters of Weir – until recently, Morg among them – were as terrified of them as most devils were, and that included the two remaining Great Gods, Byron and Lazareme. Consequently most Masters kept them sealed within the same Solidium vault wherein they kept prison pods scavenged from their grounded (mostly in the Hills of the Sleepers) and thereafter left-derelict, millennial or generational ships.

Universally, these not-so-stunningly still extant eyeorbs, as prison pods were most commonly called, contained devic Spirit Beings the Trinondevs' predecessors nailed during the Utopians seemingly interminable, pre-Earth pursuit of the Sedonshem throughout the then-known multiverse multi-millennia in the past. Hypothetically, that they'd been manufactured off planet – many on the first Weir World before Weir Star, going supernova, consumed it – explained their therefore hardly surprising durability.

To the best anyone could tell, both shut down as soon as they filled up. As much as that meant there was no immediately discernable distinction between ancient and modern eyeorbs, what if there was?

Again in theory, the ancients ones should start operating to the extent of their capacity as soon as they were purged. Yet, for those desirous of testing them as to the maximum scope of their potency, in comparison to the ones the Weirdom's self-repairing replication units churned out these days, that probability alone militated against experimentation. Curiosity didn't just kill cats.

For starters, obviously, you'd first have to release those they held. But what if the relatively modern day prison pods couldn't recapture devils first inhumed so pre-Earth long ago? There was no sensible way to answer that. There couldn't be. Why risk the pudding for the proof?

After all, who needed, let alone wanted, more devils loose in the world, the more so if they were super-powerful ones like the seven still extant firstborns? Not the Utopians of here nor any other Weirdom, if there were any left by then, which arguably there weren't by late 4824. That was as certain as sunrise, even here beneath the Cathonic Dome.

But – take this seriously please, she'd say to pre-differently-inflamed lover, Quill Tethys – should they be cleared, what if the ancient ones proved to have supplementary functions that no one either remembered or recorded next-to-endlessly long ago? What if, once vacated, they could then be used, collectively, to take out Sedon Himself? If it worked, might the risk be retrospectively hailed as well worth the taking?

Not according to any Master of any Weirdom anywhere on the Whole Earth post-Dome. Then again, virtually all the Masters of any Weirdom, ones that anyone – including the two, to-this-day, still recurring deviants, the Legendarian and the Goat, Pusan Wanderlust – could recall with any degree of confidence, had turned out to be craven crayfish, again to quote Cabalarkon's then reigning Master, Morgan Abyss.

Because Cabalarkon the Undying Utopian lay inanimate deep within the catacombs of Cabalarkon the city proper, Dark Sedon safeguarded Cabalarkon the Weirdom, his Devic Eye-Land. Its cowardly Masters were too afraid of losing his protection to do what they should have been doing all along: exerting their anti-devil goodwill and no matter how unwelcome influence, as well as their not inconsiderable might, trying anything to annihilate said Sedon and his diabolical descendants.

At least so she'd passionately complain before she got back to doing what Quill Tethys definitely did take seriously, as well as both pleasurably and, yes, passionately.

========

Pyrame dutifully delivered the Thanatoids' warning of a century past. She did so because Heat and Cold were her elders in Mithras and, despite their messenger's undeniable Lazaremist background, devils generally did as their elders instructed. Not at all astonishingly, the Moloch Sedon back then laughed it off as a fantasy threat coming from minds fermented by frustration as much as anything else.

A hundred years later, Datong Harmonia, the Unity of Balance, gave an again male Legendarian a sealed bag of clattering, but otherwise unidentified trinkets. This time Pyrame, occupying Morgan Abyss, was not to pass it, a kibisis, onto Sedon. She, rather Master Morgan, was to lock it away from him.

It didn't quite happen that way. Because of that, the message Intuit Quill gave Pyrame, so comparatively long ago in human terms, at last verged on fulfilment.

========

The monstrous, golden-skinned horrors that arched over her throne and made up its foot and armrests doubled as the House Abyss family totems. Although deliberately mutated, and therefore intentionally as well as ferociously enhanced, they were essentially dolphins. That made them mammalian, like her; save for the gills behind the ears, that is. Nonetheless, Morg declared herself an insatiable, flesh-eating shark, especially when compared to her jellyfish predecessors.

These days she wore or wielded the six Great Godly Glories as openly as she did both proudly and defiantly. Some she incorporated into her personal chain of office: a necklace of ruby-red bloodstones upon which was attached a golden triangle with a single eye staring out of it – this last, the Eye of Providence, being Pyrame's symbol more so than that of the Mastery. Others would have been woven into her garments; unless they were her garments, which was even more likely.

Dark Sedon would have realized right away which of the transmutable Tvasitar talismans was which. The ring he would have been referring to wasn't any of them. It had never been part of any Master of Weir's regular regalia either, though perhaps it would henceforth.

The Mighty Moloch must have been paying attention, likely on a nightly basis, to what the Thanatoids and their cross-tribal cronies had been doing to his Head for most of the previous hundred or so years. As a result, unless his eye-mouth in the sky was blind, which it wasn't, he had to have realized what the presumably relatively recent fabrications of Tvasitar Smithmonger, the anvil artificer of Sedon's Peak, did.

Experientially chary devils loyal to the Lathakran Empire – Lathakra being over ten decades no longer Sedon's cathartic cataract, and centuries more no longer his Headworld's Horn – used suchlike *'ringots'* to diminish, if not altogether eliminate, whatever dangers the by then spirits-only leftovers of their vanquished foes might yet present.

Plainly, regardless of how Morg did it, Sedon's Whore, Pyrame Silverstar, had to be the then most recent Master Deva thusly confined.

========

"Suckered then sucked her into it, Sed."

========

Sedon would never have been happy with such an arrogant assertion; again always assuming it was uttered. Morg-Lilith, no longer a three-thing, wouldn't have been content with it either. The consequential two-thing, a had-to-be high-level Hellion fused with a definitely top-drawer demon, would have felt an irresistible need to gloat.

"We had to release the terrifically-talented smithy first but, hey, I don't need ringots to capture devils any more than my Trinondevs do. Plus, luckily for us," she might have then provided, significantly as well as indicatively, "We need only one modern day pod per devil. That leaves all these just for you."

"I COME HERE TO VISIT CABBY MY DADDY AT THIS TIME EVERY YEAR. I'VE DONE SO FOR THOUSANDS OF YEARS. AND EVERY YEAR YOUR JERK-OFF WAR-RIORS SEEK TO SHRED ME INTO THEIR VAUNTED EYEORBS, BODY, SOUL AND MIND.

"IT'S EVER A WASTE OF THEIR TIME, NOT MINE. THEIR FEEBLE WEAPONRY IS USELESS AGAINST ME."

Existentially, eyeorbs were the last ditch depository for a great many of his devic descendants; vastly too many, if his memory really did go back to their gestation beneath Weir Star as he said it did. From First Weir's thereafter-predictable beginning of its crusade against them, to this day, and likely ongoing until neither a soul nor a spirit survived of either species, they were the major weapons in the Utopians' arsenal.

Consequently correctly called prison pods; consequently pathetically dot-ditto, at least as far as Sedon, his remaining sons and their resultantly decimated offspring must have been concerned; they topped Trinondev eye-staves, they in their tens of dozens, and Morg's Master's Mace, it in its singularity.

For purposes pretentious as well as prophylactic, hundreds of Trinondevs gathered in the Master's throne room every day she held court. There would have been at least that many there when, one way or another, the mighty Eye-Mouth usually in the sky burst into it bloody-skinned-bodily. Orbs could manifest gargoyles. In her case, her Master's Mace manifested a Death's Head, one with 3-eyes.

Right this minute, every one of tertiary them – and every eyeball glaring out of every gargoyle manifested in the throne room, no matter how many of them there were, eyes or gargoyles – must have focused on Sed's stereotypically satanic skull.

The ambush, for that was what it was, had been planned to precision. Even if no one except the two of them could be sure as to whether Primeval Lilith still existed, everyone knew of the extraordinarily persistent, love-hate relationship between the Devil and his Pauper Priestess.

Whether mad at her for not waiting in bed for him, or worried that something untoward had happened to her, he'd have to come hither in quest of Pyrame Silverstar, his main squeeze for literal aeons before she arguably acquired the lethally luscious Lily. He wouldn't have been counting, let alone caring, how many Warriors Elite were there. Neither would he have noted the antiquity of their eyeorbs.

To him, like male or female Utopians, respectively black or white as they properly were in Cabalarkon, regardless of the approaching boundless, wilfully bewildering varieties of house and personal gargoyles they projected about the Trinondevs, one eyeorb atop one eye-stave, looked much the same as any other. Hellion Morg, unless Primeval Lilith was by now the demon-dominant one, would have calculated that just as perfectly.

"ARE YOU TRYING TO TELL ME THIS YEAR IS SOME-HOW DIFFERENT?"

Morg might have waved expansively. She might have communicated with them non-verbally, via their eyeorbs, which you didn't need to be a Master or, for that matter, an Intuit to do. Howsoever she did it, she would have signalled the multitude of blue-clad, veils-drawn, armed-and-armoured Trinondev Warriors Elite assembled therein to mentally open their orbs both yawningly and consumptively.

"Not trying, Sed. I'm confirming it."

========

Or words to that effect!

****

4. Mysteries Most Maddening

On or around Imbolc Day 4824 Year of the Dome – Elsewhere on the Head

It wasn't usually but, for a brief period, her bed was bedlam.

========

Not much more than a month after Star Sedon stopped lighting up the night's sky, Harmony's High Seat rocked soothingly as it rolled along rails she'd rather whimsically set atop the Gypsium Wall. She was in nymph mode – not to be confused with lymph node – so it was hardly the first time she'd been in bed with a double-horned, fur and follicle faun. It was, however, the first time she'd been horned as in gored by one, deliberately and severely, a demon thence to obliterate.

Put better, she'd subsequently protest, she remembered it starting out as a faun. It definitely secreted faun-like pheromones, what made it impossible to resist. That she succumbed to it was therefore easy to rationalize away, if never to relish anytime afterwards. That she had so much trouble remembering his name, let alone what he looked like, if it was a *'he'* and not an *'it'*, wasn't so much explicable as it was extricable.

True, assuming suchlike soulless abominations had an actual sex and not just semblances of sex organs, what it did to her had everything to do with what it was. So did whatever it injected more so than ejaculated into her; the thingy that tried to devour her internally even as its instilling operative attempted to do a dick-dildo externally.

Semi-serendipitously, also in retrospect, something similar had afflicted her previously – albeit by herself, or itself, and more than seven centuries prior to Xuthros Hor unleashing the Genesea – when a perhaps only partially daemonic mestiza by the name of Hecate successfully took her over for a number of days, weeks or months. She therefore knew what was happening to her in approximate terms and how to deal with it in both specific as well as reflexive terms.

Altogether serendipitously, she was where she was. Snapping to that, she tumbled out of bed, dispelled her High Seat and absorbed a great whack of the Wall into herself. Gypsium was Solidium's counteragent. Chthonic critters were composed mostly of the latter whereas, as its name gave away, the Wall was almost exclusively the former.

Melting unto a pustules-popping puddle went the bipartite beastie, the entire time shrieking agonized but, to her ears, gratifying screams until it finally vaporized.

========

Especially with respect to his whereabouts, Abe Chaos was not so fortunate. Later on, however, he tried to make a nearly identical excuse for much the same spume of near-spontaneous self-indulgence. His, though, had nothing to do with fauns, half-daemonic or otherwise.

Lustfulness was upon him, yes, but it was in the form of Beguiling Belialma, Sinistral Lust of Satanwyck (which devils thought of as Sedon's Temple). It was her body-birthday and they were frolicking celebratorily. Body-birthday or not, they did that occasionally anyhow, and anywhere, and any which way. Today also being Imbolc, on both sides of the Dome, they were within her bastion of bliss above Pandemonium, the Temple's frenzied, ever-changing and sometimes all-encompassing capital city.

As usual with her, she wasn't just upon him. She was all over him. What he didn't notice, because he was too busy being all over her, was that she was bodily putting out more than herself and hence what passed for her sweat. If no souls as such, Mother Earth did impart to her existential excretions degrees of sentience to go along with an ability to shift shapes. The stickiness they oozed was, as a result, more like Mother Earth's quick-drying excrement.

In short order he'd be as hard as an immobilized statue of him could be, including nothing short about it.

========

As for Lord Order, his justification for what befell him on Imbolc Day, Belialmam 4824, did have a big hairy deal to do with fauns, on both sides of the bed.

Pusan Wanderlust was a faun; or a fauna, as she preferred. Known additionally as Trailblazer and Wayfarer, but commonly and most monosyllabically as Goat, she was also one of two deviants that kept coming back to life via her children or their children, any one of whom she'd revitalize should she have been off dancing the legless limbo while they teetered on the abyss of dying.

Unlike Quill Tethys, though, Pusan always came back in her daughters or granddaughters. She never came back in her sons or grandsons because she never gave birth to boys and neither did her offspring, thereby avoiding the imbecility that so often came with inbreeding.

Pusan's inseminating father was another onetime recurring deviant: none other than Chrysaor Attis, the celebrated golden-brown warrior many once thought of as the Universal Soldier. Attis hadn't come back since Thrygragon whereas Pusan had been around for well over 1500 years longer than Quill.

Yajur and her consequently went way, way back. The Lightning Lord also didn't mind shifting his shape into that of a satyr in order to accommodate her preference for fellow fauns. What he in his Thunder Dome – his principal domicile within the Forever Forest of Wildwyck, where she'd sought him out – did mind was how distracted she acted. Except for one thing, he would have felt insulted. Ordinarily sex blinkered fauns. When thusly engaged in it they never, ever, lost their concentration.

Pusan's inability to enjoy what she took the greatest pleasure doing struck him as so strange he read her. She was coated and it wasn't just with downy fleece. Her coat being in the process of attempting to coat him immobile, he struck her dead. Which was permissible because lesser beings didn't keep coming back to life; not consciously, with their minds and memories intact, they didn't anyhow.

He did so as he would, by electrocuting her. Next he electrified the Thunder Dome in order to make sure whatever demonic disease she'd caught hadn't brought friends. Then, because earthborn horrors spent most of their time hanging out there, he went to Hell. Where he eventually found some statuary very interesting indeed.

The temptation to do more than just say *'terminate'* was irresistible.

========

"Admirable quality," Datong Harmonia observed as she stepped out of the Weird and into Bouncing Belle's private quarters on the uppermost level of her bastion of bliss, overlooking Pandemonium, the abode of all demons, as it did. "Priapus might not be jealous but he better pretend to be."

"Should have realized you'd show up just in time to ruin my fun."

"Fun's a relative term, Sparky. So are you. And so is Abe."

"And Lust?"

"Her? You can leave her a statue."

========

Unholy Abaddon, the Unity of Chaos's solidifying statue rather, exploded. Abe Chaos shook off the stiffness even as he did the settling dust. Stifling an urge to cough, as well as to spit, he glared at Lord Ordure. No demon, not even a denim demon (as his over-coating must have been), could harden him irrevocably. He was too much a force of nature for that. But if any devil might want to suborn a demon willing to try it, it'd be his hated triplet brother.

Yajur glared back, materializing his lightning sword mercifully still sheathed and the sheath itself strapped to his back. Abe reciprocated, materializing his trident, which was actually the sheath of his Black Blade of, what else, Chaos. They must have reminded Harmony of roosters frilling their feathers and flapping their wings before they got down to the bloody business of pecking each other to death – a death so necessarily preparatory to cock-cooks plucking the loser for the pot.

For her part of the pantomime, she materialized naught. Nor did she de-materialize anything, including, no doubt disappointingly for her two immediate brothers, any shred of her glittering clothing. Instead she flashed her golden smile, thereby instantly restoring what passed for peace between them.

Ringots, Harmony likely reflected, would be useless against them. Neither would ever surrender to the other and no one else would be able to come close to disarming them. If she wasn't around, watch out Hidden Headworld just for starters. Her immediate siblings would pulp the planet, and everyone in it, even as they pulped each other until there was nothing left of anything.

She earned her godhood if only by standing forever between them.

========

Post Imbolc Day 4824 Year of the Dome – Elsewhere on the Head

Concluding Belialma had to be responsible for trying to take him out, at the apparent as well as irrational cost of taking herself out too, the three firstborn Lazaremists left Lust as is, as a statue. They didn't leave it, her in it, there, though. They took it to their father's external residence on Tympani, the Isle of the Undying One, in the Aural Sea, Sedon's Ear. No one would dare mess with it there, especially not in his Age.

As per uncooperatively usual with them, they thereupon went their separate ways; haystacks worth of tangled threads to unravel a dot-ditto, in their own way. Too bad, as winter slowly staggered towards spring and the Lathakrans inched closer and closer to Grand Elysium, suchlike perplexities continued to resist resolution. Worse, they piled the more up as, at the same time, more and more devils disappeared without a trace.

Whenever she tracked him down, Lord Order – or Ordure, as Chaos would have it – admitted frustration at his ongoing inability to puzzle them out. Then again he didn't have the persistence or the patience she had when it came to investigating anything. For a change, Abe couldn't provide any insights either.

However, his offhand remark that devils had conceded suzerainty of the Upper Head to the Lathakrans, and that therefore the conquering collective no longer had any use for ringots, did beget cattish curiosity as to why Grand Elysium's priesthood were being so obstinate. Why refuse to surrender the city? And what's with the preposterous obstructionism?

Why supply and support the roads-wrecking, crops-ruining, traps-deploying insurgents and saboteurs, the hit and run guerrilla fighters, the resistant militias and the pitiful little battles they provoked? Why bother bogging down the Lathakrans with such petty annoyances? They were only delaying the inevitable. But they were doing so to the mounting fury of the theocrats' ever-oncoming enemies. Surely there'd be hell to pay.

The stock response Elysium's elite gave to emissaries sent by the Lathakran brain trust made only marginal sense. Sure, Star Sedon shone no longer. But that didn't mean the, to them, holy city's holinesses would risk the mighty Moloch's wrath by giving it away gratis. The Thanatoids wanted it; they'd have to take it, bleeding their armies dry every puttering plod of the mucky way. They took it; they'd have to suffer the consequences of offending their virtually omnipotent grandfather themselves.

Tantal and Methandra were prepared to do just that, Chaos confided to Harmony. Once they arrived at Elysium's outskirts, they'd have their forces surround it, yes, but then they'd have them down stakes. The pair of them would thereupon enter the metropolis alone, parade bodily through it, stride unabashed into the Devil Sedon and Pyrame Silverstar's absurdly huge pyramid, and plop themselves down on their thrones – assuming they had such things, which Abe didn't know because he resolutely avoided suchlike crude displays of authority over others.

Granddaddy should feel free to object to what they were doing at any time along the way. Of course he could have done that at anytime after they first shipped their armies across the Sea of Clouds to Lathakra, half a decade shy of a century ago now. He never had before Mithramas and his star hadn't been seen since it. That said, she prodded the more: What if he suddenly reappeared and chose to do just that?

Then they'd probably walk right back out again, her brother smirked, clearly delighting in the prospect. Unless, he qualified, they rocketed out asses-backwards once Sed gave them the anything but proverbial boot to their backsides. Chaos would ensue but it was his kind of chaos, the one written in small case with lots of exclamatory squiggles.

Precisely, Harmony countered, spoiling his fun just as she had Yajur's a while back in Satanwyck. (Who else would have the nerve?) So, she posed aloud, risking repetition, why wouldn't the city fathers figure the same thing and, if not surrender as such, then stand aside and let Dark Sedon take care of the Thanatoids himself? Neither thought the question relevant to her inquiries but both reckoned it an imponderable nonetheless.

Her immediate brothers were hardly the only Lazaremists she plumbed for clues and/or hints hopefully leading to the relief of revelations. Nor were they the only tribe she consulted. To a Jack or Jill man or woman of them, what was left of the Mithradites purported the same bafflement she did. And what was left of them no longer included fourth-born Zuvem Nergalis, aka both Planter and Gravedigger, and fifth born Yama Nergal, King Harvest, two of the Thanatoids' highest born and most loyal tribesmen.

They were among the recently gone-missing devils whose absence presumably couldn't be ascribed to ringots or Abe would have told her they'd been nailed after she had Quill Tethys take the kibisis full of the reprehensible things to Pyrame in Cabalarkon. (She couldn't let them loose for fear the next time they challenged the Thanatoids and/or their highest born allies, they'd be cathonitized irretrievably.)

As for whether Lady Lust had had a chance to sic her demons on more than just the Unities, Harmony had thus far failed to uncover any proof of that. Nevertheless, when he wasn't fecundating Fecundity, which he apparently had been when Abe went to Pandemonium in order to fill the void he left behind, Zuvem had been Satanwyck's co-regent as well as a regular co-occupant of Bouncing Belle's bastion of bliss. Because of that, it was tempting to point an accusing finger at him and possibly the other two Nergalids, Yama and their bi-lunar-monthly mate, Nergal Vetala, for masterminding the hence despicable conspiracy to eliminate rival devils.

Except Vetala – whom Harmony found easily at her new residence in the former Weirdom of Manoa, on the lower west coast of the Penile Peninsula, Sedon's Mutton Chop – convincingly denied their involvement. As well as confirming Zuvem's whereabouts at the time of the New Moon at issue (*"It was his turn!"*), she was the first to ask a rather obvious, corollary question: If the others had been turned into statuary, then where were their statues?

Scrying by means of a crystal ball or some such revelatory medium wasn't a knack common to many devils. Her second-born sister in Lazareme (Titanic Metis during the Middle Sea matriarchy, or Metisophia as Illuminaries named her most of a thousand years afterwards) did have as her power focus a witch's cauldron. But she'd been taken out and stuck in a ringot years earlier.

As for Quill and his quill, Rumour of Lazareme's power focus, she wasn't about to travel up to Cabalarkon, that most perilous of places for Master Devas, and risk getting slurped into a Trinondev prison pod for her troubles. Besides, even if he no longer chose to shine upstairs, these days' altogether-dark Sedon might object, very demonstratively, should any devil other than Pyrame approach Daddy Cabby, his thought-father.

The remaining Mithradites were only moderately mollified by Harmony's pro-testations of personal blamelessness. True, she didn't support the Thanatoids and the rest of their highborn collective of Master Devas. She never had. She thought the sheer endlessness of the Era of Empires unconscionable, an appalling disgrace to devakind. All this loss of life was so wasteful, wouldn't you agree?

Yajur and his supporters did. And among the latter the Lightning Lord could count more than a few of their siblings. Dandset Typhon of Ophir-Moorset and Geld Neargon of Androgynia, a pair of sixth-born Mithradites who shared the Head's occipital regions with him, were only the two highest born. Both of these last, though, counted among the missing.

Their father Lazareme was just as disgusted. But his way was always the way of total freedom, wasn't it. He wasn't about to intervene; probably never would. You reaped what you sowed, he always said. Maybe the Mithradites' reaper, King Harvest, had simply sown the wrong sow and ended up as hardened, somewhere, as brother Abe did briefly and bouncing Belialma thus far fittingly remained.

Harmony was also quick to point out that as many or more Lazaremists as Mithradites had vanished since Star Sedon did. On top of that, she and her two firstborn brothers had been among Lady Lust's first targets – unless of course she was herself a target of whoever was targeting them.

Aha, flashed some of the more perspicacious among them, especially Belialma's fellow Apple Goddess, Kore-Coueranna, and her bull, formerly both Mithras's Bull and Belle's Baal, Cruel Plathon, a second and third born respectively. Could the Byronics of Godbad say the same thing? She heard that very enquiry so frequently Harmony finally started to wonder a dot-ditto herself.

For her aimless wondering begot purposeful wandering.

========

Harmony, with the first letter commonly capitalized, journeyed to the subcontinent of Aka-Godbad: Sedon's Mouth, Lower Teeth, Lip, Jaw and Goatee on a map of the Hidden Headworld. Harmony, without the first letter capitalized except at the beginning of a sentence, greeted her wherever she went within it. That form of harmony, harmoniousness, also greeted her wherever she went underwater-it.

She hated it when that happened.

========

With the foremost exceptions of the two Silverclouds (who continued to rule the former Weirdom of Kanin City, adjacent to Sedon's Mole, in the name of their father, but who were actually with the Lathakrans body, soul and mind), as well as some of the other higher born (who were currently imprisoned within All on Incain), most of the Byronics hid out in Godbad.

Hundreds of years before the Thanatoids threatened to invade it, their Great God of a father declared the entire subcontinent – together with its undersea realms, one of which Morgan Abyss was born in – off-limits to non-tribe members. That made it the second most dangerous place for her to go after Cabalarkon; hence her venturing into it not so much incognito – even in disguise she couldn't help being too pretty to escape notice – as either invisibly or by body-bouncing undetectably.

In truth, even though he joined them on the Mithramas day in 4376 when they ganged up on the Thrygragos whose feast it was, Bodiless Byron had been disinclined to communicate civilly with either her or her father since Thrygragon. Then again the Unmoving One rarely communicated with anyone, even his own offspring, except through his smoky mouthpiece. That'd be the always-particulate Sedona Spellbinder, as Illuminaries had her.

A second-born Byronic, one of that Great God's Primary Nucleoids, she'd come to detest upper echelon Lazaremists in particular. After all, Byronics not only acknowledged the Age of Lazareme, they apportioned adulation accordingly. Rewards wrought responsibilities, did they not.

Of course they did. Smoky Sedona would therefore appear to be quite right, as well as well within her rights, when she asserted Harmony and her family members, the highborn more so than their Lord Laziest Father, should have prevented the expansion of the Empire of Lathakra. That acknowledged, as Harmony was hardly alone to remark, her indignation wasn't altogether altruistic.

No matter how maternally oriented they might be, devils hated to lose adherents. Naturally they hated to lose them to anyone. However, they found it especially humiliating to lose them to siblings or, even worse, cousins born below them on the devic devotion meter.

Harmony reckoned, probably just as rightly, that most of Sedona's complaint gestated when the Empire expanded into her unofficial realm, the multitude of populated islands dotting Lake Sedona (after her). Because of Chaos's complicity, and hers and Order's corresponding cowardice, their fear of riling him, Lake Sedona and for practical purposes virtually all of the Penile Peninsula now belonged to an almost unbearably lowly, twelfth born Mithradite Moon Goddess.

Amongst devils Nergal Vetala was better known as Fecundity. This was due to her propensity for becoming pregnant, with azuras, once the moon waxed unto near-nothingness, then having them when it, and she, reached fully bulbous fructification. In addition to Vetalazurs, her azuras were deemed, just as unimaginatively, Nergalazurs if their sires were one or the other male Nergalid, Planter-Zuvem or Reaper-Yama.

That they'd gone bye-bye, even if Grower-Vetala hadn't, strongly intimated Sedona and her equally inaccessible father could be guilty of their disappearances. Further to that, the Lathakrans coveted the Byronics' Godbadian worshippers, so the Mithradites' allegations could yet prove well-founded.

Perhaps Harmony should count the whole tribe, over a hundred of them, prime suspects.

========

Since she never swore an unbreakable oath to stay out of Godbad, she entered it clandestinely more than a few times prior to returning to the Laughing Lands for the promised fall of Elysium. Once in awhile she manifested herself in front of a carefully chosen cadre of her more independently minded cousins in the Unmoving One.

Be it a godly or ungodly gift, her confidence was primarily due to her knees-weakening effect on men marginally more so than women. That caused her to predicate her selection process entirely on the opposite sex. A number of them, notably Chimaera Glimmenmare (Byron's Stallion), Nevair Neverknight (Byron's Paladin), and Djerrid Ruin (Byron's Bowman as well as his Green Man) only too happily spoke to her.

Devils cannot lie. Applause does not signify guilt any more than naughty thoughts invariably result in nastier deeds. She left Godbad the last time like she had every other time: persuaded Byronics, even smoky Sedona and her ultra-conservative father, whom she didn't interrogate, were innocent.

At least they were when it came to disposing of so many Master Devas.

========

Harmony finally got around to the Thanatoids of Lathakra on the afternoon before the Spring Equinox and, therefore, of 4825's New Year's Day throughout most of the Upper Head. She was pretty sure King Cold and his constant companion – whom many thought of as his Crimson Queen even though, technically, she was still Mithras's Virgin – wouldn't wittingly get rid of their own allies, especially not their younger siblings in Mithras, who obeyed them unquestioningly, but she had to be absolutely sure.

Never forget, she advised herself, Methandra much more so than Tantal had in the past exhibited decidedly, ouch, diabolical tendencies. For one thing, just before she stuck him in one, brother Tavy confessed ringots were Miss Myth's idea, not his, Tantal's or anyone else's.

For another, finding out the Thanatoids had been keeping secret the existence of an azura they'd had some time before the Great Flood, when Methandra wasn't in control of the daemonic body she was occupying – namely the Klannit creature whose homunculus Harmony accidentally fried alive on Sedon's Peak prior to the Winter Solstice – qualified as only the latest example of their innate distrustfulness.

Having endured the embarrassment of being forced to resort to blades-winged Nemesis a couple of times as a result of them, she had no difficulty recalling many more of Hot Stuff's antics during the 500-year long Middle Sea matriarchy. Astonishingly, for a good percentage of that time Miss Myth tried to set herself up as no less than Mother Earth's equal and Dark Sedon's superior. Were it not for Mithras's Midsummer, his epitome of the summer season, going Novadev-nuclear on her circa 2500 Year of the Dome, she might have succeeded as well.

Doltishly disrespectful as it might be construed, Harmony felt she had to challenge them face-to-face. It was the only way she could think of to diminish the opportunities they'd otherwise have to collaborate on some sort of derailing obfuscation that wouldn't count as a lie because they fervently believed it to be the truth. That she did it directly, and that they answered her so fast and seemingly forthrightly, satisfied her they were as blameless, and as clueless, as everyone had been.

If she was as smart as she reckoned she was, she should have been able to figure out where the blame belonged months ago. That she confronted them in Grand Elysium, within its much grander pyramid, less than a week after its guiding lights surrendered the city as unexpectedly and as inexplicably as their long refusal to do so, also might have twigged her as to the identity of the guilty party.

It wasn't so the powers-that-were could paint the city, though it did look, if not painted or whitewashed stem to stern, then what they'd missed had at least been freshly scrubbed – even the roadways looked clean. And how could she have failed to appreciate the significance, not just to her but also to the rest of her sometimes unkind kind, of the fact that Sedon's priests, Pyrame's priestesses, and rest of the city's et al, actually wanted to swear eternal allegiance to the two remaining firstborn Mithradites before they handed over the city?

That the Thanatoids not only accepted their worship after they'd needlessly caused so much prolonged strife, they granted them a blanket amnesty in return for opening Elysium's gates, strongly suggested who they suspected it had to be. If it wasn't Strife herself – Kore-Eris or Kore-Discord, the third triplet in Mithras's Second, the third Apple Goddess, Marut Kanin or Fitna Marutia as Illuminaries had her – then who else besides Sedon had the requisite might to vanish devils just like that?

Except, how could it have been Strife-Marutia? The answer to that, as someone like Quill Tethys might put it, was the question itself was *your elephant*, as in irrelevant. Rumours that she'd been Mithras's post-Thrygragon Golden Avenger to the contrary were just that: rumours designed to construct a straw man, or woman, or elephant if you preferred.

It couldn't have been her. She'd been bodily wiped out in the same year, circa 4000 YD, that Quill was born for the first time. Datong Harmonia knew it, too. She'd watched her debrained daemonic body melt away, her golden apple power focus with it, as she desperately attempted to swim across Sedon's Peak's lava lake to a two thousand year ancient, but rapidly fading portal that she hoped would take her safely beyond an enraged grandfather's grasp on the Outer Earth.

There had never been any love lost between her and Strife-Marutia so the Unity wouldn't have saved her then even if she could. The truth of matter was she'd tossed her into the molten Brainrock in the first place. For the sake of Headworld harmony, it went without stipulating. The Moloch Sedon could be such a vindictive prick and he wasn't beneath using it as a whipping post whenever he had to lash out at something.

Neither Strife nor her man of the then-recent hours, Phantast Thanatos, the devic Dream Weaver and long cathonitized third of the Thanatoid Death Gods, should have trifled with the Celestial Sphere. At least Dream's star still shone in the much more proximate Sed-Sphere. Talk about vanishing without a trace, though, that was Strife's fate. Could it have likewise been the fate of the latest batch of missing Master Devas?

The *'besides'* still held. Harmony and any other firstborns or Great Gods aside, no one except the Devil Sedon had the requisite might to plunge so many of his grandchildren into that horrendous wishing hell. Once again, must be ad infinitum by now, she had to ask herself, how could it be anyone else?

Drop the *'besides'* and that had to be her answer, didn't it.

========

Perhaps, albeit only in 20/20/20 hindsight (for devils), the Unity of Balance should have asked the Thanatoids where they and their buddies planned to invade next.

========

Almost everyone agreed the theocrats got their just desserts. Perversely, though, once word got out as to how most of them met their endgames – their best bits being eaten while they were alive and probably still conscious – its unmitigated horridness did not stir much more than a piddling pudding of disgust amongst Elysium's populace.

Moreover, regardless of how they died, common decency should have dictated against their often-grisly demise provoking so much joy. Yet that's exactly what it did, a near boundless outpouring of the hence-baffling emotion. Even worse, other than amongst their more irrefutably reactionary relatives, who must have feared they'd go out the same way, the revolting nature of so many murders barely whipped up what should have become a comprehensive condemnation of the Thanatoids.

Upon due reflection, perhaps not counter-intuitively quite the opposite happened. Many actually cheered, not blamed, the Thanatoids for what became of nearly every male, female, childish, androgynous or hermaphroditic hierophant, of any race or any genus, the ones who purported to have been born solely to interpret the will of the Moloch Sedon for the benefit of the unwashed masses. That and to receive vast riches as recompense for their righteous engendering, it also went without out stating for the record.

For the same reasons, hardly anyone accused any devil whatsoever for the vomitory verity, as fays may say, that they were so summarily slain on the very night they'd surrendered the city. Master Devas could no more breach their self-imposed bindings than they'd dare kill even potential devil-worshippers themselves. The Mithradite firstborn had promised them their personal protection in the form of a blanket amnesty, hadn't they. Devic oaths were inviolable, weren't they.

For yet another novelty, absolutely no one reckoned the followers of any devil, fanatical or just dutiful, responsible. Quite the opposite again, and evidently only moderately offensively to the pardon-granting but manifestly blameless Thanatoids, the priests' passing provided even more of an incentive to make New Year's Eve a night of boisterous revelry and unbridled gaiety.

On this matter and little else, the unsympathetic victims' fellow citizenry and the up-until-that-moment, only sullenly victorious soldiery of the Lathakran armies, all of whom had been anticipating a night of unrestrained rape and pillage, concurred. The responsible party wanted all and sundry to party guilt-freely.

Elysium's rapturous celebrants, including the devil-gods there with them, Harmony prominently among them, reasoned that while Star Sedon may not shine anymore, he (rather than it) still oversaw them, albeit as darkly at night as he had during the day until last Mithramas. The Mighty Moloch may not care overly much, let alone overtly enough, that the Thanatoids had spent the last hundred or so years making his Headworld their Headworld, but he'd never been one to tolerate apostasy, had he.

If further proof were needed, which Harmony might have appreciated, the pure brutality of so many of the executions, to call them correctly, for that's what's they were, implicated fay-fairy-fairly obvious culprits. Nearly everybody agreed nearly everything pointed to man-hating, except when it came to man-eating, demons doing the dirtily dietary deeds: big-toothed, iron-stomached, shape-shifting assassins Sedon had not only turned loose on Elysium's treacherous former hierarchy, but ones he had also transported to and from the scenes of their comestible crimes.

========

Hooray for him. Hooray for them. Let's get crazy.
****

5. Call Me Morgue

"Hallelujah, the world is saved!"
"Long live Sedon!"
"Long may he reign over us!"

========

"So long as he doesn't rain over us," Harmony muttered, cringing despite herself as the infectious chant reverberated through the teeming throng for the umpteenth time that night. "For 40 days and 40 nights, including Sedonda, the same as the do-bladder-badder did after Thrygragon."

(Back then it poured so nonstop relentlessly more that a few wondered if the Head was finally receiving the inundation it deluge-dodged when Sedon raised Cathonia out of himself in order to protect Pacifica, the Places of Peace, as the then-archipelago was called pre-Dome.)

Approaching midnight only served to accelerate the mass-mind-madness. Close-by partiers cracked or blew noisemakers, clacked swords to shields, clanged spoons to pans or, absent anything except tongues and lungs, shrieked with heartfelt exuberance. Nothing raises spirits like avoiding disaster and, with it, near certain death or lifelong incapacitation. They, spirits, were always happiest inside you, being you, and not haunting graveyards or battlefields lamenting the loss of physicality.

Devils in number, their three eyes alight with delight, were just as excited. Dark Sedon had done what the conquering Thanatoids might have if they could have, if they weren't Master Devas bound by his dictates against killing lesser beings. He'd eliminated the callous, life-squandering liars who'd been purporting to be his eye-mouthpieces for so many self-serving generations.

He had thereby given the Lathakrans a belated stamp of approval instead of the unconscionably delayed stomp of displeasure so many in not just Godbad and the Head's occipital regions felt they deserved. As a result they were as vociferously festive as Harmony felt weirdly restive.

(She'd always considered the Era of Empires an age of bullying buffoonery; had accordingly stayed out of the fray for most of its despicable duration. That it had finally ended, if it had, with victory for the most aggressive transgressors ever didn't disappoint her so much as it made her question her father's hands-off approach to devil-doings. Hardly for the first time she wished she could disobey him.)

"Too bad Jordy isn't here to record this," Wintry Moira shouted to her eldest sister over the din. "You haven't seen him lately have you?"

"Not for a few months, Chance," Datong Harmonia responded, albeit mostly mind-to-mind telepathically, in order to forestall tonsil-damage. She also addressed her, as devils were wont to do when with each other, by her attribute. "Not since I asked him to dump a kibisis full of Anvil's ringots up in Cabalarkon, Anvil in one."

"You did what?"

Just as Thrygragos Varuna Mithras had winter, Thrygragos Lazareme reserved the spring season for himself and, in his case, his second-born Life Goddesses: Flowery Anthea, Metisophia and Krepusyl Evenstar, once Mariamne Dawnstar. The most notable commonality the triplets currently shared, besides their father and their association as life goddesses with the spring season, was their non-presence, as opposed to their non-existence.

(That last was arguable. For one, Anthea – who some claimed, persistently but erroneously, was the real inspiration behind the Superior Sisterhood of the same name – hadn't been seen since shortly after she became a solid entity. For another, Titanic Metis, Quill's half-mother of record, her spirit-self, was in a ringot presumably still up in Cabalarkon somewhere.

(As for the third, Mariamne-Krepusyl, after *crepuscular*, she had renamed herself thus when Sedon moved her unofficial but effective protectorate, the Land of Daybreak, to the Land of Twilight, his Outer Nose, at the same time, near the end of the 47th Century YD, that he moved his Tongue and Cataract and thereby, perhaps not inadvertently, recharged the Era of Empires.

(The selfsame Miss Mist – not to be confused with Hot Stuff, Miss Myth, Methandra Thanatos – was among those whose disappearances Harm had pretty much given up investigating now that most everyone had concluded Grandfather Sedon was responsible for her enforced, yet non-starring, absence.)

"It isn't that loud. You heard me. I wrote you; wrote, read and wrote you again."

A fifth-born worshipped as Fata Fortuna during the Middle Sea matriarchy of circa 2500 years earlier, Chance and her triplet sisters Vishnuvita and Vanalana, as old-time Illuminaries named them maybe 1500 years earlier, split the other seasons: Vishnuvita represented summer whereas Vanalana represented autumn.

As was often the case when it came to devils, their power foci suggested their attributes. As the Growing Deva, Vishnuvita's regularly resembled a sheaf of cut-green stalks of wheat still on the rise. By contrast, Vanalana's Tvasitar talisman was a classic cornucopia brimming with the fall's bounty.

(Most would agree Vanalana's was a major league improvement on Mithras's King Harvest, Underlord Yama, whose power focus was a pickaxe, and Byron's Vanthysces, who wielded an actual scythe. Or did wield, put more Metis-like, before he was cathonitized during the Empire's expansion into the Penile Peninsula. Yama thereupon took possession of his talisman and merged it with his own.)

Moira's Tvasitar talisman was somewhat more obscure: a funny-looking figure or shape consisting of, depending on her mood, three curved lines or branches, or three stylized human arms or legs, radiating from a common centre, often a transitory – as in blinking – eyeball.

Being 3-pronged it wasn't a swastika but it was close. Technically called the Triskelion, Anvil the Artificer based it on the ages-ancient, 3-spoke wheel of fortune, thus devil-devising it consistent with her attribute, which kicked three ways: lucky, unlucky and load of hooey.

When Abe Chaos and his Lathakran pals drove what in their view were trespassing Byronics out of areas near the Cattail coastline bordering on the Head's interior ocean of Akadan, Lazareme's three seasonal sisters reclaimed the Pastures of Plenty. That made them among the highest born Lazaremists to side with the Lathakrans and from then on to assist in the expansion of their empire.

"But, don't you realize, that answers everything," the seasonally transmogrifying devil reciprocated.

It being equinoctial spring, Fata Fortuna, Wintry Moira, had been brightening up her external appearance since Imbolc Day, six weeks gone by now. While never exactly vivacious, she seldom let a physical dourness cloud her outward attractiveness and didn't today. When Chance was around, so too came hope, that most double-headed of the seven cardinal virtues.

"It does what?"

"Thrygragon, Balance. Think Steg."

"Think what?"

"Don't pretend to be as thick as Chaos or Order, Harm. Not what, who. Her name was Saudi Tethys."

"Rewrite me smarter."

They were standing together outside what had been Sedon's pyramid, the largest ever built on the Whole Earth and the one he sometimes shared with the perhaps just-as-missing half-mother of his sed-sons: the nearly eponymous, Mithradite ninth-born, Pyrame Silverstar. Like everyone around them – typically for her including many of Moira's half sons and half daughters, deviants therefore the lot of them – they were waiting for the New Year's fireworks to start going off.

"Morg can't get about anywhere; not unless she draws herself wherever she wants to go. The only way she does that … it's just like the Steg, the Saur Tsarina, Saudi Tethys wanted. Jordy's quill, my Rumour's power focus, the quill what once belonged to Quill's devic half-father … Don't you see?"

"Who's Morg?"

Why did she ever take pity on the Legendarian and occupy that mermaid anyhow?

========

"Hallelujah, the world is saved!"
It very nearly wasn't.
"Long live Sedon!"
He was still Sed-slurped.
"Long may he reign over us!"
Nope!

========

"Make it morgue, mom!"

"Hallelujah, the world is saved!"

"Ten!"

Before the crowd belted out the next second, Harmony had a pretty good mnemonic as to whom Morg was – she'd just materialized in front of them.

"Long live Sedon!"

"Nine!"

Put indisputably better, one of Weir's female Warriors Elite had; one typically shrouded head to toe in a Trinondev's dyed-blue djellaba or galabia.

"Long may he reign over us!"

"Eight!"

There was something of a sallow, albeit be-skinned death's head with deep-set and glaring, as in boring-straight-through-you, eyeballs behind the facial veil.

"Hallelujah, the world is saved!"

Didn't pal Pyrame call her most frequent shell these days, Cabalarkon's Piscine-born Master of Weir, the Death's Head Hellion?

"Seven!"

Whoa, didn't the grinning gargoyle mounted atop her handheld sceptre, its 3-eyes open terrifyingly invitingly, look exactly like you-know-who's head full on?

"Long live Sedon!"

In the waning seconds of the countdown to midnight, firstborn Harmony flashed through a number of thoughts worthy of second-born Metisophia. (Many devils addressed her ring-gotten sister, the devic half-mother of Quill Tethys, as Wisdom, as in Wisdom of Lazareme. Harmony did not, mostly because Metis liked it too much. She also reckoned herself at least as wise.)

"Six!"

Those thoughts?

"Long may he reign over us!"

The theocratic head honchos of the ecclesiastical city state hadn't delayed so long in order to have Grand Elysium's buildings repainted and/or whitewashed, the better to greet the victorious Thanatoids as they marched on to and into Sedon and Pyrame's pyramid. They hadn't had the roadways scrubbed just with sudsy water either.

"Five!"

They hadn't because they hadn't been in their right minds. Demons had been in their right minds. Translucently or somehow otherwise undetectably, demons also must have been coating them, much the same as stomach lining coats an animal's digestive system.

"Four!"

Or, expressed less anatomically, with whatever corrupted, earthen substance was coating Pusan Wanderlust when she tried to take out Lord Order in his preelectrified Thunder Dome; Lust when she did take out Chaos in her bastion of bliss; and the irresistible, pheromone-spraying satyr when he attempted to double-whammy Harmony, frolicking in her rollicking High Seat as she was at the time.

"Three!"

That might explain the awful – more like offal – condition of so many of the murder victims' remains once they were found the morning after the day they'd surrendered Elysium to the two triplet Thanatoids and their Lathakrans. Their assassins consumed them alive. They then kept them that way until their jobs were done, whereupon they shat them out only half-digested.

"Two!"

Unless, that is, demonic abdominal juices restricted what they could bodily process. In which case, being earthborn, they considerately left behind what they couldn't utilize of their meals for personal nutrition such that local gardeners could first mulch then feed it back to their Mother Nature as manure.

"One!"

Except she was wrong, wasn't she. Demons couldn't control sapient beings; they weren't devils.

Wait a millisecond. What if they were devils? Not the demons, the ones responsible, and not Byronics either. Even though she avoided the Unmoving One, Thrygragos Byron, and his second-born mouthpiece, smoky Sedona, she'd have sensed their culpability in Aka-Godbad. She hadn't. She had them down conversely; reckoned them absolutely blame free.

But who else could it be?

"Zero!"

Ring-gotten devils – had to be!

Boom!

Unless it was bang!

========

'New Year's Eve'll be a blast.'

So many of those she spoke to, people and devils alike, promised Harmony just that, once she returned from the subcontinent of Aka-Godbad the day before, intent upon confronting the two never-cathonitized Thanatoids, King Cold and Hot Stuff, with respect to the to-almost-everyone-anywhere, inexplicably missing devils.

And so it was, as in utterly evil.

****

6. New Year's Lily

20/21 Surma, 4824/5 Year of the Dome – Grand Elysium

Boom-bang!
Unless it was bang-boom!
Better make it a half-thousand booms and 500 bangs!
Unless, again, there were bangs more of the former and booms less of the latter!

========

Hundreds of fireworks went off at the shout of zero. They did so with a precision designed to do their ever-masked donor, as well as producer, proud. Hot Stuff, Methandra Thanatos, never had been shy about showing off and, as promised, they were spectacular. As also might be expected, they were just as much so fiery. Hellishly fiery!

Cathonic forces hit Grand Elysium skywards then downwards, thanks to Miss Myth. Simultaneously, thanks to Master Morg, chthonic forces did a ditto, surging ground upwards. The painting, the whitewashing, the cleaning products, they weren't paint, whitewash or cleansing solutions. They were earthborn demons in their most unformed, rawest state. And, demons being demons, nearly all were highly flammable.

Tragically, it wasn't just them who burst into flames. The immediate casualties must have been as monumental as the monuments themselves. Eruptive geysers of sewerage-like sludge that didn't immediately ignite formed instantly animalized, sometimes anthropomorphic, to the point of toothily lupine or even vampiric, grotesqueries.

Taking to the streets, often out of the streets themselves, seeking-eyes demon-dogs went on the prowl. The eyes these creatures of doggedness as much as darkness sought were third ones, those shining out of the forehead of Master Devas who'd come to Elysium to party hardily and not be eaten heartily, not to mention hungrily or even half-heartedly.

Airborne furies, none of who were as blind as bats (not that bats were actually blind), but many of who looked chiropteran and/or just as fangs-glinting vampiric, flew into the skies on identical missions. (These last included chiropteran tee-tees, who could indeed be read like an open book since it was both sides of their wings, not their tails, that contained their non-spoken tales.)

Feeding frenzies ensued. Although by then it was mostly over the devic equiva-lent of table scraps due to the fact that Morg, long distance via Quill's quill, and her spies in the conurbation, their far-seeing eyeorbs somehow concealed, must have pinpointed dozens of devils well before the countdown got underway. She'd there-upon concentrated crude clumps of thus still-oily, demonic material underneath them.

Harmony was amongst those targeted; Wintry Moira was not. Morg must have singled the latter out for herself: hence one, the *'make that morgue, mom'* crack; hence two, if perversely, the open eyeorb so disturbingly resembling Sed's head 3-goggle-eyeing them mouth-wateringly. Or once again, and this was a similarly strange notion, could it have been desperately, even pleadingly?

Why call Chance mom if she wasn't her half-mom? Would she have called Quill dad and the Unity as dumb as they come? Possibly no and possibly yes but, either way, boy, was Harmony's face red. Then it was muddier than her name was going to be once word got out she'd as good as, or as bad as, delivered Morg every bit of the wherewithal she needed to turn today/tonight into beyond merely New Years Eve 4824/5.

Folks such as the Librarian and the Legendarian could never record it as just any old spring season sprung. They'd have it for what it was, as Morg springing the deadliest trap sprung since Thrygragon. Then they'd make up a name for it, something along the lines of *'the New Years Evil'*, *'the Infernal Equinox'* or *'Elysium's Inferno'*.

Harmony instantly thought of it as Chance's Charnel Chomping even though her younger sister wasn't chomped so much as slurped into Morg's eyeorb. Then again, she was fairly-fairy-fond of fay-saying; had even fallen under the spell of a few faerie farts over the millennia: the to-her-eyes Lazareme-lookalike, Tomcat Tattle-tail, being the most seductively as well as smilingly repetitive of them.

Had that really been the catty as well as cunning trickster sidling up to them perchance to steal a kiss come midnight? And a lot more than that afterwards, not that it'd be theft by then. Talk about pheromones, he must be part satyr. Come to think of it, he did play panpipes almost as well as he played her.

In a way she could hardly wait. Then she could barely move.

========

With respect – more like disrespect, Quill Tethys might amend – to Varuna Mithras's eleventh born set of triplets, Dark Sedon cathonitized, catasterized or ill-starred Midsummer in or around the Year of the Dome 2500. His crime was detonating a volcano on the Aegean island of Strongyne (meaning Strong Women according to many, one of whom being that selfsame Quill).

This not-funnily-punning devastating, because it was undeniable, catastro-phe ended the perhaps falsely declared man-hating, Mad Goddesses' Middle Sea matriarchate on the Outer Earth. The Hyperion-titanic or Phaethon-like god-devil exploding, as if a devic supernova, explained why antique Illuminaries renamed Midsummer Novadev long after the fact.

As for the term *'Novadev-nuclear'*, devils were as familiar with the phenomena of starbursts as they were with its physics. Originally extraterrestrial Utopians were just as much so. The two races shared a consequently altogether rational fear of planet-shattering Atomics. Their attendant hatred of the so-called creative science was about the only common denominator they shared with each other.

Midsummer's pretext, had he been allowed to utter one, for blowing his top – and with it Strongyne's – would have been drunkenness. He didn't know what he was doing. No matter. Just as devils fed off the worship of their followers, Sedon fed off the worship devils accorded him. Many thousands of devic faithful died in the eruption of the Goddess Culture's sacred island. If devils had a mama's breast to suckle, which they didn't, they'd have learned at it never to mess with granddad.

(Parenthetically, as well as editorially, and in most respects sadly, though hardly irrelevantly given all that transpired in 4824/5 Years of the Dome, it hitting the Aegean's roof also brought to a dusty end the thalassocracy of Minoan Crete – a name derived from the much later-on Classical Greek word for *'strength'*.

(Crete was by far the biggest, if not quite the closest landform to Strongyne when Midsummer blew the latter island's heart into the sky. Approaching paradoxically, for a few hundred years before that happened devils and Utopians living on Crete, as well as Minoan humans on their third of the island, had actually managed to get along comparatively peacefully there.

(Along with her much lower-born cousin Pyrame Silverstar, as the radiant Queen Tanith to Dark Sedon's uncharacteristically smile-happy King Rhadamanthys, the Unity of Balance – having for a significant period strayed from her more customary hangouts in the Far East – claimed a large measure of credit for that. Since Master Devas tended to be tribal exclusivists, their joint success on Crete helped account for their unusually enduring friendship.)

Of course, even if only one potential worshipper died because of him, Sedon would have ill-starred Midsummer anyways. Unless, that is, there was another possibility. If they killed a lesser, yet fully sentient being, did they self-cathonitize? Master Devas had debated this potentially most crucial of issues amongst themselves for more than two thousand years. However, neither they nor Sedon could resolve it definitively.

Put more accurately, Sedon claimed he didn't know how to answer it and, not surprisingly, no one volunteered to test if it would or wouldn't occur automatically. Why bother? Since so far only Sedon had ill-starred anyone, and since Sedon almost never changed his mind, cathonitization remained as close as most devils could come to dying. Rather, could come with the exception of Thrygragos Varuna Mithras, who never recovered from Thrygragon or, if he had, seemed curiously disinclined to reveal it.

For a good percentage of their father's age, Novadev's triplet brothers, Equinoctial Spring and Equinoctial Autumn, served as Mithras's torchbearers. They were recognized and even engraved in stone as such on the Outer Earth, where the rites of Roman or Cave Mithraism identified them as Cautes and Cautopates. They weren't in Grand Elysium on New Year's Eve 4824/5.

Nor was Mithras's just as unstintingly loyal herald, angel or primary heliodromus (sun-runner). Iconic likenesses of the normally be-winged, leontocephalic (as in lion-headed) trumpeter could also be seen carved onto walls or pedestals within a few Outer Earth mithraea or cave temples. Out there he was sometimes called

Zurvan. By contrast Illuminaries had him as Djinn Domitian, whereas his fellow devils often referred to him as the Masochist since he enjoyed being dominated.

They weren't there because they stood in an art gallery – as part of the art.

========

Wintry Moira didn't vanish simply because it was now officially spring. She vanished into a Utopian prison pod. Like all the mortals accompanying her to Grand Elysium, the eldest of her half-children did not have that option. Yet, tellingly, neither had they been left behind to incinerate the same as the younger ones.

Along with everything else tipping the scales against Morgan Abyss, add the hateful crime of fratricide.

========

Another luscious lady, that of Luck rather than Lust, Chance's charms, ample as they were, self-evidently weren't always lucky. That didn't hold for her arms, which usually were if pregnancy was the aim. The term *'get lucky'* entered into common parlance once Rumour of Lazareme, her preferred squeeze until fucking faeries ate him shortly after the turn of the millennium, started recounting ribald stories about her during the Goddess Culture centuries of roughly 2000 to 2500 Years of the Dome.

Quill Tethys, when he saw her in person or realized she was half in bed with him, sometimes called her the same as Morg just had, as mom. There was often an element of truth about that too. While she wasn't Half-Mom Number One – second-born Metisophia, Wisdom of Lazareme, had that dubious distinction – she was, undeniably, Half-Mom Number Latest over and over again.

Harmony was among those who suspected the Legendarian would never recur if fifth-born Chance had not been occupying his conceptive mother at least twenty years, and nine months, before he came back within the by-then-dying, resultant issue. Either that or, if he was a woman that generation, something that happened more times than Quill cared to admit, she was occupying his inseminating father.

Others thought he was Rumour of Lazareme. They did so not just because the seventh-born Lazaremist's Brainrock quill adhered to him. They claimed the scar in the centre of his forehead, which itched whenever he was around devils and what only a Quill Tethys had, indicated a devic suicide. However, since there was no record of any devil cutting out his third eye and thus de-immortalizing his or herself, that may be nothing more than idle speculation.

For her part Dame Chance insisted her half-children, though by definition deviants, did not have to be potential Quills. It was an incontestable and therefore superfluous insistence. While, be it for purposes of propagation, purely for pleasure or because she wanted a change of perspective, it also stood to reason she could occupy a man as easily as a woman, she swore she didn't have to be involved in any way whatsoever for Quills of the future to gestate let alone be born.

Fate twisted fortuitously for the eldest of Fata Fortuna's half-children in that Morg must have believed she did. At least it probably twisted fortunately for those beside Harmony and her in Grand Elysium. A junior Tethys couldn't become a Quill until he or she turned twenty at a minimum. There was no secret about that. She also had to know that the first thing a dying Tethys did, the moment Quill got inside him or her – and thereby revived him or her – was cause Rumour's Brainrock quill to appear in his or her hands as if out of the blue, even if it was out of the Weird.

She somehow had to ensure that potential Quills-to-be stayed undying such that she could keep it for herself. Killing herself would be silly since, even if Chance was her half-mother, she couldn't be certain Quill was her birthfather. What she wouldn't have known, because no one could, was which junior Tethys of either sex would become the next Quill Tethys.

Nor would she have known which of Moira's over 20-year-old half-children had a Quill or a potential Quill for a parent or grandparent. That left her with little or no option except to catch as catch can. She and her witchy cohort absconded with as many of those standing in the vicinity of the two Lazaremist sisters as they could lay their hands on. If any others had wandered off before not just Methandra's fireworks began popping off, howsoever-precisely, well, hopefully they'd have shortly burnt up so toastily crumbly even Quill couldn't revive them.

Ironically, Morg and those with her, be they Trinondevs or Hellions or both, would then have to bring them to Cabalarkon, and thereafter see to it they were properly cared for; hence their fortunes twisting non-fatally. As a consequence the Utopians' lack of options actually saved their lives, albeit if only for the time being.

Presumably Morg figured it'd serve no purpose to have her lackeys take any of the younger ones to the Weirdom. In terms of percentages vis-à-vis effort required, she'd be right as well. After all, should victory elude her, chances were – no pun intended since Morg didn't play word games – she'd be dead, and Cabalarkon fallen, long before they left their teens.

To be sure Harmony's presence was a vexation. Anecdotal evidence indicated the seven remaining firstborns might be able to resist capture in a prison pod. Harmony had in the Weirdom of Kanin City a week or so before Thrygragon. That was something else the Master would have known if she'd done her research, which she must have.

They definitely would if it was already filled. Multi-millennia before devils gained debrained daemonic bodies Utopian scientocrats established it was impossible to circumvent the one devil per pod limit to their capacity. Morg had used multiple, pre-Earth pods to take out Sedon, though, and there were plenty more in the Stopstone-lined vault where those came from, so that presented no insurmountable obstacle.

Plus, as she'd demonstrated when she removed the Anvil Artificer from the ringot such that she could employ it to get the Pauper Priestess out of her and into it, it was dead easy to transfer lower born Master Devas from pre-Earth pods to eyeorbs manufactured in the Weirdom of Cabalarkon.

Harmony stood even less of a chance than Chance did.

========

Conflagrations burned things up, yes, but they also burned things off. If those things were demons and you were a Master Deva capable of not burning up as they burned off, you'd be much better off than your adherents experiencing the same incendiary miseries. And that held true for any other sentient being who wasn't fireproof, which virtually none were – none that were altogether flesh and blood anyhow.

Devils weren't, not even partially, due to the fact that subtle matter, coupled with their Brainrock talismans, only simulated flesh and blood.

========

Devic power foci worked for anyone. That said, neither Morg nor anyone else could use Quill's quill to draw anybody anywhere against his or her will. That wasn't a rule; it was a built-in constraint. It didn't so much restrict what it could do as allowed it to do what it could do. Other than suchlike inescapable preconditions to it working at all, the quill and its Brainrock ink produced a galumphing gamut of comparatively modest to positively marvellous near-miracles.

For one, it never dried up. For another, just as witches of most any affiliation did most anything in their bottomless bags or kibises, he could pack off his quill between-space the splotch pad upon which he, or in this case Morg, did their dreadful doodles. For a third, she could use it to draw anyone. And that included devils or daemons in whatever guises she knew them to be sporting currently.

Far more astonishingly, once the initial sketch was done the background automatically filled in. It did so not only with where they were but who were with them. Just as borderline-magically, Quill's quill didn't require an artistic hand at its helm. Provided you could visualize who, where or what you wanted to draw, it would do it for you. Have it put yourself in the picture, sign it and dot the signature, and you went there. Pre-draw your return and you had yourself an instant exit.

Trinondevs, so long as she knew what their shielding gargoyles looked like, would have no more objections to her drawing them somewhere than demons would. Eyeorbs did not function as prison pods in devic protectorates due to too many of the devil or devils' faithful living there. They did work in Grand Elysium, which was no devil's protectorate, not even the Moloch Sedon's.

Eye-staves were so very useful. They did much more than project gargoyles or slurp in one devil, or a dozen or more of their azura offspring, per orb. They didn't just take devils in either. They took in their subtle matter daemonic bodies and their Brainrock talismans. Plus, if you were really good with them, you could ensure they left the talismans behind for you to take with you. And Morg was really, really good with them.

So long as they were empty, all of the above were just a few of their applications. You were a thoroughly trained member of Weir's Warriors Elite then they could cast illusions near you. They could cast defensive force fields around you. They could cast gripping grapples away from you. You could levitate with them. You could far-speak with them. You could far-see from one through another.

And, although the Cathonic Dome did block their functionality, if you were beyond it you could pull off exactly the same stunts. Which of course would be the case since Trinondevs had had them for multiple multi-millennia pre-Earth. But it also explained how generations of widely faring Trinondevs and Illuminaries out there kept in touch for thousands of years before they started to return to the Head in number, circa 3000 YD, in order to revitalize the gene pool if nothing else.

Truth told, the side of Cathonia you were on only really mattered when it came to distances, which were appreciably greater out there. Some Illuminaries claimed the Outer Earth's air inhibited the usefulness of eye-staves by narrowing their range but that was no big whoop either. Besides, even if it did, intermediary relay stations overcame that.

Which in turn justified one of Quill Tethys's more caustic maxims. '*Wherever Utopians go, civilizations rise. Whenever devils follow, Utopians die out and so do the civilizations they inspired. After all, who needs civilization when you have gods – or God, as monotheists have it – to do the heavy lifting for you?*'

Of course him vouchsafing suchlike cant accounted for why the legendary 30-Year Man relatively rarely lasted his full 30-year allotment between regenerations.

========

Devic eyefire burnt anything. Trinondev force shields were no different than the Trinondevs beneath them or the demons Morg allied with herself, her Illuminaries and her Warriors Elite. Regardless of rampant conflagrations, dozens of initially fire-resistant, demonic cocoons rose out of the ground and began hardening around Master Devas, Stopstone statuary being the desired end.

Been there, done that, Harmony might have muttered to herself. As Abe had dot atop Sinistral Lust's bastion of bliss overlooking Pandemonium, Harm did ditto here in Grand Elysium. She blazed herself loose. The half-dozen Trinondevs surrounding her, gargoyles grinning garishly, their eyeorbs already open, could not be happier. Such a beautiful scalp, theirs for the slurping, they must have been cheering to themselves.

Then they couldn't be crispier.

========

The Unity of Order had a problem with King Cold. Prior to Thrygragon, the male of the two non-cathonitized Thanatoids boasted he could best him, one on one, like washerwomen did laundry, or words to that effect. That wasn't the main reason he hadn't joined the Lathakrans in their efforts to conquer the Headworld and thereby show Sedon who was beholden to whom. The main reason was his hated brother beat him to it.

Lord Yajur was nevertheless there, albeit as a 2-eyed, be-turbaned humanoid answering to the name of Sparky. Morg couldn't pre-draw him because she didn't have in mind what he looked like. Unholy Abaddon was there too. Great Byron's husband-and-wife pair of Silverclouds, Rufous Rudra and Lunar Uma, she whose attribute was more like gravity, were just as present. She did have it in her mind what they looked like.

They were attending the two triumphant, almost as terrifically powerful Thanatoids. They'd be the two who missed matrimonial bliss by the most minuscule of margins – the only time they'd had sex together was when they were demon-devoured: Klannit, the Anvil Artificer's ambitious azura, being the result. They'd also be two Master Devas who next-to-never altered their appearances. One was a gigantic iceberg with a beard and the other was an almost as gigantic fireball wearing a mask and head-to-toe garments in various shades of red.

Those therefore in the company of Chaos occupied the biggest bull's-eye in Grand Elysium. They got Morg's most especial attention. It was as if the Well of the World – the Hell-Well of Satanwyck itself – had come there expressly in order to flow underneath them. Which in a way it had, but only in the sense that it under-lay the entire Upper Head. Swelled-up thickest underneath the leftover firstborns, minus Harmony and Order, might be a better way of putting it, most agreed in afterthought.

It didn't flow upwards. What it did, after first cracking through the floor beneath their feet, was spew both rapidly and gropingly a veritable oil spout of clawing, grasping fingers – really big, really black and really, really fat fingers, ones approaching endlessly reinforced from below. Congealing statuary around them wasn't their goal. Now was hardly the time for artistic pretensions. Instead, they mashed a mini-mountain under, over and around the five of them, one that threatened to dwarf Sedon's pyramid size-wise.

Likely because she knew they could never withstand the crush, Morg didn't set any Trinondevs against them. She should have known better than to send a half-dozen against Datong Harmonia, though. Then again, she might not have known about her Nemesis persona. Either that or she considered the elite warriors expendable, which would make her as reckless as Elysium's theocrats had been with their soldiery in the three months from Mithramas onwards, those leading up to the city-state's surrender.

Harmony felt herself fracture; worse, splinter. They were pulling her apart even as they were pulling her parts into their pre-Earth prison pods. Weir's Warriors Elite would never worship devils. Sometimes chain reactions were down to her. One immediate brother fired white lightning; the other blasted black. She shot chain lightning, the northern lights in all their glorious colours rendered lethally electrocuting.

Zap! The six Trinondevs were dead, tears to shed, none hers. Still not needing Nemesis, she took to the sky, anxious to spy, Chance and her deviant half-children perchance to locate, and already thousands of faithfully theirs to avenge. Over there, goo-man demons were advancing on an already flayed-unrecognizable woman. How could she still be alive, let alone on her feet, in such a ghastly state?

Using the telescopic talents all devils had, she answered that herself. It wasn't a woman per se. It was a Master Deva; one she placed, after a second's hesitation, as a much younger and, predictably, largely insignificant sister in Lazareme. She couldn't remember how long gone Illuminaries of Weir identified the grisly spectacle she habitually made of herself. But her power focus, a flagellant's burred, knotted or, yes, raspy whip, lash, or scourge was indicative of her personality if perhaps not whatever name they did give her.

Consequently fittingly, her fellow devils called her *'the Skinless Rasp'* or variation thereof. It looked as if she'd deliberately flailed or grated her own skin off, without letting her insides fall out. Harmony reckoned she'd done just that simply because, like so many adoration-deprived lowborns, she felt the need to attract attention in hopes of simultaneously attracting adherents.

She also recalled Skinless seldom let her third eye shine forth, which must be why the seeking-eye demon-dogs hadn't spotted her yet. Then they did. Then she did. Then, like the reddish dawning of a dismal day, Harmony finally comprehended the profoundly diabolical depth of Call-me-morgue's manoeuvrings.

"Don't blast them – bugger off!"

She'd far-cried too late. The Rasp eyefire-immolated a dozen demonically overcoated sentient beings before heeding Harmony's internally heard, yet nonetheless widely broadcast shriek for devils to get the fuck out of Elysium. Many others struck her as just as intentionally inattentive. Indeed, a number of them showed no interest in leaving, most notably the one until then most conspicuous by his absence.

Non-liquid white lightning gave away his presence. That's what his '*vajra*' thunderbolts were, jolts of actual lightning, whitish as opposed to yellowish, hence Lightning Lord Yajur. Order never was absent; he'd been here all along. For some reason he'd lost interest in playing Sparky, his humanoid alter ego. Could be he'd realized the same thing Harmony suddenly had.

Clearly Chaos had. He must have. Distinctive shards of black lightning only emitted from Abe's trident and they were not far behind the vajra-bolts. The Elysium inferno intensified breathtakingly. Even the brickwork looked about to melt. What wasn't a killing field purely because the city was almost entirely made out of stone, with very few green spaces in its centre, might therefore be best thought of not as a killing floor but as a killing kiln.

Morgan Abyss and her Illuminary advisers had got it wrong, if not precisely dead wrong because for certain Morg would be long gone by now. Devils, due to their Tvasitar-trinkets, were self-psychopomps. No still-concreting mini-mountain could hold anyone if they weren't there to be held. Most highborn were quick enough to transport themselves elsewhere before becoming Stopstone statuary. Firstborn were even quicker, to retaliate as well.

That wasn't all of it, far from it. Miss Myth, Harmony punned privately, as had been her wont latterly, might be Methandra Thanatos; Miss Mist might be another of her ring-gotten, second-born sisters in Lazareme. Considering their nicknames, might it not be better to dub Morg and her guiding-lights – another pun that, not a bad one either – Master and Misses Calculation? Harmony reckoned it would.

(Miss Mist was Krepusyl Evenstar, as Illuminaries nowadays had her. She was the devic overlord of Twilight or Crepuscule, what was once the Land of Daybreak. Sedon had displaced what remained her nominal protectorate a few decades back, repositioning it as his Outer Nose on thus unavoidably revamped maps of the Hidden Headworld.)

The most obvious example of their miscalculations had to be that the Rasp got away safely even though she'd baked a dozen or more devil-worshippers and/or potential devil-worshippers. True, she'd done so reflexively. True as well, under codes of commonsense as well as the written-down laws of most nations on the Whole Earth, self-defence constituted justifiable homicide. Even when it wasn't wartime, which this was, when it was kill or be killed, the survivor usually got the benefit of the doubt.

At any rate, her actions violated that most fundamental of Sedonic decrees. As witness what became of Mithras's Midsummer 2300 years earlier, her punishment should have been instantaneous. Yet she hadn't catasterized herself – a term, meaning '*placed amongst the stars*', which mythologists first coined beyond the Dome to describe what to most Outer Earthlings was only a hypothetical phenomenon.

That meant Morg and her advisers were mistaken if they reckoned devils automatically cathonitized the moment they eyefire-burnt a lesser being to death. Or personally killed him or her any other way, as far as that went. It also meant their second major blunder related to the first in that, if one didn't work, then they must have thought the other would.

In their dreams! It was, as devils fay-said to this day, a Phantast-folly.

The Sedon Sphere still domed the Hidden Headworld. But what remained of the mighty Eye-Mouth formerly mainly in the sky had not ill-starred the self-mutilating Lazaremist. (Whom Harmony – whose memory was almost as fabled as her beauty in the eyes of any beholder – by now recollected their Illuminary-predecessors named Rastha Aragon. She further recollected they'd classified her, along with the rest her brood of invariably three, as White Godlings due to their penitential proclivities.)

The Rasp at once not joining her equally transgressive siblings and cousins in the Head's proximate, starry night amounted to pudding-proof, not that any devil was apt to doubt it, that Dark Sedon was the chief reason he ever got stellar company. Still, adherence to his dictates was so ingrained neither the Devil Himself, nor her fellow devil-gods, would ever deem her behaviour excusable.

Rather, they wouldn't have were it seconds ago. Now, though, everything had changed. Skinless should be upstairs. She wasn't. Her survival had to indicate the Moloch Sedon was mostly gone bye-bye despite their convictions to the contrary. That, it further dawned on Harmony, had to be why so many yet lingered in Grand Elysium.

The pernicious popinjays, her sibs and her cousins, were enjoying this.

========

The revelation they could get away with killing so long as Star Sedon wasn't shining compounded the carnage. One voice, female, stopped it.

"You brainless buffoons, you're killing our own. It's a set up. Do as the father-fucking degenerate says."

========

A second voice, male, resounded louder but just as crudely: "Brothers and sisters, cousins in Thrygragos, and those of you who can, reconvene in the Medusa's Meadow. The rest of you get the ice pick out of your ass and the freezing fuck out of here. Bring what you can drag, push, ride or carry with you because once we regroup, Godbad isn't next – Cabalarkon is!"

(The Medusa's Meadow, the site of Thrygragon's bloodiest engagements and, with them, Thrygragos Varuna Mithras's most momentous achievements – as well as his thus far proven-fatal fragmentation – was in the Gregarian Fields, aka Sedon's Mole. The former Weirdom of Kanin City, the devils-thought Blot on Sedon's Cheek, lay just south of the Fields.)

The second voice virtually everyone who heard it recognized. It belonged to Tantal Thanatos. Lesser devils had probably never heard the first one. Sooth said, King Cold, the three Unities of Lazareme – one of who was the *degenerate* referred to, none other than the Unity of Balance – and Bodiless Byron's firstborn Silverclouds, Kanin's current overseers, might have been the only ones there who could identify it.

It came from Hot Stuff, Mithras's Virgin. Even though Harmony had only been targeting Trinondevs, she reckoned her bang on. Killing never was the way to go anywhere – except, that is, into the mire of endless recrimination leading to personal damnation or, for devils, endless nights of looking down on the Hidden Headworld from what passed for its heavens.

Master Morgan Abyss, presumably by then back in the Weirdom of Cabalarkon, must have disagreed. Just as devils began blinking themselves elsewhere, she drew through the Weird the originally extraterrestrial drones her Trinondevs remotely controlled via their ever-so-useful eye-staves.

Drones dropping their incendiary loads, they sought to finish the job. If it could burn, it burnt. But if it died, it didn't necessarily stay down.

========

The Master and her illuminated advisors would have calculated what Nergal Vetala being there might bring to the Weirdom's struggle to last as a Utopian haven. There was nothing new about Vetalazurs and Nergalazurs reactivating the Dead. That doubtless in mind, Morg had already arranged to take out her fellow Nergalids, Yama and Zuvem, the Planter and the Reaper. Had New Years Lilith not distracted her, it's a safe bet the Mithradite Moon Goddess, whom devil-gods addressed as Fecundity or the Grower, would have been on her to-do-in-soon list.

Similarly Morg would have realized Tantal Thanatos rivalled the Nergalids in terms of prolificacy. With that awareness came a corollary: his and theirs were not the only members of what was effectively the fourth generation of devazurkind motivating the Lathakrans' armed forces. For instance, even though he expunged as facilitating energy nearly genocidal numbers of his own on Thrygragon, Varuna Mithras fathered an enormous quantity of azuras during his Age, which lasted from roughly 2000 until 4400 YD, and multitudes of them were still around.

Like devils were to theirs, azuras were genetically incapable of disobeying their fathers. In the absence of extant fathers, devils deferred to their highest born siblings, be they male or female. Azuras differed from devils in the sense that, in the absence of fathers, or firsthand paternal authority, they deferred to their mothers. In the absence of both sets of parents, which was the case with many Mithrazurs, azuras acted as if unbound because that was what they were. They might not be as fickle as faeries but they did serve whoever happened to be inspiring them at the moment.

In the current case of most of those occupying the Lathakran armed forces, the Thanatoids split their loyalties. That led lead to a strange situation whereby Mithras's Virgin commandeered the fidelity of thousands of devic offspring without having any of her own save Klannit (whom, if Harmony exemplified the overwhelming preponderance of ignorant anybodies, virtually no one except Tvasitar and the Thanatoids themselves knew existed).

Moreover, Morg may not as yet have grasped the fact that any azura could pull off the same resurrection stunt as Vetalazurs. It didn't make any difference anyhow. The azura-animated, Ambulant Dead burnt too. They just kept going until they were closer to ash than hash.

========

Harmony only belatedly took to her golden heels in accordance with Hot Stuff's arrogantly delivered directive. While she was one of many to tarry howsoever-deliberately defiantly, she was probably the first of any to realize what made up the main ingredient of the drones' teleportive fuel. It had to be identical to what Kanin City's cosmicars used over the pre-Medusa's meadow during the final stages of Thrygragon.

Her wonderful memory accounted for a good percentage of that insight. Truth seldom told, she'd surreptitiously been the one responsible for supplying a large quantity of it as part of the Panharmonium Compact she struck with everyone, including Utopians, intent upon terminating the Age of Mithras, that Great God with it. The remainder resulted from her relatively recent experiences on the shores of a lava lake spilling over with the very same ineffable Godstuff, albeit in its unrefined, molten form.

In the process of successfully withstanding the unkind attentions of her highborn brother in Lazareme, Tvasitar Smithmonger, aka the Anvil Artificer, she'd more than just rediscovered the ability to take over the body of any debrained daemon. She'd reacquainted herself with another underutilized devic knack: the ability to absorb, as if by osmosis, the caldera's Brainrock-Gypsium. Not only that, she'd perforce reminded herself that doing so recharged her – so much so that she proceeded to trounce Tvasitar regardless of her being in his own proto-protectorate atop of Sedon's Peak.

She learned here, above Grand Elysium, and remarkably for the first time, that no matter what Utopian technology had done to the miraculous Godstuff she could still absorb its essence. Which was what she proceeded to do, growing noticeably stronger by the second. Not wanting to be left out, the rest of the seven firstborns followed seriously exhilarating suit, whereupon the romp to the drones' ruination was on.

Until she began the wrecking ball rolling, they'd been trying to destroy the dodgy things with imitable projectiles of devic energy. In this they acted much like boisterous, but frustratingly inaccurate, boys and girls might when it came to smacking targets in a shooting gallery with airgun pellets and crossbow bolts, or splattering live ducks on a pond with their slingshots.

Once they started taking out, and taking into themselves, their Gypsium, the drones didn't only stop dropping their incendiary loads. They dropped out of the sky, whereupon they exploded, thus speeding along the hashes to ashes process. For Master Devas like her immediate brothers, the Thanatoids and the Silverclouds, especially those with selective memories when it came to pre-Earth encounters with space-faring Utopians, it must have seemed like decisive days of yore were back to the fore in glorious gore.

Brainrock didn't just make her stronger; it made her smarter. Harmony had herself a beautiful, possibly even brilliant flash. Naturally, when it came to her, there was nothing new about beauty, but brilliancy didn't always tag along for a jaunt through her cerebral cortex. She'd always reckoned herself at least as wise as her ring-gotten sister, Wisdom of Lazareme, and that thought was what triggered her latest brainwave.

She no more had Metisophia's power focus than she did Rumour of Lazareme's. Chances were someone did and it wouldn't be Dame Chance. Call-me-morgue had her trapped in a prison pod. Morg could also have sucked in or grabbed her Triskelion to go with Rumour's quill. But power foci worked for anyone and, if Hot Stuff didn't have Metis's cauldron, then she'd certainly know who did.

Harmony hied herself through the night, excited to scry.

========

Morg could have sucked in or grabbed the Triskelion, yes, but that didn't mean she had. Someone else might have, too.

Unless he already had a Brainrock panpipe.

****

7: Quill Killer

Equinoctial Day After Lilith Eve – The Medusa's Meadow

Immediately after their pre-Flood defeat in what chroniclers subsequently dubbed Ragnarok, still be-brained daemons acknowledged Sedon as their King. If they hadn't he'd have melted them down with cascades of the same ineffable Godstuff he used to obliterate Daemonicus, the daemons' long spouseless, yet nevertheless ever-smiling sovereign of the era.

Self-preservation therefore dictated daemonic forces, with or without the 'a', should seize the day and seek to destroy his and theirs before he came back from wherever he'd gone. Besides, even when he was around, daemons and Hellions were natural allies – Mother Natural allies.

That fact made devils their heavenly foes.

========

Sentient, even semi-sentient spirits, not being any more physical than, generally speaking, they were visible, didn't burn. Sometimes they wafted, as if smoke, every which way the wind blew. Certain sorts could waft directionally, independent of the wind. These sorts had devic parents.

They also weren't anywhere near as useless as many thought them. In truth, since they were to lower-end lifeforms what their parents were to the higher echelon, as in fully sentient species, it was mostly a matter of figuring out how to use them as effectively as possible given their undeniable limitations.

As for their parents, devils were initially spirit beings themselves. And, thanks to the subtle matter that made up their debrained daemonic bodies, as well as their Tvasitar talismans, which primarily consisted of Brainrock-Gypsium, they could still act as if they were just that. That meant they weren't anywhere near useless period. Another thing it meant was that, even without a daemonic body or a power focus, they'd always been able to get about person-to-person.

Morgan Abyss was not a pureblood Utopian. As Pyrame Silverstar had years ago shown, she could be possessed the same as any Piscine. Pyrame obviously hadn't been able to keep hold of her, however. Since she was immune to prison pods that had to be down to ringots. Clearly, her being the Pauper Priestess – in part called such because Tvasitar never made her a talisman due to the fact that she had no problem remaining solid without one of her own – left her peculiarly vulnerable to the devilish devices.

So the question became, at least it did for some devils: Were any of them, Master Deva, firstborn or even Great God, strong enough to both take her over and simultaneously resist capture in either the eyeorb atop her Master's Mace or her Tethys-delivered ringots?

Put it this way, if Sedon couldn't do it, then the answer had to be no.

Ah, but might someone else manage it?

========

One of the peculiarities of the Inner Earth was that New Years Day didn't start at the beginning of any month. Rather, it didn't start at the beginning of any month in areas of the Hidden Headworld that celebrated it on the Spring Equinox, i.e. the 20th or 21st of Surma. (Which was named after Zenit 'Blacksun' Suryad, a fourth-born Lazaremist whose protectorate, the Land of Midnight, lay in the Head's occipital region.)

Satanwyck, for example, marked New Years at the beginning of Belialmam, the last month of the Mithradic Ternary. It had, therefore, already had its party; though, particularly in Pandemonium, the partying never stopped. It wasn't called Paradise for the Damned for nada negative nought. Mind you, now that Beguiling Belialma was its ex-Sinistral, who could say what they'd call it next year.

Always assuming there was a next year for Satanwyck and its demons, that is.

========

"Mother Earth doesn't give birth to the fuckers," Fangfingers corrected the last speaker characteristically coarsely. "She excretes the malignant muck."

Many devils called him *'Fangfingers'* for reasons obvious. His Tvasitar talisman was a single glowing glove. Power foci being mutable, he regularly shaped it for wearing on his left hand simply because he was as left-handed as by far the majority of devils were. Hence why left-handedness came to be called the sinister affliction, with all the negative baggage that entailed. (Why was it, he was hardly alone in asking, right-handedness was never called an affliction, dextral or otherwise?)

Its fingers ended in what most resembled the fangs, not the talons, of a wolf, a bat or most any predacious beast. Not just devils pointed to its bizarre fingertips as verification, if any more were needed, that the fumes emitting from the Peak's bubbling Brainrock must have mind-numbed, even crazed, Anvil the Artificer long before he began crafting their power foci circa 2000 YD.

(And, with exceptions conceivably countable on one hand, those prone to making suchlike imprudent remarks knew nothing about his infatuation with a hopelessly bodiless azura by the name of Klannit Thanatos. Who, for all one of them, Harmony, knew, might by now be back in displaced Samarand – what could therefore no longer be referred to as Sedon's Tongue – re-growing into a new homo that may or may not look like mother Methandra minus the mask and gigantic pretensions.)

Something of a fashion plate, the unpleasant pretty boy was another of the not-just-lowborn Lazaremist Master Devas whose Elysium rampage provided pudding-proof that devils didn't self-cathonitize when they killed someone inclined to venerate them. His trendiness in terms of haberdashery, coupled with his mordant wit and morbid nature, often unfairly earned him the scorn of his fellow near-immortals; assuming they bothered to pay him any attention whatsoever, that is.

"We know that, fop," snorted the Rasp, his main victim as opposed to his main squeeze. "The question is from where?" Anything but a pretty girl herself, Skinless was hardly the only devil to address Fangfingers as that. She was about the only one who did so as a term of endearment, however.

Bygone Illuminaries named him Faustus Vladuca after a combination of Dacian, Carpathian, Gothic and/or Slavonic deities, folk legends or heroes. They further classed him as a Black Godling because he encouraged the sacrifice of animals; if not, due to Sedonic decree, humans or any other sentient beings. That he thus exhibited a fondness for seeing pain inflicted made them the perfect pair, not that most lovers would embrace their predilections when it came to lovemaking.

"No it isn't," said a pinkish-skinned, apple-eyed and, many would consider, delightfully proportioned stunner. "The question is what are we going to do about it?"

The newcomer speaking entered the booze tent arm in arm – and enticingly robed for a change – with a sparkling companion. Sniffing more so than hearing her, Unholy Abaddon looked up from his umpteenth horn of pilsner for the day. "I preferred you marble, Lust," he grunted borderline-nastily, if only for show.

"And I prefer you hard, not sloshed," smiled the last acknowledged Prime Sinistral of Satanwyck.

"There isn't much Ruby Red here doesn't know about fuckers fucking filthily, let alone what the planet excretes demonically," provided her escort, Lightning Lord Yajur, the Unity of Order, who'd acquired a poor, but justifiable, reputation for seeking to force humour where there wasn't any to be found. "That's why I fetched her from Tympani: to provide us with advice, not its homonym missing the *'ad'*."

"And I haven't been marble for quite a while, Abe," beguiling Belialma added, gracing Chaos with one of those provocative, come-hither winks of hers. "Quite the admirable dad the Lazareme-lot of you got. He woke up one day, saw who was standing in his statue garden, as a statue, broke me loose and we had ourselves a merry old chinwag."

"No doubt among other things," ventured Rudra Silvercloud, Byron's red-furred more so than red-haired Storm God as well as his Beast Master.

"He gave me a sympathetic ear, decided I'd been hard done by my own rebellious subjects, and I gave him a sympathetic reward."

"Like I said," the Byronic cracked, "Tits-for-tat."

"And like I said, he impressed me. Which is vastly superior to depressing me, which is what my own father used to do whenever we met."

"Mithras was schizzy," Rudra allowed. "And saturnine and Saturnian both stem from Saturn. He also played Caelus and Jupiter for a few hundred years before and after Saturn, didn't he? Unless it was Uranus and Zeus, that is; when it wasn't plain old Varuna and Mithras, I shouldn't have to admirably add."

"So he had us believe, rufous," the former Sinistral confirmed uncertainly.

(Mithras, the self-determined Great God of Truth, Light and Justice, among many other things, assumed mythic status in his own mind much more so than anywhere else.)

"Anyhow, since Byron lost his bitty little splinters pre-Dome, as Great Gods go Lazareme got the good wood compared to your guy too. I'd be jealous except Concord got the green eye and I got the red one." Actually, possibly because she usually had more interesting things to do than sleep, all three of her eyes were red. Only the one in the centre of her forehead had an apple for a pupil, however.

(The three myrionymous, second-born Mithradites each had an apple for a power focus, which was, duh, why they were known as Apple Goddesses. Long lost Strife, Mithras's Ewe for Aries as he often described her, had the Golden Apple of Discord. Hell's Belle's was the Ruby Red Apple of Concupiscence. Contrary to what Lust was implying, though, Divine Coueranna's was not of jealousy. It was the Little Green Apple of Juvenescence, called such because she started every year young again.)

"With all due kudos to your redoubtable erudition, my pomaceous spermbucket," King Cold, Tantal Thanatos – named after the Greek God of Death just as *'kudos'* came from the Greek word meaning *'magical glory'* – bellowed less despondently than drunkenly, "While it'll be tremendous to have you back bouncing in my bedroll again soon, grandfather's the Demon King and you're supposed to be his viceroy. He's gone, so if you can't stop the Earth's filthy seepage feeding on us, what can we do?"

Out of guilt as much as the fact he hated drinking alone, the always gigantic, blue-skinned, bearded iceberg had laid on the suds the others in the pavilion had been consuming with such gusto. Cold never went anywhere without kegs topped to the scuppers with the incredibly potent brew he favoured. He rarely guzzled an entire barrel by himself, however. Yet, after last night's humiliating retreat from Grand Elysium he was pails into his second.

"We smack their bottom, you big baby," answered Lust. "Rather, big sister does!"

Devic analysts such as the Librarian – the Lazaremist ancient Illuminaries named Biblio Drek – and their chroniclers, the Legendarian among them, described the Well of the World by analogy, as if Sedon had shot himself in the skull: his temple to be precise. As a result of that injection, chthonic crud underlay the Upper Head, hence Belle's allusion to its bottom.

"Except, you vacuous dingbat," objected Umashakti Silvercloud, who involuntarily waxed and waned with the moon, "We dare not do that, do we?" She also knew a thing or two about how gravity worked largely because, as the Byronic mistress of just that, she could control it.

"Heat rises. So do flames. The flames boil up, the whole Weirdom might too. We set off up the equivalent of another infernal equinox below ground, we might fricassee undying Cabalarkon, Sedon's father, in his tub of Cathonic Fluid. The old corpse finally expires for real, who knows what'll happen. We might all have to learn how to swim extremely fast and I hate water."

"Maybe Sed will wake the beastly buggery up," proposed Lunar Uma's brood brother and husband both. (Their triplet, Serathrone Hallow as Illuminaries came to call her once they heard her story, never made it to the Whole Earth. They named her thus because she'd chosen to be left behind in the Celestial Sphere once the Sedonshem escaped it long pre-Earth.)

"He does, the Weirdom's barbecued and so is its Master, with or without a different kind of fluid, the kind they use for embalming, not sauce."

"Eureka!" came a shout from an adjacent gazebo, the one wherein steamed Metis's rekindled and thereafter made Brainrock-boiling cauldron. "I found them."

========

Mid-Antheal, 4825 Year of the Dome – The Weirdom of Cabalarkon

Of the ten potential Quills-to-be Master Morgan had hauled to Cabalarkon on New Year's Lily, 'Quick', 'Quiff' and 'Quit-It' were triplets; 'Quail' and 'Quack' were twins; three brought-up-unrelated others had 'Quaff' as their Q-names; 'Quiddity' was a terribly good artist already; and Squirrelly wasn't so much a Q-name as a fact of his life.

Also in afterthought, perhaps he should have had 'Qatty' as his Q-name.

========

Antheal earned its folkloric reputation as the cruellest month. It rained, it blew, hailstones fell on Hellion hellstones, and it even snowed, more often than usual this year. Yet, on the rare day the clouds parted and the sun came out, men lowered their hoods and rolled up their sleeves. So did the generally much more modestly clad women; only, in the case of the upper class in particular, it was more often a matter of removing their veils and gloves than revealing much else.

The second month of the Lazaremist Ternary ended with what pagan practitioners of witchcrafts in northern parts of the Outer Earth's European continent called Walpurgis Night, after their wise women. West of there, in Gaelic and Celtic regions, it was called Maeve (as in May) or Beltane Eve. For Hellions in here it was one their four hell-nights, all of which they celebrated in part by lighting bonfires.

Today wasn't Antheal's last day. Today was only a few weeks after New Year's Lily, as Quaff-1 had already coined the equinoctial eve their deviant half-sister had them hied hither. Eight of the ten thus delivered were killing time chatting and telling stories, which was infinitely superior to killing each other. One was decorating his walls with drawings and paintings.

As for the tenth, he was probably off goat-dancing with Morgan Abyss. Could be, they joked, that *'Qaprine'* might've made an even better Q-name.

========

"Mother Earth," Quaff-2 continued finger reading off the tee-tee tail he'd acquired from an as-yet-alive tee-tee trapped a few hours ago in the palace kitchen, "Required Demon Queen Lilith bear mortal sedons, small case, two or three times every human generation. She did so for motives both mysteriously magisterial and mystically millennial. Meaning she wasn't in it for a good time; she was in it for a long time.

"Evidently she could only support more so than sustain Sed's Shed, and within it the Inner Earth of Sedon's Head, by resorting to suchlike, dare I say it, magical methodology. Guess I just did."

(Natives of the Inner Earth felt magic a foolish, even borderline-nonsensical notion. And so they might considering pecks of distinctly non-human sentient beings called the Head home; devils walked around it openly; psychopomp-demons or near-demons could be summoned by name; and their faerie cousins petitioned, as well as far too inconveniently often placated, herein. What seemed magical simply wasn't altogether explicable to those not in the know as yet.)

"As for why she'd want to do anything at all about a Hidden Continent that until the Genesea had been the archipelago of Pacifica, the Places of Peace, well, it could be that, as a favour to her fellow, populated planets, she preferred to keep devils contained. It could also be their All-Father threatened to destroy the whole world if she didn't. Which, come to think of it, might yet come to pass if she were to let it sink.

"At any ruinous rate, although Pyrame Silverstar claimed it was pure love, her demon being that demon had to be the secret to her seemingly forever relationship with Dark Sedon post-Dome. In other words, Pyrame having hold of lascivious Lily was what made her the fabulously female perpetual presence to the mighty Moloch's resolutely male dot-ditto."

"Shouldn't that be dick-dildo?" queried Quaff-1, the only other one there in their common room who could read tee-tee tails with some degree of accuracy.

"Thanks for the heads-up," #2 said to #1. "You're right of course. I'll make a menial mote mentally. Still working on my Jordyisms, don't you know?"

"That's not all we know," complained Quaff-3, a young woman like Quack, Quick, Quiff and Quit-It. "And one of them is we know all about Sed-sons from #1's tee-tee tail. You said yours was different."

"Hey, a guy's got to practise. Otherwise how can I keep getting laid?"

Unlike the other potential Legendarians there, Quaff-2 showed no knack for musicianship, dancing, singing or bardic pursuits such as writing then reciting fine poetry or enacting pantomimes. If he was going to make it on the troubadour circuit the same as the rest of them already had – which, to perform, was why they'd joined their jointly devic half-mother in Elysium – he'd have to do so as a raconteur or storyteller.

"And a guy's got to get laid," agreed Quail, Quack's dapper, always colourfully dressed twin brother.

"Don't look at me," said Quiff, called such because of her forelock, not because of her promiscuity. "I don't do relatives."

Her predilection for, as Q-troupe's cruder members put it, spreading herself around sexually was well-known from previous gigs. Here, though, at least thus far, she'd only favoured their minders, most of whom belonged to the Weirdom's so-called Sarpedon underclass.

"Yes, yes, we know all that too," said Quaff-3 impatiently. "And don't look at me either, Quail. Not unless you get down on your knees first. I'm the marrying kind."

Lauded throughout the Upper Head for her abilities as an actress, Quaff-3's off-stage, non-thespian antics as a walking divorce writ attracted almost as much attention. Sometimes, it seemed not just to her, celebrity tittle-tattle bruited about by paid or unpaid scandalmongers put as many or more bums in seats than talent, a decent text or good theatre did.

"Six divorces in as many marriages sort of says that, doesn't it," Quail acknowledged, feigning disappointment. Nothing ventured, nothing gained.

"Marrying messily," contributed Quack, who was far more snarky than ducky, as in lovable, "Yet getting out of it alive, no matter how many times you do it, still strikes me as beanbags better than being the prematurely burying sort."

Quack was also far more of a silk-throated songbird than her Q-name indicated. Quail was similarly gifted, although it had to be said she was something of a Plain Jane to his Handsome Harry. Web-footed fowl were like that. Evolutionarily speaking, the males of most species were flashier-looking than the females. That's what made them desirable. What rightly reproduction-oriented ducky would want to mate with a dullard drake?

"What can I tell you?" #3 put to him. "I collect rings. At least I'm not polyandrous. Besides, someone has to look after the little ducklings when I'm on tour."

"Ew," Quiff squealed in mock disgust. "He proposes; you accept; you'll both end up with idiots just like all these Weirdoes, capitalized, that the Sarpedons wheel around."

"We're not related," Quick snapped automatically, as if it was expected of her. "Having the same half-mother doesn't count if she's a devil."

"And our dad's still alive," added Quit-It, the last of the triplets born. She got her Q-name because their mother was fed up giving birth – *'You can quit it now, babies'*. She didn't get it because Quit-It was always being naughty when they were growing up – *'You don't quit it, you're quilt dead'*.

"At least he was the last time we saw him. He never became a Quill and neither did his father before him, though they were both bilged bastards."

"Oh let's not go over all that again," said Quack. The troupe's popular singers, Quail and Quack, were avian-humans from Godbad's Goatwood, Sedon's Beard. "Just because they never wore caps with a quill in them doesn't say they weren't Legendarians and besides, Chance could have been possessing one of them."

"Or your grandmother could have been him," said Quail, unable to resist going over it again. "You said her name was Jordan. One of you is even named after her, right."

"So are you," said Quiff, the one whose first name was Jordan.

"Not after your grandmother I'm not," Quail reminded her.

"Can I please go on?" all-but-begged Quaff-2, the practising-to-be-Jordy, though his given name was Gordon.

"Only if you skip to the end," #3, the serial monogamist, said to the #2 tail-teller.

"In those days," he obliged her, zipping well ahead, "There were as many black-as-night male as there were white-as-light female Warriors Elites."

The tale the tail came into being telling, via its bum-bumps, sprinkled ridges and pimply nodules, tactile striations and varying vales, was only a few months old. Be that as it may, the voracious rodents were creatures of the *'once upon a time, long, long ago'* school of narrative, both in terms of incising and vocalizing. As for the tale it would have told when #2 pulled its tail, the tee-tee must have been traumatized by its capture because it bit its own tail off the moment Quaff-2 started pulling it, hence its escape.

"Every one of them would have been holding onto their eye-staves; most would have already activated their household gargoyles, as emanating from the eyeorbs or devic prison pods atop them; and nary a solitary soldier among them had ever, except in their wildest dreams, fancied victory, let alone survival, a probable outcome of their long-awaited confrontation with the approaching impossibly mighty Moloch Sedon."

"It's the throne room version," supplied Quaff-1, the older, already practising teller of tales and reader of tails. "Not the storeroom version like mine."

(That version of the previous midwinter's calamitous proceedings had the Devil Sedon eyefire-requiring Master Morg unseal the Solidium vault containing prison pods stuffed shut pre-Earth, ones that been retrieved and deposited there-in. Magnanimous Moloch that he had next-to-never been tempted to evince until that day, he thereupon freed the multitude of devic spirit beings internally salvaged within the same orbs, or pods, ancestral Trinondevs used to capture them off-world during their seemingly interminable pursuit of the Sedonshem.

(Empty eyeorbs of First or Second Weir World manufacture neither should nor, for Sedon milliseconds later, could be confused with empty eyeorbs produced in decrepit, post-Dome Weirdoms like Cabalarkon's. Wherever or however he was trapped – in the throne room, in the storage vault itself, or in virtually any other scenario – the end-result was identical: no more Sed-Star shining upstairs.)

"So it is," #2 confirmed for everyone. "Morgan Abyss would have been holding her sceptre, her Masters Mace, the symbol of her authority. Likely she wouldn't have caused her personal gargoyle, whatever it is, to manifest and thence harden around her as yet, if she ever did. She would have fashioned its eyeorb into the approxima-tion of a Death's Head, however. Folks didn't nickname her the Death's Head Hel-lion for zero multiplied by zippers, as the Quill-Jordy might fay-say it."

"Good one that, 2."

"Thanks again, 1."

"Stop with the mutual admiration society already, you two," said #3. "You don't, I may have to hurl, as in puke."

"Don't tell me you're pregnant already," said Quiff.

"I told you, I'm saving myself for marriage."

"I told you Quaff-3's no Tethys," reiterated the non-ducky singer sarcastically. "Tethyses always have a procreative imperative."

"I do too and I am three. It's my last name. What's yours, Quail – Dickhead?"

"Actually it's Kestrel."

"I know that four. Or is it five by now? I'm confused."

"The All-Father of devazurkind," Quaff-2, exasperated, motor-mouthed, "Went from being totally unimpressed with Weir's eyeorbs to being wholly frag-mented by them. Whereupon his subtle matter, formerly constituent particles instantly slurped into the selfsame feeble weaponry he had so ceaselessly scorned.

"That's it – The End!"

========

Vanalal 1, 4825 Year of the Dome – The Weirdom of Cabalarkon

Morg didn't have a Q-name; not one she admitted to at any rate. She had gills behind her ears, however. Which made her an aquatic and its 'q' counted. She wasn't the marrying sort either, not yet, though she did collect rings. They weren't wedding bands; she wouldn't have her first, and hopefully last, of those until next month.

Azky, after Azkeecyoos, Lazareme's male healer, aka Sturgeon the Surgeon, was the traditional time for marriages. She was all in favour of tradition, especially the Utopians' tradition of not only hating Sedon and all his unkind line, but trying to destroy them. She was also flexible. Marriages purely of convenience were fine by her. She liked Squirrelly best but Quiddity could draw better than any of them.

And for some reason, Rumour's quill hadn't been doing its job properly for well over a month.

========

Thus far spring had been noticeably colder than usual. In Cabalarkon City, and indeed throughout the countryside, the hell-night bonfires Hellions lit yesterday evening in order to help blaze in Vanalal, the third month of the Lazaremist Ternary, and with it the pastoral summer season, had finally been allowed to die down. In spite of the unseasonably miserable weather, the metropolis's maypole ceremony, which she made a point of overseeing in her capacity of Master of Weir, was due to start at noon.

Right now, though, Morg was figuratively crying *'Mayday, mayday!'* and Quiddity was doing his best to respond in a pole-free manner – albeit not a pen-free one.

"If you'd let me use the quill, mistress," he said to her.

"I'm no man's mistress; no woman's either."

"If you'd let me use the quill, Master," he rephrased.

"Not a chance, Quid. You saw her, you draw her."

"That was six weeks ago and you saw her too."

"Maybe my idea of perfect beauty has changed since then."

"That shouldn't make any difference. Harmony's gorgeousness personified. Imagine what perfect beauty is in your mind and Rumour's quill will do the rest."

"You ever heard of Harmony being a man?"

"Squirrelly's got you that bad?"

"Don't be impertinent, boy. But, yes, he does. He's a regular spellbinder."

"There's a Byronic called that, isn't there?"

"Sedona's never male either; not that I've ever heard anyhow and I'm from the Gulf of Aka."

"If I draw her, what I remember of her, what'll you do?"

"Trace it, obviously."

So he did, with an ordinary stylus. So she did too, with Rumour's quill. Rather, she did it with its ever-replenishing Brainrock ink. Nothing happened. The background didn't even fill in when she retook the tracing and splotched it out on her splotch pad. Devils were messing with her much more that she was Squirrelly, who reminded her of renditions she'd seen of Thrygragos Lazareme that the real Legendarian had done of his Great God grandfather, on both sides of the bed, in decades and centuries past.

"Any more bright ideas?"

"Didn't I warn you not to be insolent, Quid?"

Maybe her, pick one, annoyed, haughty and/or threatening tone set him off; maybe something else did – perhaps his own pent-up frustrations, perhaps an urgent need to act decisively for the perceived purpose of self-preservation. Whatever the case, a third eye suddenly sprouted in the middle of his forehead.

As predicted, eyefire didn't blaze out of it. Morg squelched a smile. She hadn't expected it would. After seemingly endless trials, which they'd begun shortly after the Legendarian brought the kibisis stuffed with ringots to the Weirdom for her to deposit in its Stopstone vault, she and her Illuminaries had been right on that score at least.

Apparently – if not, at the conclusion of their experiments, absolutely beyond any shadow of a doubt – devils could only unleash eyefire when they had a power focus. Albeit only by the same theoretical token, that strongly suggested they had to be disarmed before they could be ring-gotten.

She stifled her grin a-budding because, distressingly, and scarcely for the first time in recent months, it dawned on her they were definitely wrong on a much more crucial score. The devic spirit beings she sent into potential Quills-to-be, from what she now regarded as her ringots, were supposed to keep their shells docile, at their command, just as the devils themselves remained at hers.

That had been the case with the priestly powers-that-were, whom she'd done a ditto to in Grand Elysium mere days after Mithramas. Then again, none of them had come near a power focus until they'd carried out the delaying tactics she'd assigned them while she had the city booby-trapped with her goopy, yet nonetheless exceedingly inflammatory allies.

This one had – Rumour of Lazareme's. Hers!

========

He attacked, grabbing for it.

Quiddity was at least twenty years younger than her but Piscines were hardy folk. Long daily swims kept them fit for life whereas Quid was a pampered artiste incensed by a possessive devil that saw a way to escape captivity. Morg also lifted weights regularly. He did too, albeit a much a different sort than she did, though to his credit nowhere near thirty a day. That would have killed a non-Quill years before he turned thirty.

Ursine Bardol, that was the Lazaremist's Illuminary-given name. She knew that because she'd stuck him in a different shell before interviewing him, truth compelled to tell. And, yes, he was a monstrous bear of beast-man when he had a de-brained daemonic body and a burl-on-a-big-branch Tvasitar-trinket to keep him godlike. He had no more had either then, when she interviewed him, than he did now.

First order of business was to dodge the lunge. Next, in rapid-fire succession, she chopped him on the back of the head as he went by, applied a couple of swift boots to the solar plexus in order to get him down, and a couple more to keep him that way. Finally, just for good measure, she booted him in the head, one foot at a time, once, twice and, because she was enjoying herself so much, thrice.

(Unless, and this was a thought almost as chilling as the weather had been lately, it was the demon within her enjoying herself.)

Quid was out. Activating one of the now-empty ringots she habitually wore, she extracted Bardol. Winded, she sat down. Remarkably, it only then occurred to her that she'd dispatched Quiddity all the while holding Rumour's quill in hand. Likely, she probably rationalized, she'd been subconsciously afraid to let go of it.

Then it vanished.

Then she whirled, saw Quid's corpse, what she'd reckoned his unconscious body, rise onto its haunches, dazed look in both eyes and Brainrock quill in his hand instead of hers. Whereupon, before the Jordy-degenerate's latest regeneration could splotch out its splotch pad and dot himself to safety elsewhere, she was upon him.

She killed him again – not that she'd particularly wanted to kill the kid in the first place. She just didn't know her own strength. Or his innate weakness, as the case may be. She did him in this time with a twist of the arm, a bones-snapping jerk, and a kill-quill-jab that penetrated the forehead into his cerebellum.

Nib entered skull at the exact spot where Bardol's third eye had so briefly shone, if not blazed. She stood back; watched as his blood, braincells and bone-bits drained onto her dayroom floor. So this was what defending the Weirdom against all comers came down to, she must have realized, howsoever-bemusedly. She might be losing it, her soul if not necessarily her mind, but she wasn't about to risk losing Rumour's quill.

Holding onto it made her a stone cold killer; a typical devil's bargain that. One day she'd accidentally or intentionally kill one of Chance's half-children and nothing would happen. One day someone else would kill someone somewhere else and she'd be without Rumour's quill forever afterwards.

Or until she killed herself and saw what became of her, which she'd never dare do because she might not be a Jordy-in-waiting. Besides, the Legendarian might not be dancing the limbless limbo between-space when she up and topped herself. He wasn't, even if she was a potential Quill-to-be she would be Morg in the morgue irrevocably.

It was pointless to draw any of the other firstborn, not even one of the two non-cathonitized Thanatoids, who almost never changed their outward seemings. They'd be doing like Harmony. They'd be occupying someone. She drew them anyhow. The backgrounds behind one did fill-in for a change. Too bad it was Abe Chaos.

Unholy Abaddon sometimes changed his appearance on an hourly basis. Today he looked huge and hairy, just like he had on Equinoctial Eve. He was smiling, as if he could sense she'd just drawn him. Not for the first time she wished she could draw him hither, into the land of Trinondevs and dozens of empty, pre-Earth prison pods.

Rumour's quill didn't work that way so she put it away and summoned Squirrelly instead. His quill always worked.

========

Snow threatened outside. Inside, for a few minutes anyhow, all was warm.
****

8. Her Gargoyle's Strife

Vanalal 1, 4825 Year of the Dome – The Weirdom of Cabalarkon

The southern songbirds, Quail and Quack Kestrel, tenor and soprano respectively, vanished before noon on a chilly Beltane Day.

========

Informed of it at the maypole ceremony, Morg went off with her advisers for a few minutes private consultation. In 20/20 retrospect, they quickly realized how they must have pulled it off. After Quiddity, though, the real issue was not how or even where they'd gone. It was that they'd obviously done the opposite to what cost the unlucky Quid his life, twice. The devils inside them hadn't asserted themselves over the Kestrels; the Kestrels had somehow managed to overwhelm the devils.

Once away from prying eyes, she materialized Rumour's quill and, out of curiosity, if only to see where they'd got to, she drew the two fled avian-humans from memory. Rather, Rumour's quill drew them from her memory. Much to her delight and surprise it worked properly this time, filling in a bar of some sort as their background. They were speaking with some warty old witch, one of their wise women probably, though why the bar was in a cave, instead of up a tree, and why they weren't wearing their flying feathers, she couldn't be bothered to wonder.

Her people, fuelled though not warmed by rumours of the viral variety, were shivering in a drizzle interspersed with snowflakes by the time she returned to the maypole ceremony. Put-upon for months now by wintry weather that just wouldn't quit, they were clamouring for answers. After one of her mouthpieces confirmed the twins' disappearance, Morg herself stepped forward to briefly address the crowd.

Stunningly, in a hitherto unheard of display of regret for this Master, if not any previous Master, Morg accepted blame for it. She had sadly miscalculated the totality of their capabilities. They were avian-humans but were they also closet Garudas? Definitely. Were they devic spies she'd invited to stay in the Weirdom after their troupe's escape from Elysium? She'd find out.

If they were, what could they pass on to their masters? She'd find that out too. Devils weren't the only ones who had spies. Was there anything more they should worry about, besides catching a chill? Not from devils, the cowards are terrified of us and their armies will take years to rebuild after our Elysium masterstroke.

If you've any other issues, my spokeswomen will gladly hang around for a few more minutes, though not from a scaffold.

Thanks for the umbrella. Good thing I wore my woollies, eh?

========

What was much, much worse, Morg and her advisers had already figured out, but couldn't comment upon in public, was that she should never, ever, have entrusted the Q-troupe's continuing complacency to devils; this despite the fact that she'd only learned this morning they were beyond her ability to control 100%.

That she didn't dare admit it wasn't just because the existence of ringots, let alone knowledge of what they could do, were a state secret either. When it came to attempts to obliterate devils, the idiots of Weir forgave almost everything including failure. Some things they almost never forgave, however.

As witness the disgraceful treatment of the Sarpedon underclass for over 1500-years already, the unavoidable humiliation of having to put up with Sedon's patronage, as a trade-off for their own survival upon the Whole Earth, left such a bilious aftertaste they'd round on anyone they perceived as compromising their apocalyptic aspirations by persistently poor decision-making.

Anyone relying on devils for anything, even peace, therefore didn't risk rebuke, they risked retaliation. At the minimum, dethronement awaited any Master thought guilty of such an unpardonable transgression. *'Thought'*, not *'judged'*, was the optimal word as well. When it came to Utopians, mind-over-matter explained virtually everything others might deem either miraculous or magical about them.

At least it did in any Weirdom where an applied brand of mass-mind consensus didn't just empower its Master. It did where it actually powered the machinery that kept everything that did work still working. And that remained the situation in the first Weirdom established on the planet, that of Cabalarkon. Which, in terms of a preponderance of purebloods, was also the last true Weirdom.

That said, or more like left unsaid, the enlightened liars who made up her inner circle of scientocratic, Illuminary, Hellion and Trinondev advisers purported to back up Morg's admission of guilt by ignorance – as well as omission, when it came to predetermining Quail and Quack's capabilities – with irrefutable facts.

Question any of them and they'd claim that, the Kestrels being avian-humans from Sedon's Beard, the twins in effect just sprouted feathers and flew off between-space. Suchlike hollow-boned men and women often were Garudas and Garudas were self-psychopomps. They could travel through the Weird at will. Everyone knew that.

(Sedon' Beard was the heavily forested area in the southernmost section of the subcontinent of Aka-Godbad. In part because it grew out of Sedon's Chin, like the Devil's own bushy goatee, cartographers commonly identified it as Goatwood on maps of the Hidden Headworld. Cartographers really were clever chaps.)

All right, so they didn't exactly sprout their flying feathers. They pulled them out and put them on, the same as most folks put on clothes, but you get the picture. As for where their feathers came from, well duh, the aquiline men and women travelled through the answer to that. Obviously, when they took them off, Garudas didn't store them in a wardrobe or a suitcase the same as a sensible fellow like you might reckon they did. They kept them between-space.

What's more, they didn't need witch-stones, kibises or something similar to keep them there. They did so naturally. I mean, if tee-tees can grow tails that told tales, or tongues somehow connected to voice boxes that allowed them tell other ones out loud, ask yourself this: What's so odd about Garudas growing feathers between-space, being able to conjure them at will, and then buggering off unseen by anyone?

You might as well ask our noble Trinondevs where they kept their gargoyles when they weren't materializing more so than displaying them. All right again, they kept them in mind, or in eyeorbs if you prefer, not between-space but, hey, you can always call a spade a spade if you want. It still works like a shovel, so what's the big shaggy dog difference? Or the tiny bald poodle one, as far as that goes.

Are there any more questions?

========

What the enlightened liars couldn't as easily dismiss was why, a couple of hours after the mucky maypole ceremony ended in soggy indifference, Quiddity threw himself out of Morg's airborne beetle – what she called her lady-buggy. That didn't stop them from speculating, though.

It didn't prevent the therefore trebly shocked, potential Quills-to-be of Q-troupe doing so either. Quid promised Quick he'd be at the ceremony, attentively. She'd dressed accordingly, in not very much at all. (One couldn't comfortably cavort in winter clothing, could one.) Yet he'd missed it and now he was dead. How come?

One remaining Q-person didn't participate in their at times appreciably teary nattering. That'd be the fellow who, even though he didn't have three sea-green eyes, sky-blue skin and sunshiny, golden hair, did resemble centuries' worth of paintings or drawings of Thrygragos Lazareme decorating walls and corridors near, in, and/or leading into the Masters throne room.

That'd also be the fellow who'd confided in Q-troupe's two Legendarian-wannabes, Quaffs 1 & 2, that this year the Master would be dancing around the maypole for him alone. Which, since for whatever reason the Master didn't dance it period, may have made him the biggest storyteller of the babbling batch.

He didn't participate because he wasn't there. He might not have even if he had been. Likely he could care less about Q-troupe.

========

Unless they were deaf, others there had no choice in matter. The fly on the wall, the spider in a web behind the curtains, the mouse beneath the most comfortable couch in their common area, the bedbugs inside it and even an azura with a knack for mirrors, including the handheld glass Quaff-3 used when she was touching up her powder and face-paint, couldn't help but overhear them.

That last wasn't just following her parents' instructions. She was using #3's makeup mirror as her personal mirador, or viewpoint, on the off chance her missing lover had been taken there after he disappeared. She didn't particularly enjoy mindfucks so this would be her physical lover from the centuries prior to circa 2000 YD, the centuries during which they both had sexually responsive bodies.

Unfortunately unlike his, hers was never a debrained daemon, hence her recent reliance on fleshy, but far too fragile, homunculi.

========

"Maybe he got jealous of all the attention the Master's been giving Squirrelly."

"Qatty isn't getting attention. He's getting laid."

"Hey, I was getting to that."

"For someone with Quick for a Q-name, you sure were slow."

"Suicides leave notes. Quid didn't, not that we've seen anyhow."

"What are you saying – that the Master and Qaprine quit goat-dancing long enough to off him? Why bother?"

"Maybe they invited him to join in and he got caught on a horn. And I don't mean of a dilemma."

"So they tossed him out of her aerial jalopy to disguise their dreadful deed?"

"Sounds right to me."

"Sounds asinine to me."

"The thingy with the eye-staves sticking out of it like the spines of a sea urchin, or a porcupine's quills, that's a jalopy? I thought it was a modified cosmicar."

"Jalopy's what Tomcat calls it. Don't ask me why. He uses all sorts of weird words. Says they're future-speak but I think he just makes them up as he goes."

"And the Master calls it her lady-buggy, or Battle Beetle, on account of it does look kind of like a beetle when all the eye-stave portals are shut."

"Cosmicars are bigger, like a bus."

"What's a bus, a kind of kiss?"

"It's what you got on your chest, 3."

"That's a bust, 2 – like you, from what Quack told me."

"A bus is one of those long, step-up lorries with all sorts of seats and windows for their passengers to look out of. The Sarpedons will them around the streets and out into the countryside when they're taking Weirdoes sightseeing."

"Will, or wheel?"

"Will the wheels to go round if you prefer."

"I thought that was an ambulance."

"That's what they use when they're carting them off to hospital, or out to the Hills of the Sleepers if they can't do anything else for them."

"Ambulances got bells not boobs."

"Size-wise, busses are to ambulances what cosmicars are to the Master's jalopy. And they don't will them around they drive them around."

"On wheels, by willpower."

"I'll go along, as well as around, with wheels. The Sarpedons are will-sapped, not will-filled like the idiots of Weir."

"Old buggery! Looks like we're in for a blizzard."

"Whatever happened to all those showers bringing all those flowers?"

"Hey, snowdrops are kind of pretty."

"Maybe we should ask Qatty what happened to Quid."

"And you'd believe a guy whose last name is tattletale even if he spells it, in Sedon Speak, Tattletail?"

========

"Of course he didn't snuff himself." For a hideously warty beldam the speaker had a disconcertingly mellifluous, even beautiful voice.

"How can you be so sure, Harm? You weren't watching them in the fumes. You were watching us. That's how you realized we were alone."

========

"Trust me, pauper. The Piscine witch killed him all by her lonesome."

"I'd watch who you're calling a witch, Unity. Ever heard the saying *'that's like calling a Utopian guy black*'? Or haven't you looked in a mirror lately?"

"Ugliness is in the eye of the beholder, you ungrateful, sexless toad," said the Unity as well as the Harm in question, this despite the fact she was addressing a very well dressed, Handsome Harry of a drake-man (as opposed to a mandrake plant).

The speakers were sitting around a table in a curtained-off corner of a huge, mostly underground, smoke, steam and even mist-filled barroom, namely the Dinq Doinq Danq Cavern Tavern. They'd come to the DDD in order to rest after a harrowing couple of hours.

They weren't sampling its wicked mushroom wine – although inebriated leles dancing naked nearby obviously had, in quantity. Instead, they were sipping Cathy, a form of distilled Cathonic Fluid that devils in particular loved. A restorative potion heavy on powdered Brainrock-Gypsium, its taste was so foul the Kestrels, even though they were akin to fowl, had trouble stomaching the wretched concoction.

Harmony's humanoid host was an ordinarily beer-guzzling, long no longer handsome hag, hence Quail's mirror crack. Astonishingly to many, the nearly toothless crone still somehow managed to make a living hooking out of the DDD, which lay in the south-easternmost edge of Marutia, Sedon's Cheek. Moreover, since loveliness incarnate rarely singled her out for purposes possessive, she did so entirely on her own merits.

"And, just in case you've been out of it for so long your brain's more addled than it used to be, Hellions are witches. They've the hellstones to prove it. Also in truth, or at least as an arguable aspect of it, she did it two times. As for two-trillion-timing Tommy, he and her ignoramus Illuminaries only helped the bitch, if you prefer, cover her precious butt-end."

"Two-trillion-timing Tommy?"

"Tomcat Tattletail, toad. He's a faerie trickster. I spotted him in Elysium just before Hot Stuff set off her pyrotechnics, what set off the Elysium Inferno you'll have heard about when you gleaned your shell. We call him that because he's the *'love them and leave them'* type. There's a lot of the Legendarian about him. This version might even be his son or grandson."

"*'Love them and leave them'* is a euphemism if ever there was one," remarked still-2-eyed Pyrame Silverstar, simultaneously Quack Kestrel, who only ever had two eyes. "Take it from me, Balance, you and your fabled memory are sickeningly out of whack when it comes to that fucking faerie prick.

"You're not only his favourite victim; you can't wait to be victimized again. That means you and his mother – assuming he had a mother he didn't suckle dry and eat – are probably the only ones who call him anything except variations on asshole. Me, when I'm not calling him a prick or an asshole, I call him an unmitigated jerk."

The Pauper Priestess likely trusted their cross-tribal, yet nevertheless enduring, friendship would allow her to get away with a couple of perceptive comments, ones carefully couched within the parameters of acceptable teasing. A snap glance into the beldam's eyes told her she'd trusted wrong, that she'd hit a serious sore spot and inadvertently reopened an unhealed wound.

The Harmony-hag's eyes suddenly flickered thrice. "So says Sedon's Whore."

Quack was quick enough not to look hurt on Pyrame's behalf. Instead she shrugged. Then she seized upon something the Unity had just mentioned and sensibly switched the subject: "Arguable because Quid looked to have become Quill by then?"

Even though she'd intuited the answer already – who else ever had to be killed twice? – she reckoned it a timely strategy. Asking rhetorical questions definitely beat yanking Harmony's chains any more than briefly about an all-too-familiar-looking faerie fart prone to future-speak. Which was something else Thrygragos Lazareme did fay-fairly-frequently, as he, Harmony and Tomcat Tattletail might put it.

"That's how it seemed to this malevolent Master of yours, priestess," said Harmony, vanishing the third eye in her host's forehead almost as instantly as she'd so shamefully let it flare. "I know because they were already talking about it when I tuned into her. And I didn't do that until I knew you and the Neuter were safely out of Great-Granddaddy Cabby's Weirdom."

(The fumes they were referring to emitted from Metisophia's cauldron, her power focus. Methandra Thanatos confiscated it after ring-getting Wisdom of Lazareme during the Lathakrans' rampage through her nominal territory on the Cattail Peninsula most of a century ago.

(Said fumes didn't provide audio. However, azuras occupying rodents and much dinkier creepy-crawlers had been infiltrating the Weirdom since late Surma, the first month of the Lazaremist Ternary. Devils thoroughly in tune with their otherwise incorporeal offspring could thereby listen in on conversations they were overhearing at the same time they could see what they were witnessing.)

"And it's neutral, not neuter," Quail objected; rather, 2-eyed Geld Neargon objected via Quail's mouth. He did so in his own unmistakable voice, though. "So stop calling me *'the Neuter'*. I may choose to look toadyish sometimes, when I'm out and about, but sexless or neutered I'm not. You want to talk true, cousin? Then I'm insulted you could think me either/or. I bear my own azuras. Can you say the same thing?"

"Don't know, never tried, have I?" one shell said to another shell in her occupant's voice. "That doesn't mean I couldn't. We are all gods and goddesses after all. It might even turn out to be entertaining, once. You'll have to show your technique to Hot Stuff when she returns. Parthenogenesis might appeal to her."

"It isn't a virgin birth. If anything, it's more like autogenesis or self-propagation. I actually fuck myself."

"Oh, I do that too; particularly when it comes to tumbling Tom, as my pointy-headed pal ever so precipitously just reminded us. Only I don't get any azuras out of it."

(When Silverstar walked amidst her fellow devils as herself, not possessing anyone, she often lost her face and retracted her ordinarily silken, tinsel-silvery hair. She did not go around headless as such, though she regularly did do so topless. Instead of adopting anything animalistic to take its place, which many of her fellow devils did in Egypt immediately before, during and for a short while after the halcyon days of the Middle Sea matriarchy, she altered her skull into the shape of a tetrahedron.

(In this imitable – for metamorphs – but idiosyncratic form, the upper sides of her head met at an apex like that of a capstone on a three-faced pyramid, if such a thing existed. In her case, each of its upper faces sported a solitary eyeball along the lines of an Egyptian '*wadjet*' or, even more precisely, the all-seeing Eye of Providence.)

"No one but you would want to be so boringly independent, toad," the Pauper Priestess put to her/their brother/s, Quail-Neargon, if only in hopes of shoring up her relationship with the powerful, but overly sensitive, firstborn again. "Actually, now that I think about it, allow me to rephrase that: Who else except you is such an unpleasant contrarian no one would want to have children with you any which way?"

"That's hog-hooey, Pyrame, and you should know it. Certain sorts of Ophidians do it all the time in Ophir-Moorset."

"Which is on your eastern frontier as I recall," said Pyrame, speaking to the hermaphroditic toad occupying Quail.

"More to the point," the Unity inserted poignantly, "It's also irrelevant. Ophidians can't bear azuras; they can only bear other Ophidians."

"There is that," Neargon allowed.

"Plus," Harmony added, "I fail to see how anyone else could bear my azuras."

"Bollocks, Balance. You could if you grew a dick and impregnated someone prone to fertility like our ever-earthy Silverstar here."

"All this talk about Ophidians strikes me as less risqué than risky," Pyrame cautioned, ignoring the oral barbs the Harmony-hag and the internally androgynous drake-man were tossing across the table at each other. Cathy restored vigour but it also seemed to reinforce devic competitiveness and concomitant clannish acrimony.

"How so?" Neargon bit; perhaps at last appreciating he really was coming across as an ungrateful toad. Harmony had probably hoped to extract a couple of her own siblings when she rescued the Kestrels. That she got a pair of Mithradites instead might tempt her to return them to Cabalarkon; something she could presumably do as easily as she got them out, by merely reversing the procedure.

"From what I understand," Pyrame-Quack carried on, "Old Eden's pre-Golden Age experiments into the building blocks of life resulted in almost all of the Head's non-earthborn exotica. Tee-tees are among the least intelligent whereas you could make a case that Garudas and Ophidians are way up there at the other end of the scale. Intelligence doesn't eliminate instinctive animosity. So, if only because eagles feed on snakes and snakes love eating eagle eggs, those two species hated each other from the get-go."

"Then it's a good thing we're not possessing Garudas."

"And a much better thing the murder-minded Piscine doesn't realize it," noted Harmony, sounding relieved not to be slinging spoken mud anymore. "Otherwise, she might figure out how we really got you out of Cabalarkon and try the same stunt herself. It's not as if, thanks mostly to me, she doesn't have the wherewithal, is it?"

"Beat yourself up some more, Unity," said Quail-Neargon cheerfully. "I'm starting to enjoy it."

"If I might finish," Quack-Pyrame interceded, before the conversation got nasty again. "They are from Goatwood, there's no question both have ridden Garudas stacks of times, and their surname probably means some of their ancestors were Garudas. Quack was even engaged to one once. Since our hold on the twins is tenuous at best, it might not be wise to excite them overly much.

"And that's all I'm saying. Until I get back into All down on Incain and you get yourself a replacement body, and a new power focus, we need them."

"No more than they need you, pauper. The Master has Jordy's quill, don't forget."

"We won't," Quail-Neargon promised her, with a wink directed at Quack. "For about the half-second it takes the happy harpy here to whisk us up to Sed's Peak."

"There's no way to break it to you gently, toad," said Harmony, disinclined to hold back the bad news any longer. "But I'm afraid that's not going to happen anytime soon, let alone in half a second. Anvil turned on me so I returned the joy and stuck him into one of his spare ringots. He was in one of the ones I had Jordy bring up north for you to stash in the Weirdom's Stopstone vault, pauper."

"That explains that then," Pyrame muttered lowly, as if it wasn't one of her proudest moments, which it clearly wasn't. "The Piscine got me out of her somehow and it wasn't mind-over-mind like even the most ordinary U-blood does to keep us out of him or her in the first place. I reckon she must have got me into Quack the same way. Except by then I was a veritable puppet on a string she was manipulating mentally.

"Distance is probably the only reason I'm not hers to command anymore. Which is 'all' the more reason, pun intended, you should take me down to Incain straightaway. I owe her big-time, bad time. Once I'm reunited with the She-Sphinx, I can guarantee her a mighty fierce payback. We'll do a Kanin City on her candy ass."

"You'll be welcome to her, pauper. But not until she's no longer the Master and that won't happen until we finish discrediting her in the eyes of her people."

"I'm in All she won't need discrediting, she'll need disinterring."

"I wish it were that simple. I really do."

"What else aren't you telling us, Unity?" Neargon challenged her.

"Just disabusing anyone of any comparison to Kanin City post-Thrygragon. Put moderately more obscurely, the Melusine-Piscine's been the Master of 'Where-The-Fuck-Is-He?' since at least New Years Day."

"Amazing what a knife to the throat can do."

Quail-Neargon had twigged to Harm's Cabby the Daddy reference rather more swiftly than most highborn devils would have expected of him; this even though by most counts the Trigregos Sisters bore him three broods higher than Pyrame, whom Harmony and the Thanatoids, despite their occasional sparring, tended to treat as a near equal.

"You said Hot Stuff is somewhere else," he chanced, grasping at the thinnest straw of hope. "Might that somewhere else be where she hid my noggin neutralizer?"

"Sorry to say yet again, toad," the Balance-bag answered him, aware that that was what he called his power focus when he was feeling humorous or at least sardonic. (The proper term for it was an Alchemical or Elemental Mitre – mitre deriving from his father, Thrygragos Varuna Mithras.) "But it might very well be the same somewhere else Hot Stuff destroyed it."

As witness the number of ringots – 20 to 30, maybe more – that the Legendarian delivered to the three-thing, Morgan-Pyrame-Lilith, just before last year's Mithramas; the empire's Master Devas, particularly the Thanatoids and its three other supportive firstborn, disarmed then captured devils who refused to submit to them two or three times a decade on average. That didn't mean they followed up by destroying their power foci. Then again, it didn't mean they didn't.

As Harmony had no problem recollecting from her dealings with the traitorous Strife-Marutia after the failure of the Crimson Conspiracy, in the early decades of the 40th Century of the Dome, there was only one way to destroy Tvasitar talismans. That was to return them from whence they came.

Other than by increasing the number and fervency of their adherents there was also only one way for devils to increase the magnitude of their abilities. Hardly coincidentally they just happened to be most readily available in the same place – the self-replenishing lava lake of molten Brainrock atop Sedon's Peak.

"I do, however, happen to know where there is a spare power focus."

"Then give it to me."

"Why you and not Pyrame?"

"Because she doesn't need one, never has. I do."

"I wish I was as sure of that as you are, toad."

"Tell you what," said Harmony, appreciating Pyrame's concern about losing her demon after most of five millennia. "I'll look into it."

"Very funny, Harm," said Pyrame, figuring she was referring to Titanic Metis's revelatory cauldron.

"I do try."

========

Hymeneal Day, 4825 Year of the Dome – Cathedral Grove, Goatwood

Vanalal, the merry month of maypole ceremonies, all too depressingly fast gave way to the marrying month of Azky.

========

Quack Kestrel and her Garuda guy got together again. Then they got together conjugally on the ides of Azky, one of the eight months of the year where the ides fell on the 13th day. Azky being what it was, and thirteen being regarded as an auspicious or lucky number throughout Hidden Headworld, marriage-minded avian-humans regarded it as the perfect date to tie the connubial knot, hence Hymeneal Day.

It wasn't a twin wedding. Her twin was there, though, as her Garuda guy's best man (as opposed to his best bird, who was also there). Along with Quack's bridesmaids, her hens of honour, and the groom's attendants (his cock-tenders, as they were more correctly called in Goatwood), be they aquiline or born-flightless the same as the Kestrels themselves, he'd agreed to lend his illustrious pipes to the prothalamium, a chorus celebrating marriage.

He also promised to sing a solo aria during the epithalamium, an ode he and his sister had co-composed a couple of years back for a different bride and groom. They'd both received accolades for it then so Quack's hubby-to-be, who was there then, insisted he sing it again at their wedding.

(In retrospect, it was a good thing not everyone who applauded at its premiere was able to attend the repeat performance. Otherwise it might have been forgotten.)

Hymeneal Hall was high up in the interlocking branches of a cluster of titanic trees. Many devils were in the huge common, aerie or aviary surmounting Cathedral Grove, at the redwood heart of Goatwood, Sedon's Beard. Some like the host, Goatwood's Green Man, Djerrid Ruin (to whom Garudas prayed), were there in their regular forms – his being facially aquiline but bodily arboreal when he was around Garudas and suchlike avian-humans.

Others were there possessively. Nowhere near all of them were Byronics, though they were the only ones outwardly there as themselves. Among those others was the Unity of Balance as well as Panharmonium, a dream she never let die. She hadn't so much buried the hatchet with the Byronics as agreed to keep it padded for the nonce.

The assassin didn't step out of the Weird on a witch-stone. She simply appeared atop the candlelit altar just as Quack and her betrothed, a rapturous raptor if ever there was one, were reciting their nuptial bindings. As subsequently established, or mutually conjectured, by the survivors, that she was a she mostly came down to a matter of inescapably fleeting impressions.

The prohibitive murderess had neither face nor any visible hair. What she did have sticking out of the top of her reflective skull appeared to be nothing less than a curved, polished, crimson blade. That her skin was glassine or mirrored was another universally held recollection.

Her necklace seemed to consist of ruby red droplets dangling off a chain composed of golden links. Her short, thigh-high and sleeveless gown might have been made out of rich brocade. It might also have been varying shades of red, though like everything else about her it gave off the aurous aura of Brainrock-Gypsium.

To some, what she held in her right hand could have been a short eye-stave, mace or sceptre. The object's bulbous, crowning skull-shape could have been akin to a Death's Head. Equally so, it could have resembled Sedon's head full on. Upon reconstruction of the events multiple post-mortems later, most concurred she chucked an oversized apple, one that didn't just glow golden, into the midst of the wedding party.

It looked to be an actual golden apple, the symbol as well as the power focus of the most disreputable Mithradite Apple Goddess ever. Rather, it looked to have started out as that. Then its stem suddenly flickered alight and began to sparkle like a New Years firecracker. It was as if the apple had transformed in midair; become what it immediately proved to be, an antipersonnel daisy-cutter.

Its stem might only have been a secondary or failsafe fuse, there for show alone, because the abominable device exploded upon impact. Thus given impetus, its mutilating, metallic innards pin-cushioned everyone within a 10-foot circumference and many more beyond that.

The deadly darts that tore out of the effective nail-bomb and through, as often as into, their victims amounted to a double whammy. Evidently they'd been dipped in some sort of baneful toxin before they were packed into the bomb's casing – Ophidian venom being the consensus culprit in this respect. Those struck that didn't perish from the resultant lacerations straightaway, did much more agonizingly slowly from the lethal whatever-it-was they carried.

"Spies must die!" the solitary slayer shouted as she tossed the golden apple.

She was gone as quickly as she'd come.

========

"That was Strife," one once-disguised as well as disgusted devil, Pyrame Silverstar, said to another, Datong Harmonia, after they gave up trying to re-enliven their hosts, the same ones they'd been occupying since Maypole Day for fear of something exactly like this happening. Someone capable of causing the Elysium Inferno would inevitably seek to turn loose ends into garrottes.

"Either that or it was a seeming," said the devic Dand of Androgynia, as he or she, or both, angrily plucked the poisonous projectiles out of Quail's hence risen but now toad-headed corpse.

To see a dead man, with or without a batrachian cranium, standing where the best man stood might have unsettled those survivors who didn't have 3-eyes. Except by then the only survivors still standing, or wafting in Sedona Spellbinder's case, were those who hadn't fled already.

Master Devas the livid lot of them, until that day most had excelled at preserving the lives of their shells. While it made perfect sense to help keep their adherents alive and reasonably well, their knack for enhancing longevity was one of the many reasons devils continued to be worshipped as gods and goddesses.

'You have to earn your godhood', the Lord Laziest Lazareme often admonished his offspring, quite rightly too. But frags (fragmentation bombs) like the one that just went off in such a confined area did an intentionally excellent job of rendering even not quite dead bodies irretrievable.

"Not a seeming, toad, a fucking gargoyle. That was the Master of Weir. I recognized the mace."

"Her gargoyle's Strife? How can that be, Harmony?"

"Not her gargoyle, pauper. Her!"

"No wonder I couldn't take over the witch-bitch," said Sedona, who, as the smoke from one of the candles on the altar, had been virtually beside the bomber when she appeared out of the Weird. "She's already possessed!"

"Unless it was me trying to get into her simultaneously, cousin," Harmony reconsidered after recollecting her previous dismissal of Strife as the perpetrator of all that had gone wrong since Star Sedon disappeared from the night's sky the previous Mithramas. "Maybe we ricocheted off each other."

"You're only as fast as lightning, Unity," the highest born female Nucleoid countered. "I'm as fast as thought itself. And I'm telling you Strife, Fitna Marutia, Kore-Eris, Kore-Discord, Mithras's ewe for Aries, howsoever you want to call her, she's back and the Piscine has her."

"Does that mean you're finally with us, sister?" asked Lunar Uma (Umashakti Silvercloud), firstborn to second-born. (Along with their father and her brood brothers, Vayu Maelstrom, and Chimaera Glimmenmare, who often changed sexes as quickly as he did shapes, smoky Sedona made up Thrygragos Byron's Primary Nucleus, a four-part conglomeration capable of cathonitization.)

Spellbinder hesitated, as if to consider her response, though it was difficult to tell when dealing with a vaguely humanoid shape composed of greyish particulates; a therefore contained but insubstantial pillar of pallor, put mnemonically. "Let me speak with father, Gravity. I'll get back to you."

And so she did.

========

Midsummer's Eve, 4825 Year of the Dome – The Weirdom of Cabalarkon

The 13ᵗʰ of Azky was more than Hymeneal Day in Sedon's Beard. It was the night of the full moon. A week later it still shone, full as ever, above the Weirdom of Cabalarkon. Even odder, every night of late it had risen with a different face glaring as much as staring down on Sedon's Devic Eye-Land.

Illuminaries recognized many of them. In keeping with ages-old notion of 'Brother Sun, Sister Moon', most were female, the likes of Umashakti Silvercloud and Nergal Vetala. Tonight, though, it featured that of a completely hairless man. Tomcat Tattletail (aka Squirrelly, Qatty and Qaprine) identified it at once as Unmoving Byron, the Great God that had been all head and no body since 366 years pre-Dome.

"Don't fret it, Tom," Morg attempted to reassure him. "He won't ruin your fun and games any more than any of the third generation would. I've the only ace we'll ever need to keep the Weirdom safe and sound. Although, if you'll pardon a pun, it might be better to say 'out of Harm's way'."

"Harmony would never hurt me."

"I didn't say she would, did I."

****

9. The Dystopia of Cabalarkon

Mid-Azky, 4825 Year of the Dome – Tympani, the Isle of the Undying One

So many weeks worth of nights passed without sight of Star Sedon, many reckoned the mighty Moloch had been killed on Mithramas 4824. Six months later, increasingly vociferous outrage on the part of not solely Master Devas throughout the Hidden Head-world looked to force a different kind of reckoning.

After all, knives to the throat only work if mass murderers like the amphibious Master Morgan Abyss convince those they're blackmailing, robbing or otherwise coercing that they're prepared to use them. She hadn't convinced anyone she had the hellstones to do anything of the sort. Ergo, it was way past time to call Morg's bluff.

And who better to do it than he whose nominal Age it was, not to mention he whose third of the year was coming to a still nippy end north of Sedon's Eyebrow?

========

"It's not about devils, darling dumbass," Thrygragos Lazareme, aka Thrygragos Everyman, responded to his eldest offspring howsoever-eccentrically. They'd been bandying about the possibility of Strife's survival; more, about the possibility she was Mithras's much bruited but, until Hymeneal Day, never seen, avenging angel.

Since circa 4000 YD Harmony had been among the vast majority of devils that believed her attempt to swim the caldera full of bubbling Brainrock in the aftermath of the Crimson Conspiracy's collapse resulted in either her successful escape to the Outer Earth, albeit strictly as a possessive spirit being, or else her abolition.

Now, though, she'd begun to put forward the notion that she'd returned some-time after Thrygragon – hence the seemingly endlessly ensuing Era of Empires – only to be captured relatively recently in a ringot. This led her to speculate further that Strife had displaced Pyrame Silverstar just prior to Mithramas and that there-fore she currently possessed Cabalarkon's Master Morgan.

Her father, when she finally got around to consulting with him not long after the daisy-cutter horror show in Goatwood's Cathedral Grove, quickly developed a totally different hypothesis. "Well, it is and isn't. I reckon it's more about daemons, with or without the '*a*'. I'll look into it."

"You'd go to Cabalarkon?"

"I said I'll look into it, not go anywhere near that unspeakable scar on the landscape. Now let me get back to sleep, perchance to dream."

"That sounds poetic."

"Better poetic than prison-podded, I always say. And so should you. Care to join me?"

"Not tonight."

"You sure? My back's royally buggering up again so I could do with a massage. And those octopod chain-tips of yours are positively succulent in the right places."

"I'm sure."

"Then where's Sparky? And no, I haven't all of a sudden gone batrachian on you. I've a job for him."

"Why him and not Abe?"

"You do know why Illuminaries eventually came to name him Unholy Abaddon, don't you?"

"Of course I do. It means *'destruction'.*"

"It also means *'destroyer'*, as in Shiva the Destroyer, of the Hindu Trimurti. I've never met any of them personally but from what I understand their aptly named Number Two wields a wicked trident, the same as Abe does."

"And rides a psychopomp-dolphin, just like Apollo."

"Very good again, Harmony. You and that memory of yours truly are fabulous fonts of coincidental correctness. In the Outer Earth's Biblical book of *'Revelations'*, Abaddon refers to the Angel of the Abyss. And by that I don't mean Morgan Abyss; I mean Apollyon."

"As in Hell."

"Or the mouse god Apollo, a name that also means destroyer. But I'm thinking of *'abyss'* in terms of *'the bottomless pit'*. And that doesn't necessarily refer to Satanwyck or even to the Hell-Well as such. In other words, subtlety and Abe have incompatible philosophies. Besides, he's already on assignment."

"Then why not me?"

"Ahimsa, honey."

"As in *'do no harm'*?"

"In this case, more like *'don't send Harm'*, capitalized."

"Oh my God, you're going to have Odour kill Tomcat!"

"Thanks for the compliment."

========

Devils, not even Great Gods, were able to lie. That incapacity didn't mean they had to divulge everything truthfully, just not falsely. Harmony's statement, back in the Danq on Beltane ('I'll look into it'), fit that category. If anything it was a tease, perhaps even an inadvertent one. No matter how the Pauper Priestess took it, Harmony knew Metisophia's cauldron could never be considered a spare power focus.

It was so very useful Methandra would never let it out of her possession.

========

Much to her retrospective regret, Pyrame Silverstar identified boatloads of admirable qualities in Morgan Abyss at an early age. They made her a worthy shell for an ambitious devil with oceans of notions, to coin a phrase she felt appropriate for an aquatic. None of those notions included Morg eventually bearing Sedon's sedons, small case as well as plural. The mighty Moloch mostly in the sky enjoyed fresh conquests too much for that. Besides, Morg may well have been a morgue when it came to fertility.

Pyrame's oceans of notions did include Morg winning the Challenge of Weir and thereafter sitting on Cabalarkon's throne as the Weirdom's Master. So, a decade or so earlier, the marvellously female perpetual presence took her over and proceeded to do just that. After she successfully masterminded the Piscine's victory, Phase Two involved examining and reactivating as much of the Utopians' exceedingly ancient weapon systems that she could.

In keeping with the era, her intent was to carve out an Upper Head queenship she could rule independent of Sedon's Elysium. Not having much of a constituency to call her own, she hadn't got very far in terms of empire building. However, one of the less personally useful devices (because All of Incain was already hers to command) she got going again controlled the Mandroid Monster Maker long distance.

Utopians, in maybe a hundred millennial or generational ships, began arriving on the planet a decade before the Great Flood. They didn't need to be Illuminaries in order to appreciate that Mandroids could be exceedingly treacherous. Wisely they incorporated performance-mediating overrides affecting All into Cabalarkon's Citadel of the Thinkers, the first structure they completed during the stone city's construction.

Encroaching idiocy accounted for why subsequent Utopians forgot what the overrides did. However yet again, and very much ironically as far as Pyrame was concerned, since she was occupying Morg when she reactivated the controls, the Weirdom's insidious Master not only recalled what they did but also how they worked.

Once she apprehended the pauper had escaped Daddy Cabby's cyclopean confines within Quack Kestrel, Morg wasted little time wirelessly disconnecting, via the telecommunicational medium of Brainrock-Gypsium, the She-Sphinx's synaptic recognition processes. To her therefore abiding dismay, when Harmony took her, still in Quack, to the Prison Beach the day after their getaway, Pyrame found out All of Incain wanted to welcome her back as food rather than as her mistress.

Rejecting that, because she quite liked her, Harmony didn't know what else to do with the morose Mithradite. So she returned her to the Dinq Doinq Danq Cavern Tavern. Once ensconced there, Pyrame promptly began nattering, as always through Quack, into the earholes of devils who were still out and about and partial to imbibing there, be it for Cathy, mushroom wine, beer or spirits.

The Master of Weir must pay the severest penalty for humiliating her and the Thanatoids. Even though she was *'temporarily'* denied access to the She-Sphinx, she could still show them how to exact their revenge. They did as she advised they would rapidly recoup their reputations, their entitlement to unquestioned godhood, and the nourishing exaltations they were fast losing, all over the Hidden Headworld, due to Morg's desperate machinations and their wholly inadequate response to them.

Mindful of Lunar Uma's admonishment of Lady Lust on New Year's Day, no one paid much attention to her. So, having prevailed upon the still outraged Unity to *'lend'* her – and not the sex-shifting Dand of Androgynia – the power focus

Harmony regarded as a spare (Tvasitar's Brainrock anvil), Pyrame in Quack went to Eardrum Isle.

Crocks were cracked; plots were hatched. Not long thereafter, Magnus Minus, Minotaurus of Minius, made his grandiose return to the realm of mundane reality.

How that came about was less of a story and more of a lesson.

========

The Lord Laziest Lazareme was nowhere near as myrionymous as any of the Apple Goddesses. Other than Thrygragos Everyman, his most widespread tag was that of the Lackland Libertine. Somewhat belying the *'libertine'* aspect of such a snide sobriquet, he almost never got as soused as Unholy Abaddon frequently did.

When the reputedly firstborn Great God was awake, father and son shared a mutual delight in the DDD's pilsner. In that they were hardly alone and Pyrame, via her long association with Demon Queen Lilith, or whoever made up her daemonic body, was privy to most things daemonic.

That included how they got the minds needed to upgrade their primitive, even primordial, brain functions to a level as close as they ever came to full sentience. They snared them from minutes-earlier, deceased men and women, many of whom probably fancied their spirits would be on their way to either heaven or hell.

Beer-guzzling sybarites dropped dead everyday, if not every hour, on both sides of the Dome. Reasoning – perhaps even knowing it for certain – that the souls of dead drunks would gravitate to it like wasps to discarded salmon skin, Pyrame had the Unity of Chaos boost barrels of the wondrous elixir from the DDD and take them to the Hell-Well's crusty hollow beneath Sedon's Devic Eye-Land.

Following her instructions, he liberally sprinkled libations of pilsner over the hitherto seemingly lifeless, underground plains of what Lazareme characterized to Harmony as the bottomless pit. Sure enough, shortly thereafter Abe Chaos had himself a companionable Minotaurus of mightily minute vitality, one who by virtue of his origin, if not anywhere close to a superior intelligence, doubled as a daemonic demiurge.

Sooth said, the Minotaurus – called such due to the bull's horns, head, fur and proportionately oversized genitalia he sported – fancied himself a latter day Daemonicus, a demon king lacking subjects but completely capable of fashioning them. Even more importantly in terms of Pyrame's impressive plan forward, this Magnus Minus, a name he gave himself, was a native son.

While it was a dog-demon's bone of contention as to whether Morg even had any creature-creative talents in the first place, because it was his birthplace he had to trump her in the demiurgic department; at least he would with respect to that source of chthonic crud, the nearest to Cabalarkon. Since the highborn Lazaremist, Dand Tariqartha, howsoever-unofficially, already over-lorded the other main underworld in the Upper Head, that of Subterranean Temporis, that left Morg with only Satanwyck from which to recruit malicious, not to mention mainly simple-minded, subordinates.

Abe willingly accepted the assignment to keep the dysfunctional dipsomaniac entertained, very much bibulously. Being a total anarchist, free drinks made it about the only kind of assignment he would accept. Notwithstanding his babysitting duties, just for fun he also enjoyed helping to fashion the demons Magnus Minus breathed into and out of what passed for liveliness on their part.

In order to do so, the Minotaurus mined the motile muck that made up what he'd also named Minius, after himself naturally, the Subterranean Land of therefore much more than just Mandroids. What they in the process turned up, quite by accident, resulted in Thrygragos Lazareme coining yet another aphorism: *'Fortune favours flukiness'.*

After that unexpected turn-up for the Librarian's subsequent books, Absudyl-become-Minius igniting ceased being a matter of eventually. It became imminent.

========

Midsummer's Eve, 4825 – The Masters' Glade, Cabalarkon

Had he appeared on the 30th of Antheal, Beltane Eve – had he appeared beyond the Dome on May Eve, aka Walpurgis or Witches' Night, in Northern Europe, to be absolutely accurate – one might presume quite reasonably that the entity just now manifesting himself in the woodlands beyond Cabalarkon's Masters Palace was a form of Brocken Spectre.

This well-documented phenomenon can be described as the magnified shadow of an observer, typically surrounded by rainbow-like bands, thrown onto a bank of cloud in high mountain areas when the sun is low or the moon is rising. Of course, even though the Mystic Mountains, Sedon's Crown, loomed a fair distance to the north, the Weirdom of Cabalarkon was not in a mountainous area as such.

Neither was the moon rising. It was a Great God. So too was this particular non-Brocken Spectre. "You'd be the Pan in Pandemonium."

========

The speaker, he in a purple robe with ermine fringes, seemed to step out of the woods deep within the palace's backyard parkland. Barring the third eye, the two usual but just as sea-green eyeballs, the sky-blue skin and the long, wavy, sun-bleached hair, he bore a striking similarity to Squirrelly's standard guise, the one he'd been sporting for months now. That the latter had been assuming a different semblance since dusk mostly came down to getting into the spirit of the night's rites.

"Oh, hello, granddad," said the Pan at issue, abruptly ceasing his intoxicating, albeit non-alcohol-fuelled, tooting.

There wasn't much point in carrying on anymore anyways. Upon seeing who'd just emerged into the clearing, this Pan's already half-naked flock of fervid followers broke off their until-then dizzying lunging and leaping about the glade in a circle. All except one had rushed toward the outsider and were now kneeling or prostrating themselves before him.

The one that didn't get abjectly awestruck all of a sudden had a Q-name that wasn't Squirrelly, Qatty or Qaprine. She got hers because of the forelock she was born with, not due to the onset of the promiscuous behaviour so many potential Quills succumbed to in their late teens. You didn't need to be a bona fide Legendarian, just related to one, for a procreative imperative to kick in.

As for the rest, it was as if they'd almost instantly become a suitably, if silently, chastened assemblage of parishioners in an outdoors basilica or, notwithstanding the lack of a dome and with trees replacing minarets, one of those relatively new-fangled mosques that were springing up mostly in Arabia and points east on the

Outer Earth. They were murmuring under their breath so lowly the three on their feet probably couldn't tell whether they were blithering prayers of praise or mewling pleas for forgiveness.

"I didn't realize you were watching," added the one that, dependent on who was addressing him, might have answered to Squirrelly, Qatty or Qaprine.

"So now you do. And don't call me grandfather, you scum-sucking fraud. You're the latest Dusted Daemonicus, the craven, onetime King of Daemons crawled out from under some cowpat somewhere now that their acknowledged king's gone and got himself put out of circulation for predictability if nothing else. The panpipes give you away, churl. They're glowing."

"So they are. That doesn't make them mine. Fact is they're my half-mother's. She's why I'm your grandson, gramps."

"Grumps would be more accurate. You're no more the recurring half-son of Lady Luck and roguish Rumour than you're the legitimate Legendarian's kid by whomever, maybe even himself as herself. I'd have you arrested for impersonating a preening popinjay if I agreed with that sort of thing."

"Now you're talking about yourself. Kid's kind of funny, too."

"Feel free to laugh till you drop dead, trickster."

"When did you get here?"

"I didn't. When you can already far-see, it doesn't take a great deal more effort to also be far-seen."

(Kid was funny because, self-admittedly, if a fellow with the last name of Tattletail could be believed, he was a metamorphic faerie fart. Unless it was a very, very good costume, Squirrelly had gone goatish, hirsute, capric or caprine fully physically for tonight's caprice, caper, romp or, as he'd have it, jumped-up jaunt of tomfoolery.)

Pan was often confused with Sedon Himself, as the Outer Earth's inspiration for, as well as embodiment of, the Devil, singular and capitalized. He didn't cart around a 4-pronged pitchfork as Sedon sometimes did, much to the embarrassment of a large majority of his second and third generational descendants, but he did have a human torso and head matted with soft fur, with a goat's hind legs, horns, and ears.

Much the same description fit a supposedly fantastical woodland creature generally depicted as having the pointed ears, legs, and short horns of an upright goat as well as a fondness for unrestrained debauchery. That creature would be a faun or satyr. As both Harmony and Pusan Wanderlust would attest, though not as happily as they might have up until a few months ago, there was nothing imaginary about suchlike rustic ruffians in here.

Nor was there anything make-believe about faeries. However, unless they were large and invisible, or minuscule and flitting dodgily underfoot, both of which they could do or be, the erstwhile ecstatic inebriates who'd been cavorting about the clearing were not faeries. They were members of the Sarpedon underclass.

Now uniformly on their knees, or wallowing even baser, the besotted idolaters were typical U-bloods. U-men were black-as-midnight on a starless night at the time of the new moon whereas U-women were the reverse, white-as-light on a salt flat at noon on a sunny day.

Other than the changeling satyr and the 3-eyed devil he addressed as grand-dad or gramps, the only non-Utopian there was a surviving member of the thus far tragically unlucky Q-Troupe, a certain Jordan called *'Quiff'* to distinguish her from other Jordans in the group. Ever so rudely having just been snapped out of terpsichorean heaven by an irritating dearth of pulsating piping, she was now breathlessly flashing double-takes between transformed Squirrelly and the numinous newcomer.

"That's not you," she gasped confusedly. "It can't be you, not if you're you only masquerading as a satyr and he really does have a third eye. Which he can't have, can he? Not here, not in a genuine Weirdom. And why the fuck are the Sarpedons grovelling in the dirt down in front of him? They don't do that when you look like that."

"They think he's God," the pretender provided nervously, though not yet outwardly panicky – another word derived from Pan.

"That's Thrygragos Lazareme?"

"I'm also called Thrygragos Everyman for a reason, child. In case you were skipping classes when your parents or teachers got around to me, no matter what their race is whoever sees me thinks I'm their God. I call it my ungodly gift when I'm feeling anarchic, which I usually am. How come you're not reduced to reverence yourself?"

"Because you're a man and I'm from Shenon, Witch Isle. We don't have male deities; at least we don't in the quarter-queenship I come from. And I didn't think Utopians had deities period."

"Not deities, Entities, capitalized and plural, a man and a woman, the sun and the moon if you prefer, though it's nowhere near that straightforward. To them I must look like the Male Entity. I won't have black skin because neither of the Entities had black skin, and I'll only have a pair of eyes, but I might be bald and gnarly and have a big beard that keeps me decent since I could be naked.

"To put it unappreciatively, as you may or may not know the idiots of Weir leech off the Sarpedons. That saps their willpower the same as if it was syrup out of a maple tree. It also leaves them simple and, in my experience, simpletons almost always have gods. In a Weirdom empowered by imbeciles, the Sarpedons have just enough sense left to keep their predisposition to idolize anyone, let alone the Dual Entities, to themselves.

"Rather, they had. The cat's out of the bag now; unless it's the squirrel. Devils will be queuing up for a shot at their adulation from now on, which might be good news for their continued existence. But, hey, their secret's safe with me and I won't tell if you won't. He might, though. Let's see, shall we." The Great God made a signal like chopping a hatchet.

"You bastard!" screamed the Pan-pretender, catching it.

It was too late for him to start laughing now. Seemingly out of nowhere, a bolt of white lightning whacked him where he stood.

Ostrich-like, the Sarpedons sought to bury their heads in quivering amazement. Not one to suffer astraphobia, the young, potential Quill-to-be managed to stay on her feet. Nonetheless, if humans or Utopians could cause earthquakes by shaking in their booties, hers and the Sarpedons' shuddering combined might have done just that.

"You bastard!" she echoed, as the faunlike piper dropped to the ground, acrid smoke billowing off his crumbling body. "You killed Squirrelly."

"Perhaps, but only in the sense that I didn't have a mother," Lazareme's sending acknowledged. "You lot, get dressed and then cart that thing off to your Master before it turns into a basket of venomous vipers or, worse, viral vomit. Tell her it's my wedding present. You can keep the pipes if you want, granddaughter. I don't think they'll bite."

Some of the Sarpedons shrouded Squirrelly's corpse in their retrieved robes, picked him up and started back through the parkland towards the Masters Palace proper. Before she could follow them, or it, gave Quiff some additional instructions: "Be an angel and take a message to their mass-murderous Master.

"Advise her I'm a big fan of Mother Earth. Brother Lunatic is too," he further stipulated, pointing upwards at the Byronhead still hovering moonlike high above them, high above the reach of Trinondev eyeorbs too. "Both of us appreciate her letting us walk all over her – not that he can walk per se, him not having legs anymore. Plus, we'll readily admit the planetary puppeteer and her misbegotten marionette have been playing a pretty good game since Mithramas.

"But, you know what, all they've succeeded doing is getting our dander up, which is also quite a feat since I can't recall him ever having hair. The pudding proof of that is he's mobile and he's Unmoving Byron. I'm awake and I hate being awake unnecessarily. I especially hate it when I have to do something other than, you know, eat, drink and be merry for tomorrow you will die or, being mortals, one of your friends might.

"Any other year I'd be hosting my own Midsummer Night's dream shebang. And, from the looks of you, you'd make a dreamy she to bang. So, hear the deal and pass it on to your morgue of a pissant Piscine: Mistakes have been made, savage slaughters started both before and after conflagrations committed and, yes, not all the atrocities were marriage-massacres.

"She wants to chance the inevitable termination of a Sedonplay, fine. Fools have always rushed in where we devils sensibly fear to tread. Just leave us out of it, okay. She releases the prison pods she has containing our kin, the ringots she has containing dot-ditto as well as dick-dildo, any Tvasitar talismans she's collected, and she can keep Father Sedon as long as he lets her.

"I mean, Hell's Teeth, if he can't look after himself then who can? She doesn't, well, lightning isn't all that can strike twice."

"More marriage massacres aren't going to happen tomorrow," Quiff protested more ignorantly than bravely. "The Master's not going to marry a dead man."

"I don't doubt you're right, girl. But she won't have to, will she. Not if he is who he says he is and she knows what to do with him. Which she will do if she's a real Hellion and not simply some re-brained, demoniacal dominatrix's doxy, as a certain pissed off pauper priestess too often yelling in our earholes of late insists she is.

"I'll be watching."

========

Come daylight the Devic Eye-Land's weather still sucked. Come noon the Master of Weir still married Tomcat Tattletail. Quiff was right, though. There would be no marriage massacres this day.

It was the reception afterwards that proved a killer.

****

10. The Coming Chaos

Midsummer's Eve, 4825 Year of the Dome – The Weirdom of Cabalarkon

As for the panpipes, power foci transmuted. Q-troupe's mutual half-mother's Triskelion was no different in that respect.

========

Outer Earth monotheists propagandized that those who venerated Moloch (a word that originally just meant *'king'*) propitiated him by baking babies in ovens, among other distasteful things, and/or roasting them on spits over open flames. Even if that were once true out there, it was about the furthest thing from the truth in here. No devil, especially not his or her All-Father, the Moloch Sedon, condoned human sacrifice.

Despite this, suchlike containers remained poetic metaphors for many at times divergent items. A seething furnace of fury, for example, referred to a battlefield, where grown up babies, if only size-wise, slice and dice each other in hand-to-hand combat just because it was expected of them. At the opposite extreme, a bun in the oven meant a pregnancy on both sides of the Dome. A faerie in the oven, though, had a completely different connotation; one that, as Thrygragos Lazareme predicted, Morgan Abyss knew all about.

Fays came in whatever size appealed to them at the moment, including gigantic. As a result, faerie-ovens occasionally had to be specially built. Blacksmiths and arms-makers long ago devised adjustable, reusable ones made of super-hardened metal. These were available commercially, particularly in Crepuscule, Sedon's Outer Nose, which was as often, or more often, known as the Land of Twilight.

(The same territory had once been on the other side of the hidden continent, where it naturally went by Daybreak. Regardless of its name or placement, faeries proliferated there in such number it was frequently thought of as Faery or Fairyland. That was a misnomer, though. There wasn't one fairyland. There were as many fairylands as there were types of faeries and there were despicable dozens of those.)

While it's easy to conjecture how authentic faerie-ovens could be used for unauthorized purposes, they weren't designed for making offerings. Closed but not altogether sealed, with only a minimum amount of air holes in order to maximize combustion, the mini-furnaces were intended as one-fay-at-a-time cremation chambers. Indeed, when properly utilized only dead fays were laid inside them.

They did make a hash out of fair folk but it wasn't for eating, not even by their invariably carnivorous cousins, the demons of not just Satanwyck. What they made of them could be used for tephromancy (a fancy word meaning divination by examining ashes leftover from a sacrifice). But again, that would be a waste. Faerie-ovens certainly weren't intended to kill anyone. Quite the contrary, the resultant pixy powder, as some called it, revitalized fays, albeit overtop non-faerie folk, ones already alive but thereafter in no way themselves anymore.

Even though it was barely lightening outside, Hellion familiars, their crows or ravens, were already cawing the coming morning. Despite daylight's looming arrival, Master Morgan had some of the Sarpedons build a balefire in the open air of her palace's central courtyard. (Many considered *'balefire'* nearly synonymous with *'bonfire'*. The only real difference was the former was generally judged bad whereas the latter was regularly reckoned good. Aware of the distinction, Morg thought a balefire ideal for immolating fays.)

She sent others rummaging through nooks and crannies situated in or around the blocky Masters Palace proper. Their task wasn't quite so readily accomplished. They had to locate a generic faerie-oven, one that could be lengthened or shortened, fattened or narrowed, dependent on the faerie's dimensions at the time of his, her or its most recent expiration more so than ultimate death.

Morg figured at least one was there somewhere and as usual she imagined she was right. (Not all that unusually for her, all things considered impartially, she'd calculated correctly as well.) While she was waiting, she dispatched trusted Trinondevs out to the glade some distance away in the palace's backyard parkland wherein Squirrelly, whom she knew to call Tomcat Tattletail, was struck down.

They came back with their prison pods still empty. This perplexed her so, after she dismissed them and was sure they were alone, she once again had the Jordan called Quiff go over last night's events in detail, repeat verbatim as she did so the message Lazareme's sending had her bring to her. That done, yet still not satisfied, she had the devil she'd stuck within Quiff on New Year's Day come to the forefront.

"So, Drek," she addressed a now consequently 3-eyed Quiff using the devil's Illuminary-given name, "Can your father deliver the goods?" (Illuminaries had prodigious memories. Consequently, they'd called the Lazaremist Librarian Biblio Drek mostly out of disdain for his precious books.)

"He certainly can for my tribe, whereas the Unmoving One's presence above the clearing indicated he and his Byronics have signed onboard. The Mithradites are more problematic, particularly the Thanatoids of Lathakra. They're under no obligation to obey either my father or Great Byron. Nonetheless, they would never have advanced so far in terms of expanding their empire without my father's tacit approval.

"In that respect, as you're no doubt aware Abe's hardly the only one of my brothers or sisters marching at their side. Long before the Silverclouds took me out in Kanin City, the majority of my siblings in the Cattail, as well as a few of the biggies from north of the Gypsium Wall, had thrown their support behind them.

Harmony and Lord Order didn't, but they've shown remarkable forbearance this last century or so."

"They obviously didn't do anything to prevent you being ring-gotten."

"That's a bang on the bongo drum that is," he agreed via Quiff. "I was Lazareme's appointed ambassador to Kanin City at the time; had been since Harmony, Pyrame Silverstar and All of Incain liberated it from the mainly hybrid Utopians who ruled there until just after Thrygragon. It being one of the oldest occupied cities on the Whole Earth, and me being a historian at heart, I rather enjoyed living there too.

"In any event, you have a falling out with the powers-that-be in another country, you might expel their ambassadors. But you don't beat them to a pulp, rob them of their glasses, and incarcerate them indefinitely. Since that's what Rufous Rudra more so than Lunar Uma did to me, I reckon the Unities would have rescued me for sure."

"Except …"

"Precisely. And to be fair to the first two, just in case they're listening, they did have an enormous, not to mention ambassadorially unappreciative, if not altogether ungodly, obstacle preventing their intervention on my behalf."

"Their third, your biggest and baddest brother, went over to the Thanatoids almost immediately after Sedon moved Lathakra to off the Cattail Coast and they invaded it."

"In my mind Abe's the key to everything. He is Chaos after all. As much as Order might want to, you can't tangle with Chaos and expect to preserve any semblance of harmony. I do hold one thing against the Silverclouds in particular, however. They didn't stick me in the Prison Beach's mother of all Mandroids and tell my father why. That's how Master Devas and even Great Gods are supposed to punish transgressors."

"Why would they? Your fatuous father doesn't believe in depriving anyone of his or her freedom. Either he or the superlative Harmony would have had the She-Sphinx release you as soon as they heard about it. That'd go for everyone else they ended up ring-getting. You take control, you don't want to give it back two seconds or two days or two weeks later, do you?"

"Just so again. Far more fatuously than our father ever gets, some of us would have gone straight back home and sought to reassert our authority over our people. We succeeded then the Thanatoids would have to backtrack in order to put down the resulting rebellions. They did that they might be tempted to try to cathonitize us next time."

"And without Sedon around to release you, it'd be forever catasterized, as opposed to castrated."

"Not that there's a great deal of difference. They're both for life."

"You're making a very strong case for me to do as your father wants."

"But for one thing. To play the devils' advocate on behalf of my fellow cowards, no matter how hard or how easily we were ring-gotten the first time, there's no guarantee we'll be in a rebellious mood the next time."

"Bah! I'm on top of the situation and my people know it. That's why they still support me. The Infernal Equinox was a tremendous triumph and it won't be our last."

"Fays say hubris is humus, Master, and as far as I'm concerned they're spot on the spittoon. Thanks to your daemonic paintjob, the conflagration you suckered my dimwit siblings and cousins into setting off three months ago entirely engulfed Grand Elysium. Uncounted hundreds and probably thousands of Lathakran soldiers burnt to death in it, yes. But how many more innocents were wiped out at the same time? Tens of thousands, at the minimum, is my guess. How can you justify that?"

"To quote the Male Entity just before he had the Female nuke Weir Star: *'Innocents do not worship devils!'*"

"And to quote you: *'Bah!'* If, as I suspect, your goal was to see if devils self-cathonitized when they killed someone, then it was an act of evil, pure and simple. If, as you'll protest, it was an act of war, well, you convinced yourself the Thanatoids intended to march their men over the Hills of the Sleepers after Elysium surrendered. But how could you have been so cocksure certain of that?"

"Sedon didn't want any of us to come anywhere near here long before he simultaneously lowered and raised the Dome, out of himself. Truth told, which we always do, he forbade us access to what was then a huge island centuries before your Utopian predecessors even arrived on the Whole Earth the last time we know about for sure. Ergo, his proscription has nothing to do with Trinondev eye-staves and everything to do with where they built their first damnable Weirdom: namely, overtop of Cabby the Daddy's to date final resting place."

"You're not telling me anything new, Drek. Sedon's terrified one of your psychotic higher-ups, his firstborn or Chaos most likely, will finish off his father and that that in turn will finish him off. That happens, the Dome goes bye-bye and it's back to the Great Flood for the loathsome load of you."

"I'm not arguing with you."

"You're not shaking in Quiff's booties either. My Illuminaries claim the Genesea eradicated hundreds and, yes, probably thousands of your siblings and cousins along with their shells. Are they wrong?"

"You couldn't prove it by me. I didn't become the Librarian until Brother Tvasitar looked deep into my transcendent soul and crafted me a pair of 3-lens eyeglasses as my torrid talisman. But surely that's all the more reason to heed one of my father's favourite aphorisms: *'Let sleeping dogsbodies lie'*. He meant it to apply to him, but it should go double for sleeping Utopians of the Sedon-thought-father variety."

"What's so torrid about eyeglasses?"

"You think molten Brainrock's cool?"

"Not to the touch, no, I suppose not."

"Then leave my alliterative amusements alone. I might be accounted humourless but I'm good with words."

"Sorry."

"Apology accepted. Anyhow, if you were to ask me, and you have, next to taking Grandfather out in the first place, unwarranted overconfidence has to be your biggest failing. For Masters of Weir suchlike superciliousness may not be as inexcusable as collaboration with devils, but you can't tweak the noses of Master Devas such as the Thanatoids or Abe Chaos and expect to get away with it for long."

"Trust a Librarian not only to come up with a word like *'superciliousness'* but to make a fay-saying out of it." He glared at her. For a devil who apparently didn't have a power focus she sensed him striving to keep his eyefire leashed. Which harkened back to her earlier perplexity.

'Curiouser and curiouser', she thought but didn't say. Instead, persuaded of her personal immunity to everything and anything he could throw at her, she swallowed her gall as much as her pride and apologized once more: "Sorry again. Pray, do go on. I may not look like it but I'm all-ears." She thought that was funny.

"With gills behind them." He thought that was funny. It was her turn to glare. For the briefest instant a very nearly invisible, but decidedly glowing, halo or aura of some sort flared into view all around her. If he thereby learned the reality behind her gargoyle he didn't let on. Following her lead, he carried on with nary a blip.

"To re-rail my train of thought, you don't rub their noses in anything. You pile-drive their nasal bridge-bones straight into their brainpans and don't let up until they burst out the other side of their skulls. Dad's no genius but you haven't got anywhere near the power to do that and he knows it. The Thanatoids are never going to forgive you, and nor should they, but one word from him and Abe stands down."

"And without Uncle Unholy, the domino-effect clicks in," she understood. "No more Lazaremists, no more Byronics, and without any more firstborn allies from the other tribes to endorse their ambitions, Mithradites will turn on them the same as they did their father on Thrygragon. For the Thanatoids it's all fall down, go boom time."

"That's how I see it. It's probably how dad sees it, too, and if he is watching, he'll be listening. So, got a response?"

"I said bah and I meant bah. I'm no sheep but, in case you haven't figured it out yet, your father's bluffing big-time. You see, borderline-presciently, even if I do say so myself, the first thing I did after I took out his father last Mithramas was render the Catacombs of the Sleepers, beneath the Citadel of the Thinkers, no longer Sed's thought-father's last resting place. And – you're right – in my not at all humble opinion, that might prove my best move ever."

She must have reckoned she was bang-on about that as well. Cabalarkon had never lost its raison-d'être the same as the Inner Earth's other Weirdoms, Manoa, Godbad and Kanin City among them. So long as Daddy Cabby – he in his spill-proof sarcophagus brimful of animation suspending, yet life-preserving Cathonic Fluid – remained safe wherever she hid him, she felt confident it never would either.

The Librarian didn't see it that way and told her as much. "I beg to disagree. You're jeopardizing your Weirdom's last gasp shot at salvation, Master. Yours too. Devils won't let up and you can't outlast immortals. You must realize that. Sure, they won't invade themselves, but they will gnaw away at your people's resolve relentlessly. Smells, sensations and tastes can be far-sent as easily as sights, sounds and thoughts.

"You don't take dad's deal they'll drive you so crazy you'll eventually have to make good on your threat to kill Cabalarkon. And the second you make a move for him, dad will know where you've hidden him. One way or another he'll beat you there, whisk him elsewhere and that'll be that for you and your imbeciles."

"I will never kowtow to devils. Neither will my people. Even if it means an end to their existence on this forsaken planet, the purebloods would never stand for it. You better make your move now or you might as well forget ever making one again."

"How did you figure it out?"

"Wasn't much to figure out, was there? My mother's a Melusine Piscine. Females from her branch of the amphibian-human race may be the mermaids of not just every sailor's lonely longings, but they're not changeling selkies or fairy-nixies. Once you get over the fleshy flaps between the fingers and toes, and the gill behind the ears, about the only thing abnormal about them is how they can be bipedal on land and fishy in water.

"The explanation's identical to avian-humans and their Garuda feathers. They can keep their legs or tails between-space. I'm only half Melusine so I can't do that. If I want to go for a long swim, and I do most days, I put on flippers. But Tomcat's a fucking faerie. He told me so himself.

"Faeries eat devils. Most of them also eat their birthmothers. Tom says he did. Of course he could be lying but, if he's not, then that's a fay-fucking-fair indication Wintry Moira wasn't his conceptive half-mother, wouldn't you say. She'd be asking for gastronomic problems if she went into a faerie fucking, wouldn't she?"

"Squirrelly was a member of Q-troupe. Quaff-1 hired him because he was a multi-instrumentalist and Quiff gleans we needed one."

"He didn't hire him until after Mithramas. I know. I checked with some of the others. I'm sure your inner Quiff will verify it if you'd care to give her another quick glean." He didn't. Or, if he did, he didn't interrupt her.

"At first I thought the same as your putrid pappy apparently said he did back a couple of hours now. I thought he was a Dusted Daemonicus. Illuminary-annals say the pre-Sedon-released, but pre-Ragnarok-deposed, Demon King ate an otherwise nameless, as well as forgettable, Pan-like devil not long after your Anvil the Artificer crafted a power focus, a syrinx no less, for him 2800-odd years ago. Allegedly this Daemonicus is indestructible. Reputedly also, he didn't digest the devil he ate so much as fused with him, which makes him double trouble.

"At any rate, I could have inadvertently let him out of one of the comparatively modern day prison pods we had stored alongside the really, really old ones I vacated in order to nail your rapacious grandfather. I've never been overly confident about that but, just to be on the safe side, I sent a few of my handpicked Warriors Elite out to the glade where your Great Gods did in my Tommy Truelove.

"They've pure U-blood so they can't be possessed any more than the Sarpedons can. They didn't scarf up any bodiless devil wafting about it. Nor did they come back with a devic power focus. That said, a few minutes ago I sensed you wanting to blast me. Devils might be able to take most folks over without a power focus but they can't eyefire-burn anyone without one.

"Ergo, you've a set of panpipes in your pocket – Quiff's pocket, put more accurately – or somewhere close-by. So, like I said, use it or lose it."

"Look," 3-eyed shell pleaded on behalf of both her and the occupant providing her with that selfsame third eye and a man's voice. "I'm not saying dad knew which one of us you stuck inside me." Not that he had any choice in the matter but it was beginning to sound as if he regretted doing as Lazareme instructed him.

"I'm betting he didn't but even if he did, he told me to be an angel, not a hero. He can call on the equivalent of a whole brood of heliodromi. They weren't there – not that they could function here – so, in their absence, he appointed me his munificent mailman. That makes me generous, a giving not a taking personage.

"Besides," he additionally blustered as much as she appeared flustered, "I try to take you over, what happens? Zip, that's what happens. You've stuck Strife inside yourself already, so there's no more room. She was in one of the modern day prison pods you opened in that iniquitous, Solidium-sealed vault where you keep your pre-Earth trophies, for want of a better word, the ones you salvaged from your millennial ships.

"Or, if she wasn't, then she had to have been inside one of the ringots my impossibly beautiful, but sometimes dumb as they come, eldest sister sent up here in that kibisis she had Jordy deliver to Pyrame just before you ring-got her out of you. Since it suggests Anvil had ringots centuries before any of us knew what they were, I kind of doubt that. The reality remains unchanged. The one devil at a time rule applies when it comes to possession as much as it does to eyeorbs."

(In contrast to hyperbolic angelologies found mostly on the Outer Earth, the word *'angel'* just meant envoy or courier. A heliodromus or sun-runner was a term taken from the ages-old mysteries of Mithras. Devils used it to describe the generally highborn offspring of one Great God traditionally charged with taking messages between his brothers, their offspring or even Dark Sedon, when he was in the night's sky and not holding court in Grand Elysium's now thoroughly scorched pyramid.)

"You devils and your long range telepathy, you're so full of yourselves you make me sick. How dare you call me overconfident? Fuck bah! Let's go with hah!"

Morg didn't exactly shoot the messenger. She did, however, use an empty ringot to suck the Librarian out of Quiff. That had the expected effect of knocking out the other messenger, his human host. Her she did shoot – with a syringe full of dope in order to keep her that way.

Patting her down, Morg came up with what had been the missing panpipes. She'd by now formulated a plausible theory as to what Tvasitar Smithmonger made them into initially. The ease with which she tactilely reversed the pipes into that singular shape as good as confirmed she was right about that too. Tomcat must have picked it up where Chance dropped it, outside Sedon's pyramid in Grand Elysium, before following her back here to Cabalarkon between-space on New Years Eve.

"That explains that." She shook Lady Luck's talisman, her 3-bladed, propeller-like Triskelion, at the air itself. "Come to mommy, you contemptible daughter-diddler."

She didn't anticipate Thrygragos Lazareme would reply, not with a far-spoken sending let alone in prison-podable person. No doubt much to her never-disclosed relief, when no response came after a few minutes, she silently congratulated herself on the roll she was on then sat back and waited until Tomcat's corpse was ash.

That took surprisingly little time. He was done and dusted mere hours after dawn brightened into a brilliant summer day, one perfect for their wedding. Shortly after biblically bolstering themselves for the day's ceremonial ordeals, they stepping-stoned to the main hospital, where they watched Quaff-1 die.

Of the 10 potential Quills-in-waiting Morg had brought to Cabalarkon on New Years Eve that left … well, there was bound to be some debate about that.

========

Not only didn't Master Morg accept his offer of what amounted to a return to how things were prior to the Infernal Equinox, she didn't heed the old maxim: 'Never shoot the keyboard player!' Lazareme thereupon decided he'd have to rewrite it in order to better reflect what the emotionally bent Master of Weir did to Quiff-minus-Drek. He proceeded to do that too: 'Don't demon-dust an angel!'

Then he went back to bed.

========

Midsummer's Day, 4825 Year of the Dome – The Weirdom of Cabalarkon

In temperate climes such as Cabalarkon the Devic Eye-Land, there was never any assurance the sun would shine on Midsummer Day. Nor, for that matter, could anyone guarantee with absolute certitude that it would on any other day of any other year. A mite more than three months into this one, though, days had pretty much given up being unpredictable weather-wise. In some respects oppositely, they'd become increasingly predictable, depressingly so, in terms of their sheer, inclement miserableness.

Although the days had been lengthening as per usual after the winter solstice, it was as if the sun itself had taken a holiday. Even the idiots of Weir knew whom to blame. Devils were dreadfully talented when it came to witching weather. Equally so, Masters were positively lousy when it came to anything to do with atmospheric crankiness.

Unlike hereditary royalty on the Outer Earth – at least when it came to their personally self-serving, but disingenuous mythology – they weren't much use when it came to the healing crafts either. In truth, compared to their doctors or sciento-crats, Masters were only marginally more effective than Weir's idiots in that respect. Fortunately for Cabby's Weirdom, still relatively competent Utopians hoarded medical knowledge. It remained perhaps the most coveted and best preserved of all their originally extraterrestrial learning.

Devils did much worse than witch weather. For disbelievers as much as never-believers, they excelled at causing a plethora of foul phenomena. A culling of rodents and other vermin, their fleas hopefully with them, mosquitoes and other biting bugs, and whatever other suchlike infectious pests they could target via traps, insecticides and their invidious ilk, couldn't prevent the deaths of thousands. Despite the devils within them, count Quit-It, one of Quiff's triplet sisters, and Quaff-2, in their number.

Significantly, unlike when Quiddity died the first time, neither of them rose on their haunches, Brainrock quill in hand. Of course only Morg's closest advisors, the Misters and Misses Calculations who'd helped mask Quid's meditated murder, much more than defensible homicide, as suicide, knew these non-events constituted significances.

One of them, the now only semi-late Squirrelly, was with Morg in the quarantined infirmary when Quaff-1, technically their quarter-brother, went the way of other members of the conceivably, if perhaps not necessarily conceptively, cursed company: Quiddity, Quack, Quail, Quit-It, Quaff-2 and, in a manner of speaking, Quiff herself. Funnily enough, not that there was anything particularly funny about death, he was smiling much less broadly than usual.

Cognisant of the fact that Quaff didn't have the option of a remedial, fay-fair-ly-fully-restorative balefire, it could be he was being uncharacteristically reflective. Then again, like demons, faeries were all body and no soul, so it was questionable he could feel anything like empathy or sympathy for anyone. Nevertheless, as she closed Quaff's recriminating eyelids, that old bugaboo for cats, curiosity, got the better of him.

"Wasn't he was the most likely Quill-in-waiting?" he posed.

"That he was," Morg acknowledged. "So long as Jordy's off dancing the legless limbo it should go without saying."

"Quaff-3? No, she's still walking about freely, isn't she."

"And with a devil keeping her inline, not that devils seem particularly preserva-tive when it comes to our pathetic assortment of pseudo-relatives. Quick – devil or no devil in her, she grew increasingly despondent after Quack and Quail dis-appeared. So she tried to hang herself; almost succeeded too."

"You stopped her?"

"Quiff and the Quaffs did, cut her down and had their minders call one of my Illuminary-insiders. I reckon the devil I gave her somehow kept her ticking until I got there, but she was in awfully rough shape by the time I did. I said I'd do my best for her so they left us alone while I gave her the royal treatment."

"I've heard of that. It's a laying-on of hands, right? Except, Masters aren't sup-posed to be any good at it and you're not even a Utopian."

"Far more pertinently, I'm not an Althean. I got the devil out of her before any over-juiced smartass started wondering how she could still be breathing. That was when I reverted to the manual method of revivification for Quills-in-waiting."

(Altheans were witches belonging to a strangely-to-some, scientifically oriented sisterhood primarily concerned with panhumanistic health and welfare. Named after Amal-Althea, Lazareme's goatish, female healer, they didn't so much worship at her feet, or hooves, as practised what she preached. That boiled down to: *'Life still held mysteries; solve them!'*)

"Only the hands I laid on were over her nose. I held them there until, sure enough, she sprang up, knocked me ass over teakettle, and with Rumour's talisman in no longer palsied paw to boot. Except I did the booting before she got to the scooting. Then I smacked her around a mite more and took it back for myself."

"Everyone says she'd attacked you."

"Weren't you listening? She did, with suicidal strength as well, thus the ass over teakettle routine, wherever that came from."

"Testicles."

"Come again?"

"Prim and proper folks don't like saying bum over balls so they say ass over teakettle instead."

"Do they really?"

"Actually, I just made that up. Of course, now that I think about it, balls over bum wouldn't apply to women, would it?"

"Depends on the woman," she smiled. It wasn't a particularly pleasant smile. Piscines, even half-Piscines like her, tended to have shark-sharp teeth. "At any rate, I fought her off and that's how she ended up so badly bruised. Only a madwoman would attack a Master of Weir, don't you know. Especially one who'd just saved her life."

"You just never mentioned it wasn't until after you finished the job she began."

"I deliberately held off killing her a second time, yes, but there were no witnesses so why would anyone pester me? It's not like they needed to know."

"That she wasn't altogether Quick anymore – that a quick kill had resulted in a Quick Quill."

"Or that my rings weren't just for show, that too. She was ranting and raving, frothing at the mouth and screaming about the unspeakable evils I'd done to her, Quiddity before her and Q-troupe in general. None of that was sitting well, so I had her gagged and trussed up in a padded cell at the nearest secure sanatorium.

"It goes without saying that I stuck a devil back inside her as soon as I safely, and secretly, could. Needles also to slay, as she herself might put it in better days, she's been under the very best care the Weirdom can offer ever since. I'm surprised I hadn't thought of it before, quite frankly."

"Under constant surveillance too, I imagine."

"24-hours a day, toilet in full view, Sarpedon nursemaids and mollycoddlers on call to keep her fed and watered, with soap and scrub brushes as required. It's called a suicide watch and there's no shortage of volunteers for the armed job either. You aspire to join the elite; you have to start down low and dirty, on guard duty. It builds character."

"No beer, what a horrible way for a Quill Tethys to go."

"You missed the point. She's not going anywhere."

"I did get that far, Morg. All I meant was …"

"Then you should have said it. But, irrespective of whether you did or you didn't; to what you meant to say, I say tough tiddlywinks. Devic half-mother or no half-mother, where I come from you make your own luck or you're supper. Q-troupe's just seems to be all bad, so sad. Besides, Jordy thinks our best brew's rotgut anyhow."

"Abstinence does make the heart grow fonder," Squirrelly commiserated.

"And keeps the beer gut non-existent. She'll thank me once I get around to finding her a replacement Quail."

========

As the Librarian implied, there'd be hell to pay for trifling with not just the Than-atoids of Lathakra. Hell on Earth paid part of it.

========

Antique Illuminaries' named the devic epitome of Midsummer 'Novadev'. Circa 2500 YD, his boozed-up explosiveness cost Methandra Thanatos the Goddess Culture's sacred island of Strongyne, Strong Women. Perhaps in commemoration of his betrayal of the 500-year Middle Sea matriarchy she championed, Miss Myth, Mithras's Virgin, chose the 24th to belatedly heed Lady Lust's advice to King Cold on New Years Day. She turned Paradise for the Damned into an inescapably blazing inferno.

If demons could cry *'mayday, mayday'* in Azky, which they could, though Hellions throughout the Inner Earth probably sensed more so than heard it, then it went unanswered. The supremely self-assured Master of Weir may have heard it in addition to sensing it. She may have wept as well.

But, if she did, her tears likely came from the Demon Queen within her (always assuming there was a Demon Queen within her). Either that or her eyes misted over because she was so delighted to finally be saying *'I do'* to Tomcat at their wedding ceremony. If her Melusine of an amphibious mother had been there, hers would have too. She never wanted Morg to die an old maid. Might grandchildren be on the horizon?

There wasn't much of anything anyone could do about Satanwyck anyhow. The Weirdom's tragically depleted panoply of extraterrestrial wonderments did not contain fire suppressants capable of covering countryside approximately the same area as Cabalarkon, if not more, and that only in terms of its uppermost territories. Even if it did, which it might have at one time, it certainly didn't contain anything that would allow said chemicals to be transported, let alone teleported, halfway across a hidden continent in anywhere near enough time to mitigate the literal devastation.

Something else did, however; rather, some things did. These things were neither extraterrestrial in origin nor Utopian in terms of design or manufacture. Morgan Abyss, she and her advisers – be they scientocrats, Illuminaries, Hellions, Trinondevs, all in one, all in some and none in others or, giving credence to rumours that Morg practised geomancy, Mother Earth herself – just didn't realize it yet.

As for why they weren't used to extricate the Librarian, lowborns – even if they were relative highborns like Biblio Drek – didn't warrant the same consideration firstborns and even higher-born Master Devas did. While they weren't eminently expendable like Thrygragos Varuna Mithras judged his own azuras on Thrygragon, they didn't rate listing on the rescue-at-all-costs register either.

Not while Harmony wanted to keep what else ringots did hush-hush they didn't.

========

Quiff kept the syrinx just as Lazareme suggested she should. She also played it the next day, at her own wedding reception – though by then, as he'd promised his maypole admirers weeks before he was struck down so cold-bloodedly in the woods, it was Squirrelly playing it at his own wedding reception.

Morg hadn't gone batrachian overnight. In a manner of speaking Quiff-now-Squirrelly had, however.

========

Notwithstanding clear blue skies above, he (ex-she) unintelligently chanced lightning again by playing outside in the palace's spectacular garden-cum-woodlands-cum-wildlife-preserve much later that same day. He was stomping and piping jaunty jigs like a man possessed, which he wasn't. (Since there was no point wasting a devil by sticking him or her inside a faerie, Morg hadn't bothered this time any more than she had when he showed up in Cabby's Weirdom and revealed his heritage to her.)

So contagious were the rhythms he was putting out, even the park's feral cats and its resident squirrels, of the four-legged variety, had given up stalking or pelting each other and were themselves jauntily jigging. Suddenly an ear-splittingly loud, incessantly clanging alarum rang out from the vicinity of the Citadel of Thinkers, which lay across the megalithic metropolis's vast *'People's Plaza'* from the front of the Masters Palace.

The closest thing the Weirdom came to having a centre for higher learning, plenty of Morg's Illuminaries and some of its scientocrats went to what, for them, passed for employment within the Citadel. However, as soon as they announced their upcoming wedding, weeks ago now, city officials declared today's solstice a holiday. That meant it was closed for classes, teachers, students, most workers and all visitors.

Oh, a few aspiring Trinondevs would be pacing the hallways on counter-devil duty, house gargoyles manifest and empty eyeorbs at the ready. However, along with some Sarpedon functionaries such as equipment monitors, minor technicians and animal keepers, they should be the only ones inside the massive, cyclopean edifice. Consequently, no matter what triggered the alarm bells – if, for example, the Citadel had come under attack from azura-occupied lab rats – there wasn't much danger of it causing many, if any, casualties.

Much more urgently, to the Weirdom's malefic Master's mind, a large, thickly walled and anchored-immovable chamber, one sealed with Stopstone-Solidium to prevent entrance or egress via the Weird, lay beneath it. From time approaching immemorial, in terms of the Inner Earth of Sedon's Head, Trinondevs and their Masters kept packed prison pods and other captured or confiscated objects of devilish interest locked therein.

Regardless of whether she'd sensed Methandra setting Satanwyck's surface on fire, in a belated tit-for-tat strike three months after the Elysium Inferno, Squirrelly's bride of a couple hours earlier had been expecting something even more untoward than bolts of targeted lightning happening today. After all, weddings were supposed to be the happiest day of one's life. When else would devils choose to escalate the challenges their hateful leadership devised in order to wither away the fragile goodwill the Weirdom's populace continued to bear her?

In their distressing chinwag this morning, the Lackland Libertine's loose-lipped Librarian had essentially spelled out Lazareme's strategy now that he'd taken to running the madhouse instead of the Thanatoids. Undermining her authority by showing up her inability to counterattack with anything except bluffs and powder-puff punches amounted to the long, short and curly hairs of it.

Evidently the ghostly dancers – devic far-sendings the macabre many of them – had been anticipating the disruption as well. The abominations aborted their merrily mocking hopscotching and just as silly be-bopping the instant the once again Lazareme-lookalike ceased his pulse-pounding grandstanding. The apparitions promptly sat down, or up, in the very air itself as if waiting for the next act to begin.

Their insubstantial, but grotesquely perceptible, and deliberately stinky presence indicated Thrygragos Everyman had gone ahead with the midsummer shebang he'd boasted of to Quiff (pre-he) last night. Moreover, like a veritable maestro of confusion, he'd had the Master Devas who came to Tympani broadcast their repugnant revelries to Cabalarkon the Garden.

They were here. They'd been in the Weirdom's tri-towered Cathedral of Light, fronting the south side of the plaza, for the marriage ceremony. They would probably be in bed with them tonight, when they sought to consummate it officially. Overall, devils lacked much in the way of an imagination but they shone wretchedly at wreaking reeking havoc, to fay-say some.

Morg went to the catacombs beneath the Citadel inter-spatially, on pre-planted hellstones. She manifested her Strife-gargoyle but that was more misdirection than anything else; a red herring calculated to distract or delude her foes from her real weapons. What she was no longer wearing or wielding just between-space; what she'd also found in the same, between-space-blocked vault; what she's thereupon fashioned into her garments and chain of office; they didn't only forestall devic possession.

They could be used to kill the blighters.

========

Consider the earth's surface akin to a piecrust. Pastry chefs poke piecrusts with forks to see if they're done. One always contrarian Master Deva, wrongly reckoned by many the firstborn of the firstborn, didn't poke the earth's crust with a fork; he used a very much enlargeable trident. He also didn't fork it from the outside; he forked it from the inside.

The earth's crust underneath the Master's Garden shook and shook some more. A hillock rose. Its summit split. A 20-foot trident partially extended through the resultant cleft, barbed, pointy prongs first and them twirling on upright axes as if metallic dervishes on a curved crossbeam. Doors and windows cracked open up and down them; four and twenty thousand blackbirds burst forth like plagues on parade.

No, the one ghost there who wasn't a sending reconsidered, it couldn't be anywhere near that many. It just seemed like it. They weren't all black either, just mostly black. And they weren't blackbirds. They were demons, had to be – very, very toothy and hungry looking demons.

To say chaos followed worked both capitalized and regularly written.

****

11. Countering Chaos

<u>**Midsummer's Day, 4825 Year of the Dome – The Weirdom of Cabalarkon**</u>

By the 'equivalent of a whole brood of heliodromi' the Librarian, Biblio Drek, meant his father had at least three designated couriers or sun-runners. They weren't triplets – put better, their triplet siblings weren't each other – but they could flit or ghost about invisibly, with or without power foci, the same as every other devil could.

In point of fact one heliodromus called himself Djinn Ghoster. His Tvasitar talisman was similar to the Neuter's in that it was headgear, a turban in his case. He'd been ring-gotten. Ergo, he didn't have it anymore. He'd also been inserted, past tense. He got out of his unaware and probably unwilling host the best way possible, without getting sucked into anything else.

He still didn't have a power focus but he was looking at one that, with a little judicious jiggling, would do as well as any.

========

Master Morgan Abyss stepped out of the Weird into a huge, artificially hollowed-out, subterranean cavern. Part of the tunnel system that over time became the Catacombs of the Sleepers, the Utopians who founded Cabalarkon City telekinetically carted, via their multipurpose eye-staves, an even-then Stopstone-sealed chamber from one of their grounded millennial or generational ships to here.

They did so shortly after the Moloch Sedon raised the Cathonic Zone out of his own essence and effectively trapped them beneath the henceforth Dome or Sedon Sphere. Since long before the time of those space-faring Utopians, the chamber was used to deposit and contain objects precious to devils more so than to anyone else.

Morg never altogether satisfied herself as to whether that era's galactic veterans constituted Utopian cats among devic pigeons or it was the other way around. Equally so, she never quite forgave herself for sticking Pyrame Silverstar in an avian-human called Quack. Even if Quack wasn't a Garuda, suchlike sloppiness deserved a face-rearranging slap and/or an hour or two in the blocks, with Squirrelly throwing hopefully thoroughly rotten tomatoes at her.

Save for the Devil Himself, Pyrame was the last devil she should have let out of her possession. At the minimum, she should have kept her sealed in a ringot deposited inside this very vault, along with most of the ancient eyeorbs holding

Sedonic shreds and perhaps twice that many new and old prison pods containing captured or transferred Master Devas. Even less riskily, she should have kept her sealed within a ring on her finger.

Morg had heard it said that life is one big crapshoot. If so then she was on a pretty good roll; had been, with one or two minor setbacks, since Jordy showed up just before Mithramas, kibisis and its ringots for Pyrame and her demon, inside the Master of Weir, to dispose of in there.

Six months back the Pauper Priestess was the one that got disposed of, how-soever-temporarily, in one of them instead. Still, Morg had also heard tell that when tossing bones, or dice, what goes around comes around. Sometimes it comes back to haunt you. Other times you're given a second shot.

She hadn't been expecting to see the topless, bodily beautiful, tetrahedral-headed, Master Deva there, she in her strapped up sandals and Egyptian- or Etocretan-style sheath or flounce skirt. She doubly hadn't expected to see her trying to smash her way into the vault with an arm ending in a heavy and unwieldy-looking anvil, one whose glow was so dazzlingly incandescent it came close to blinding. That, though, was precisely what she was doing.

As to the first, that shouldn't have been at all surprising. No other devil was immune to capture in a Trinondev prison pod. As to the second, even though it had clearly been supercharged with Brainrock-Gypsium, it may or may not be Tvasitar Smithmonger, aka Anvil the Artificer's actual anvil.

Not that that made much difference; any devil could use any other devil's power focus. Indeed, anyone with a measure of sentience could use any devil's power focus – witness her and Rumour's quill, or Tomcat-Squirrelly and Chance's Triskelion. Nonetheless, although at one time Pyrame Silverstar sported a goodly number of trophy talismans, as far as Morg had heard she never needed one in order to stay solid before. To see her thus armed – this was no time for puns – therefore approached the shocking.

Yet the one plus the two begged three questions. Make it four. Was she really immune or was the Demon Queen she animated until Morg took her out the invulnerable one? That'd be two, if you were counting, which she was, flashingly fast. Would one of the vacated, pre-Earth orbs work on Pyrame or would an empty, terrestrially manufactured one do just as well now that she was Lilith-free?

That'd be four, wouldn't it? Or did that make it five? Just to be sure she asked herself if the Pauper Priestess had sunk so low she was now doing Lazareme's bidding?

For bare beginners, there was only one way to find any of that out. She materialized her Master's Mace. A representation of Sedon's head didn't glare out of its top either mouth-wateringly or pleadingly; a Death's Head did. She'd freshly evacuated the eyeorb this morning, in preparation for Thrygragos Lazareme, or the source of the last night's Tomcat-killer thunderbolt, should either/or dare to pop by for a repeat performance.

It was hardly the only first or second Weir World prison pod she'd readied while Tomcat-Squirrelly was being done to dust. Months back, the devil she'd stuck in Quit-It, unless it was Quaff-2, was Monk-Eye, as devils called him, a Byronic ring-gotten around the same time as the Librarian had been in Kanin City.

This Monk-Eye wasn't just something of a monkey, as in prankster, who took an exceedingly immature delight in driving Biblio Drek buggy, as the Librarian himself put it when she first interviewed him, he in Quiff, not long after New Years Day. Head to toe, and with all parts in between, the Byronic's favourite form was that of a genuine, resolutely male monkey. That, along with a twisted sense of humour, he teased, quite seriously, accounted for most of the reason he called his power focus a '*bazooka banana*'.

Three months ago, his assertive jest, her own Jordy-like wit, and another word for a different sort of '*buggy*', a jalopy, gave her ideas. Quiddity sort of hadn't leapt to his death out of the result of those ideas and Brainrock powered it, which meant it could slip between-space.

She wasn't going to tell, or show, the 3-eyed, yet bizarrely Cyclops-like, one-woman devic wrecking crew any of that, though. Completely misreading what the lone adult, fabulously female perpetual presence was doing there, she proclaimed instead: "You're a fucking idiot, Pyrame. Did you really think I'd leave the undying Utopian in such an obvious place?"

"Not anymore I don't." Her words came vocally; this despite the fact the Pauper Priestess had no mouth on any of her head's three, singly eyed, uppermost sides.

She vanished. It was as if she'd never been there, though the dents in the vault's exterior belied that perhaps wishful whimsy. Plainly Lazareme didn't intend to fight just a war of nerves. He intended to fight one of verve too, with Pyrame as his thought-invulnerable strike-force.

Where were the Trinondevs supposed to be on patrol down here anyhow? Had they seen her and skedaddled? Skull bones may have to roll instead of knucklebones, even if most dice were made of ivory these days.

The ground grumbled, a minor earthquake only. Then it shook some more, rocking much more robustly this time. Lightning wasn't the only thing that struck twice. So did temblors. Although they were fairly common in the Upper Head, there was no way for her to be sure, especially from down here, if devils were responsible for it.

Nobody would bet against it, she felt positive. Everyone blamed the tsunami that smashed up Cabalarkon's main seaport a few weeks ago on Umashakti Silvercloud but they couldn't verify that either. It might not even have been devil-doings. Still, if Lazareme really did employ Pyrame to sucker her over here, then had someone else cause an earthquake to bury her – Nakba Ramazar, the Apocalyptic of Catastrophe or Sudden Destruction, perhaps – she counted her lucky stars that her Utopian predecessors were astute enough to realize the entire archipelago of Pacifica was prone to tectonic extremes.

They'd probably come to that conclusion by looking at how the native Edenites or their Golden Age successors constructed other cities and/or monumental edifices on islands hundreds, if not thousands, of years before Sedon linked them as a consequential hidden continent. Copying their techniques, they quarried then pieced the Weirdom's cyclopean stonework together without mortar. As a result, only dust, not the roof itself, fell on her.

If it weren't for the mysteriously AWOL Warriors Elite, she was still on a roll – for about five more seconds. That's how long it took her to hellstone-step back to the garden party. By the time she arrived general disarray didn't rule. Admiral Chaos (capitalized, first name Abe) did.

And the ghost who wouldn't have been an apparition even if he were visible was making his move.

========

As an actress Quaff-3 was extremely self-conscious, which could explain why she'd been carrying around a handheld vanity mirror for months now. In a way, the self-pronounced serial monogamist's concern for her appearance made her and Djinn Ghoster an ideal pairing. Very few devils were as fastidious as Lazareme's always-accommodating heliodromus.

That she had started to smell ever so slightly off might have been a significance everyone except her managed to miss, however.

========

Stopstone-Solidium was Brainrock-Gypsium's counteragent. More of the one offset less of the other. Cabalarkon City was built over the Subterranean Land of Absudyl, it of the Mandroids, a cross-continental extension of the Upper Head's Hell-Well. Nonetheless, bubbling pools of the miraculously self-replenishing Godstuff abounded throughout Sedon's Devic Eye-Land. (Which was no doubt part of the attraction for the then only recently earthbound Utopians to found and thereafter build their first Weirdom here.)

The wedding reception took place in the meticulously landscaped garden-slash-grassy-field where Utopians held the maypole ceremony every year on the 1st of Vanalal. Regardless of whether Pyrame popping into the Catacombs of the Sleepers was intended to draw Master Morg there, the cloudless and hence seasonally warm day – for any except this extraordinarily disheartening year, and not just weather-wise – proved a deliberately irresistible lure for hundreds of Utopians.

Devic sendings couldn't physically harm anyone. A combination of the noises they made and the noisome odours they gave off served only to keep the more faint-hearted members of the invited public away. To a man or woman of them, Illuminaries, scientocrats and Trinondevs purported themselves made of sterner stuff. Unfortunately, far too much of it had already been spilled on the expansive lawn leading up to the foot of the grandiose staircase coming down from the back of the palace.

Many of the guests and guards stood stupidly motionless, as if stunned petrified in disbelief as much as in dismay that a devil dared invade Cabalarkon; worse, that a devil could get away with invading Cabalarkon. Lifesaving panic had hit many more. Some had already found refuge inside the palace but most were still seeking to flee to it, or beyond it, on two feet or on all fours if they were too badly injured to do otherwise. A disturbing number just lay where they fell, possibly already dead, whereas a few could do little else except seek to slither away from the locus of the attack.

Of those heroically holding their ground, none were holding their own because no one was even challenging the 3-eyed lunatic. Everywhere she looked blue-robed Trinondevs desperately strove to rip what looked to be mobile variations of fantastical roof-spouts off the tips of their eye-staves. The blackish and probably brackish horrors clinging so tenaciously to the eyeorbs that focused Utopian brainwaves, and thereby made eye-staves work, accounted for why they were so disconcertingly unprotected by their house or personal gargoyles.

The living equivalencies had to be dire demons of some description, earthborn and maybe even relatively newborn abominations. Their Stopstone or Solidium prevented the Trinondevs opening their eyeorbs. Unopened they couldn't first shred then suck in the Unholy Unity's spirit being self, daemonic body and Brainrock power focus. An overabundance of chthonic crud trumped an under-abundance of Godstuff every day of the week and that included a Master's wedding day.

She was torn between awed appreciations of her Trinondevs' steadfastness in the face of Chaos incarnadine, as well as incarnate, and the fearsome devil's clearly non-suicidal bravura at entering an uncorrupted Weirdom jammed chock-a-block with empty eyeorbs and protected by a Warrior Elite unmatched at using them. Then, eyeballs finally adjusting to the scope of the tumultuous hurly-burly, she was cured of any more such squishy sentimentality.

Her groom of not so long ago lay on the up-chucked ground in front of her ungodly uncle. There'd be no faerie-oven for Tomcat *'Squirrelly'* Tattletail this time. Not unless the voracious, seemingly still semi-mercurial fiends left enough, for them, indigestible but salvageable piles of gnawed bones and slit sinews, moderately solid puke and non-diarrheic crap, behind after they finished devouring him.

As for Abe Chaos, he'd assumed close to what must be his most fiercely formidable guise. Commonly long-bearded, darkly hairy, and broad-shouldered, he had additionally rendered himself a giant maybe eight feet, maybe nine feet tall, scarlet-skinned and absolutely massive. Evidently not yet registering her, he folded his arms in front of his chest and almost casually, even dispassionately, surveyed the havoc his arrival and the release of his protean, apparently kept-starved or never-fed demons were causing.

At least eight arrow-like sparklers, their tips lit and blistering, poked out of the tangled mane of muddily woven and matted hair ringing his head. To both compliment and compound his apparent but weirdly aloof ferocity, he looked to be dressed in bearskin minutes removed from a grizzly he'd out-wrestled in a bear pit and skinned alive with his bare hands.

He wasn't holding his trident or *'trishula'*. It was behind him; its three prongs and lower curvature framed him. It was as if he'd rammed the whole thing upwards, out of the ground instead of into it, which would account for the temblors. Its fork-ends, on its only partially emerged shaft or *'danda'*, protruded at a ratio of maybe three times his already impressive size.

She was almost pleased to see him. "I was hoping for Harmony but you'll do fine – for starters."

"Good, because with an attitude like that I no longer feel inclined to ask you to move all your ringots to one hand."

"Huh?"

"Dad sent me here to disarm you, Master. Guess I'll take them both now."

The black bolt smote her harder than its whitish kin did Squirrelly last night.

========

She skipped the wedding and scheduled reception afterwards.

========

Superficially her excuse seemed suitably prima-donna-like. She complained that none of the perfume her minders offered, as a replacement for her own now sadly spent stash of fragrance, flattered her sufficiently. That she'd spent her stash had everything to do with why the Sarpedons offered her a replacement fragrance.

She dismissed them characteristically haughtily. When they heeded her for a change, happy that they could attend the Master's connubial carousing without fear of reproach, she went off to visit Cousin Quick. She didn't know she wasn't Cousin Quick anymore. She therefore didn't know she might be mama or grandma, daddy or granddaddy Quick either.

She didn't even know why she paused at one of the natural fountains of up-whelming Brainrock on her way to the sanatorium. Nor did she know why she ever so slyly mixed some of the miraculous substance into the compact containing her face powder. There was a reason for her ignorance. It was the same reason Djinn Ghoster got out of her without anyone realizing he had.

Outwardly, but for the worsening body odour, nothing much had changed in the few weeks since she left the hospital, stricken as she had been with the same malady that ultimately claimed Quaff-2, unless it was Quit-It. She was still occupied too, except now she was only bodily Quaff-3.

She was no zombie. She was just a too fast drying-up husk of humanity.

========

"Quick?" She asked the forlorn figure lounging on the cell's cot.

Hearing her arguable cousin's voice, Quick perked up. They were separated by padded bars but she could see her unhindered, gave her a speedy once-over visually, sniffed the air a couple of times rather rudely, and then cracked a bemused grin: "Jordy, of the paterfamilias variety, though I'll understand if you mistake me for the materfamilias variety. These incarnations occur far more often than I care to admit. Who are you?"

"Is it that obvious?"

"Glassy eyeballs; a pallor that makes U-women look tanned; a pong that mephitic demons would die for, if they weren't as good as dead and buried and then newly risen already. The word '*exsanguinous*' comes to mind but that wouldn't be fair to Sangs. They tend to take better care of their shells.

"Truth told, which I always endeavour to do; no Valkyrie would ever choose any of my proper descendants to be a Valhallan. Not unless it was to join their marching band. Which, believe it or not, has happened. Of course his mom just happened to be a Valkyrie. Fact is she killed him a second time just so she could stick a Sang into him."

"Seems to me I recall you telling my parents that once. Something to do with Thrygragon wasn't it?"

"Also something to do with its aftermath; how Kanin City's extraterrestrial goodies, along with its then royal family, one of whom eventually became me, ended up in Cabalarkon. But that's enough about me. Or about my erstwhile carnations, put more comprehensibly. I'm all of a sudden much more intrigued by you.

"Which parents are you talking about? Surely not Quaff's because you're just animating her. And there are so many different kinds of azuras I could die of thirst before guessing which one you are. Speaking of which …"

"My father's as fond as pills as you are, maybe more."

"Impossible. And that doesn't narrow down the criteria in any way whatsoever. Gabbling kegs of devils love their beer or ale or mead almost as much as I do."

"He carries barrels of the stuff with him wherever he goes. Rather, his minions do. Some of them are also really good at chilling it on account of they're icemen."

"A Tantalazur, eh? You said parents. Surely not Lady Luck."

"Nor Lady Lust either. My mother's the impossible one. She reckons what happened to her can be ascribed to some sort of daemonic parthenogenesis, meaning she had me even though it was the demons that ate dad and her who had sex. I'm the world's first and only pre-Genesea azura."

"Klannit Thanatos."

"So much for it being our secret. Did Harmony far-send you that info?"

"You'd be surprised what tales tee-tees and/or their tails are born telling. It almost makes me want to believe in God the Dabbler, the same jokester who sprinkled the earth with dinosaur skeletons in order to make us think he didn't create the planet in six days, which everyone knows she did.

"But, other than that, you're right. We have been in communication, mind-to-mind. I was an Intuit too once. So I'm good at that. That hackneyed, hem-worn adage about old dogs and new tricks doesn't apply to me because it's the young dogs who learn them before I come along to take over territorial pissing duties."

"How'd she figure out you've come back in Quick? No one in Q-troupe did and we live here; lived here in Quaff's case."

"Since you did, or do, you might have heard that another meaning for '*bug*' is '*listening device*'. Utopians have all sorts of the buggers, pun intended, in their toolbox of techno-tricks and Harm's always been good at thieving her enemies' thunder. Which, now that I think about it, might pass for another one, a pun in a pun-bun so to spun."

"How so?"

"It's always struck me as a stretch to get northern lights or chain lightning out of a golden neck torc. Yet that's what you-know-who made for her after he made his anvil for himself and the six Great Godly Glories for his father, uncles and mothers. I mean, if he'd fashioned her the manacles and broken chains, fine. Even the Scales of Justice earrings she wears would work. But she made them herself."

"A golden torc, what's it good for – a noose?"

"She stole her triplet brothers' thunder because she stole the idea of it from their black or white thunderbolts."

"Very good, Klannit." Jordy-Quick gave her a perfunctory clap or two before obliging her with a typical Legendarian denouement. "Bugs as bugs, there's your mnemonic. She's been sending hundreds of her azuras in hundreds of bugs into the Weirdom for months now."

He, as a she, waited for her, Klannit in Quaff's ambulant corpse, to applaud. Reciprocity revealed itself unforthcoming. Just as well. Something was troubling him-become-her and it wasn't just the almighty itchiness of the scar that developed in Quick's forehead the moment he incarnated as her. That, which only happened when devils were close by, had been troubling him, her now, since he came back as she.

"Wait a minute. How did she get rid of the guards?"

"I'm not at liberty to tell you."

"Because I might tell Morg."

"You wouldn't want to, but you wouldn't have any choice in the matter – if we don't hurry up and not get caught before we get away, it should go without fay-saying. Trinondev eye-staves are so very useful; you'll have heard that as well as said it, probably many times over. Only trouble is I've no way of doing that."

"No way – not no idea?" Then she twigged. "Wait a minute. That's why I mixed some Brainrock into Quaff's face-paint."

"I provide the idea; you provide the way. Let's quit jawing and get to drawing."

Quaff-Klannit went to reach Quaff's compact through the food tray opening in the cell door. Then she apparently thought better of it and instead wangled it invitingly out of Jordy's reach. "No, you wait a minute. My dad's Illuminary-name is Tantal, as in tantalizing. Can you draw your quill back here and yourself away before they come back and nail us both, me with their sticks' pointy ends?"

"Hey, I was Quick."

"Good. Then draw my beloved first and once we have him, we can all bugger off together."

"Your beloved?"

"Tvasitar Smithmonger. Or didn't your tee-tees get that far?"

"Just wanted to hear you say is all, lover," said a suddenly 3-eyed Quick in a certain smithy's gruff voice. "Hand it over."

"Tavy!"

========

Presumably what occurred next was more of a bolt from the blue to Chaos than a literal one to Master Morgan Abyss.

========

It must have been. This if only because his black-blade blast, admittedly – in retrospect, more like manifestly – as filtered through its trident shaft of a sheath, then through his back and out of his abruptly outstretched arms, did not do to Morg what Order's vajra-jolt did to satyr Squirrelly the night before.

She electrified, yes, but not with all the crisping and crackling he would have expected. Neither did she drop to the ground, let alone drop to it stone dead. Nor did she do so convulsing, which would have been moderately less satisfying but a result notwithstanding. Truth told she jerked, briefly, but stayed standing. Then something appeared above her not so much out of the blue, though it did that too, as out of the Weird.

The Unity did not yet know to call it the *'All-Eyes Contraption'*. Neither did he immediately conceive of it as a hovering, mechanical porcupine complete with eye-stalks akin to ommatophores. However, the Master's Brainrock-powered and hence teleportive jalopy did have dozens of eyeorbs sticking quill-like out of it on the ends of otherwise unmanned eye-staves.

Then, as if recoiling, reloading and rapid-firing bazookas, they began discharging prison pods in their hundreds. Opening in midflight, they shredded Chaos exactly as their anciently scientocrat- and/or Mother-Machine-made ilk had his grandfather Sedon. Even as they were landing, they were still sucking the Unholy

Unity's spirit being self, daemonic body and power focus into their multiple be-tween-space repositories.

What occurred next nevertheless must have startled Master Morgan Abyss.

========

Wide-open eyeorbs in effect imploding internally acted as vacuum cleaners or siphons not just with respect the unholy Unity's spirit being self, daemonic body and Brainrock power focus. They also shredded and sucked the protean demons assailing her Trinondevs and, more specifically, their eye-staves into multiple be-tween-space repositories. She thus freed up her Warriors Elite such that they could belatedly manifest their protective house or personal gargoyles.

Although this was an expected by-product of her bazooka bursts, it was also barn door and escaping cows stuff. Worse, it finally dawned, as dusk approached, on Morg that the trident hadn't been glowing the way power foci usually did, especially when they were being utilized. Something on the ground did, dully – Tomcat's pan-pipe. Before her eyes it morphed into a triple-bladed propeller, Chance's Triskelion, whereupon it rotated speedily into the Weird, thereby vanishing.

Something else did a ditto, though this she sensed more so than witnessed. It went away too, put better. She could be sure of that because she sought to material-ize it and zip times naught appeared in her hand. Once again she had to wonder what had become of nearly top of the totem pole Trinondevs and basically bottom of it Sarpedons.

Only this time she had to wonder what had become of the ones guarding/minding Quick-cum-Jordy rather than the ones patrolling within the vicinity of the Stopstone vault beneath the Citadel of the Thinkers. With the Tomcat-Quiff irretrievably gone again, had Quick died a second time? Had Quaff-3, the only potential Legendarian left in the Weirdom other than herself, died a first time next to simultaneously?

Had Rumour's quill gone to her or had there been another Quill-to-be killed elsewhere? Had Harmony, or whoever, discovered that and killed him, or her, a first time after somehow executing Quick, via the Weird, like the evil bastards did Squir-relly last night? Devils never cathonitized when they killed either 30-Beers or Pusan Wanderlust but, as she demonstrated by tricking them into setting off the Elysium Inferno, they didn't automatically ill-star themselves when they killed anyone, let alone Quills-to-be, anyhow.

Almost overwhelmed by events, she ordered still terrified attendants running towards her to salvage what they could of Tomcat-Squirrelly then hellstone-stepped to the sanatorium. An empty cell, no Quick, no guards nor any minders could be seen anywhere. She took herself to the quiet of her throne room. No guards were there either.

That was okay, though. She'd declared today a holiday in honour of her mar-riage, so no one was supposed to be on duty here. But there were also no more stop-stoned statues about the place. That wasn't okay; that was totally wrong. This was getting even more depressing than the weather had been since New Years.

'*It's supposed to be.*' She had another thought. Like the first it wasn't her thought. It was far-sent to her – and by the same personage, rather than person per se. '*Heard it was me you were hoping for. Well, here I am. And hearing me you are. Know what they say about folks who hear discombobulated voices, Master? Guess what? If you're not crazier than your Hellion Sisterhood's everyday average hoot owl yet, you soon will be.'*

"Harmony?" Morg asked the air, as well as herself, aloud.

'That'd be Disharmony to you, Call-me-morgue. You've put me off satyrs evermore and no one's seen the Goat since Order had to kill her, also thanks to you. You might be wearing or wielding the six Great Godly Glories. Our pal the Pauper Priestess says you are, and devils always talk true, so I believe her. But they're no good at deafening you mentally. There's only one sure way to do that. Want to borrow my neck-torc? It'd make for a fabulous noose.'

Morg clutched her ears; tried to concentrate on more pleasant matters. It did no good. Another voice, with another set of thoughts, assaulted her. *'Naughty notions those, Piscine, even I'm approaching scandalized. What will you do if you can't scrape up and reheat enough of Harmony's favourite fuckhead to sodomize, sorry, solemnize, your wedding night? No worries. Minius is full of raw material and if you're looking for pointers, hey, I'll be there for you.'*

Pyrame Silverstar spoke into her head next. *'That was Lust, in case you mistook her for Chastity or some such. Our eldest sister, who isn't as chaste as she pretends, would like to pass on a few words of wisdom too – except she doesn't talk to strangers, not to mention most of us.*

'Firestorms are popular. She specializes in them, as you may have gathered by now. Always presuming demons can cry mayday in Azky and you can hear them. But, just in case you can't, she assures me Satanwyck did go up, in a proverbial blaze of glory, rather nicely. And now it's going down, down, down even more nicely.

'Good thing Order forewarned Dand Tariqartha, as your Illuminaries called Cousin Chronocollector all those centuries ago, of what we were up to in his subterranean neighbourhood. He ensured Temporis was sealed against roaring infernos. Wish I could say the same about Minius but I can't, can I.

'Hopefully Hot Stuff's manufactured conflagration will burn out before it gets that far. Its Minotaurus is almost as stupid as your idiots – stupider, since he lacks any imagination whatsoever. And he'd never think to waste beer putting out a fire. Magnus Minus was my idea by the way.'

'But scattering my brain into his constructs,' interrupted a male voice, one Morg had last heard in the palace's garden, *'That was mine.'*

'I offered to splatter it,' Yajur contributed jovially. *'But that's for the future.'*

'You wish, dickless.'

'Now, now, boys,' Beguiling Belialma tut-tutted the male Unities into silence. *'It's a good trick, though. Even you'll have to admit that, Master. Of course it only stands to reason; which is something Abe almost never does. We animate debrained demons so why shouldn't we be able to simultaneously animate dozens of demons, ones that never had brains to start with, with dribs and drabs of ours. We are gods, aren't we?'*

"In your dreams," thought as well as said the Master of Weir.

'Woof! What's that stench?' wondered Rudra Silvercloud, not bothering to identify himself. *'Oh, it's what's-her-name, the actress from Chance's travelling troupe of troubling troubadours. Saw her perform in Kanin City once. Then I had her perform a couple more times for me alone, without her clothes. Didn't have to get married either. Of course I already am that, aren't I.'*

'I did not have to hear that, beast,' transmitted Lunar Uma, the sister-wife of reference, also not identifying herself.

'And here's Ghoster,' Harmony interrupted the sometimes warring couple, *'Our Djinn, not Mithras's jinni. He looks kind of funny wearing a beanie with a propeller on top of it for a turban.'*

'And, by gosh and by golly,' said Pyrame, *'Isn't that Anvil externalizing himself out of Quick-Quill? Of course it is. And isn't he a handsome rogue? Haven't seen him since next door to forever. Oh dear, he's getting such a royal bollocking Jordy's ass is going to be ablaze for months to come.'*

'Tavy won't need bellows to light his forge anymore,' said Sedona Spellbinder, not wanting to be left out of the taunting tediousness. Being all smoke she presumably knew something about fires. *'Or keep it going. All he'll have to do is fart.'*

'How dare he invent ringots and not tell daddy,' Order concurred.

'My, such treats we're having today,' said Chaos.

'Disharmony here again, Morg. And in the interests of averting it, after her drooling over Tavy like that, you can have Pyrame back for free. No noose needed.'

There was no such thing as capital punishment in devic realms on the Hidden Continent of Sedon's Head. Murder, though, warranted the harshest punishment any tribe or nation dared carry out. In this respect, the Legendarian might pun some, unnatural deaths resulting from war, rebellion or self-defence naturally didn't count. While that suggested there was no such thing as war crimes, the fact of the matter was none of this necessarily applied to the Weirdom of Cabalarkon.

Utopians didn't believe in capital punishment either. Nowhere that reckoned itself civilized did. But, to Morg, the implication of Harmony's words couldn't be clearer. It remained to be seen what would happen to those who would never worship devil-gods if Cabalarkon fell. Trinondevs and other pureblood Utopians, regardless of mental competency, should be quaking in terror rather than rallying behind a failed Mastery.

Harmony was offering not just her a way out. She was offering her people a way to forestall extinction on the Whole Earth. And here was her father to confirm it.

'For a tailless Melusine, you're awfully scrappy. I'll give you that. But, when it comes to us, you're nothing except crappy.' (Besides being fay-fairly-good at fay-saying, Thrygragos Lazareme must have been listening in earlier that approaching unbearably long, long day when she told the Librarian about her parents.)

'Release whomever of ours you have left, stick the Great Godly Glories back where you found them and submit to Silverstar. Allow yourself to be repossessed, Mother Earth's Primeval Lilith or whomever with you. You'll lose your freewill again but there'll be no further retaliation on our part. Agreed?'

"Agreed."

========

Quill Tethys couldn't draw anyone anywhere against his or her will. He or she could, however, draw damn near anything – and with damn near any utensil, including fingers, or any combination of condiments, so long as he could smear them. Inanimate objects, provided they weren't sentient, could never object to him transporting them wher-

ever and sentient ones, even if they were immobilized, could always give their permission, be it mind-to-mind or vocally.

As for drawing quills with face powder, when mixed with the ineffable Godstuff of Brainrock-Gypsium, it did the trick as well as Rumour's quill did.

****

12. Save Us from the Glowing Rain

Presumably what occurred next was more of a proverbial bolt from the blue to the Unity of Chaos than a literal one to Master Morgan Abyss.

========

Abe passed out – off Tympani, Eardrum Isle, that of the Undying One, in the Aural Sea of Sedon's Ear.

"Shall I drench him, dad?" Harmony asked her father, bucket of suds at the ready, rapidly recovering from her own jaw dropping jolt of surprise at seeing her most rambunctious brood brother collapse like that.

"And waste all that fantastic pilsner?" Thrygragos Lazareme responded, evidently unconcerned at what had just befallen a third of his firstborn. "Bugger that for a game of horseshoes. Pour everyone a round and give the rest to me."

"You're going to let her get away with that, Lackland?" a space-hogging giantess queried disrespectfully.

The pointlessly oversized Mithradite did so apparently intentionally, as if to add insult to impertinence, after declining Harmony's offer of the Dinq Doinq Danq's finest pills. Unflappable, doing her best imitation of a gracious hostess, the lone female Unity – from all reports the first Master Deva born, albeit only by a few seconds, of the Trigregos Sisters – merely smiled and moved on to their next guest.

(Except for one thing, the pavilion's very existence might belie the notion of Lazareme being the Lackland Libertine. That one thing? It wasn't on land as such. It was between-space. Harmony had promulgated a theory, validated by a subsequent dearth of any additional devic disappearances, that the uncanny sorceress who used Rumour's quill to pinpoint Master Devas, and thereafter sic her daemonic thralls on them, couldn't detect anyone if they were hiding either inside someone or else in the Weird.)

"She speaks," exclaimed Lord Yajur, the Unity of Order, who was too orderly to drink alcohol period.

"Not to you, Sparky," said-speaker snarled.

Even though she stood amidst a group of exceedingly potent allies with her face impolitely hidden, Methandra Thanatos did design to speak to highborn and their fathers. Despite persistent rumours that the Undying One was actually Thrygragos

Varuna Mithras, that Thrygragos Lazareme had been using his stoned then severed head – crushed, hollowed-out and stuffed with goose and eagle down – as a pillow on his bed since Thrygragon, of the latter only the Unity's firstborn father was present.

Hooded, masked and robed in varying shades of red, that she sometimes referred to her power focus as a firebrand, or matchstick, only partially accounted for why devils often referred to her as Hot Stuff. Her fiery attribute accounted for most of the rest, that and the temper that went with it.

Along with the Great God, his three Unities and herself, the Virgin's triplet brother Tantal (King Cold of Lathakra), her anything-but-virginal brood-younger sister in Mithras (Beguiling Belialma, ex-Sinistral Lust of Satanwyck and current belle bouncing in Lazareme's bed, which she denied had as a pillow Mithras's head made comfortable), the two Silverclouds and the Silverclouds' sister Sedona Spellbinder (a second-born Nucleoid, the one that could speak for the Byronics' father, the Unmoving One himself) were the others there.

Together, in the opulent tholos or beehive-shaped pavilion perched as if on nothingness between-space, they had just witnessed Morg's Brainrock-powered jalopy appear out of the Weird. They had done so via their far-sight artfully combined with the revelatory vapours emitting from Metisophia's captured cauldron. To a one they mirrored Harmony, gaping in horror as its eye-staves mimicked burping blowguns and the prison pods they shot made like demon-inhuming spitballs.

Not just Abe's earth-wrought simulacrum, his phantasm given Stopstone flesh, went the way the Moloch Sedon must have gone on Mithramas. Although he managed to reflexively retract, retrieve or otherwise rescue his trident, shredded too were the dinky delinquents he psychically animated, and his embodied eidolon brought with itself from Minius, in order to neutralize Trinondev eye-staves.

A collective shiver of more than just anxiety, of no less than impending mortality, swept through the gathering when Abe passed out from the strain as well as, presumably, the loss of his ever-so-cleverly scattered brain cells. How could anyone this side of Grandfather Sedon bring the Unity of Chaos so low?

This Master of Weir was beyond merely scrappy. She was truly redoubtable; their most dangerous foe since the Dual Entities last time-tumbled into the linear timeline devazurs experienced. That realization explained Methandra's initial burst of scornful outrage. It also explained Lazareme's lack of an immediate reply.

He hated making decisions. As for challenges, either to his authority or to his potency, such as both were, he generally ignored them. Fortunately, as if he'd willed the eye-pleasing distraction of her entry, a newcomer gave him more time to formulate a comeback. Her arrival did something else as well. It provided him with the kernel of a solution to the double dilemma of 'Call-me-morgue' and what technically speaking wasn't precisely the Weirdom of Cabalarkon anymore.

"How about me?" Pyrame Silverstar, back to being a silver-haired Middle Sea stunner, ventured as she sauntered in from off the outdoors statue garden.

"You did well," Methandra allowed, Pyrame being about the only lowborn to whom she would deign to speak.

Next in line for Harmony and her bucket of beer was Rufous Rudra Silvercloud, Bodiless Byron's Beast, his highest born son as well as Storm Lord. He chugalugged his horn so fast he had it emptied and held out for more before Harmony moved on to his sister-wife, Umashakti-Gravity.

"Cabalarkon isn't where I thought she'd hid him," Pyrame reported. "But those are the Godly Glories. I'd stake my reputation on it; hence also me scarpering."

"Better your reputation than your life," Yajur observed.

Like the others there, he knew from grim experience what the Thrygragos and Trigregos Talismans could do to Master Devas, if perhaps not their fathers. Varuna Mithras having got hold of the former on Thrygragon almost won him that day. Befuddled by the latter, Taurus Chrysaor Attis damn near cost him it.

Pyrame ignored the Unity; said instead: "Got some new statuary out there, I see. I was wondering what became of the Masochist and dad's torchbearers." (Devils called Mithras's preferred heliodromus, and primary herald, the Masochist whereas his torchbearers were Midsummer-Novadev's triplet brothers, Mid-Spring Tammuz and Mid-Autumn Osiraq)

"Ours more so than theirs," acknowledged Tantal, referring to the statuary, as he nodded at the four Lazaremists. Another space-hogging giant, the icicle-bearded, blue-skinned and labrys-armed, humanoid glacier took two horns of the DDD's wondrous elixir as if to compensate for his brood sister's refusal of one.

"Abe was supposed to bring us the rest, along with the Master's arms, but she outsmarted them yet again. And now *he* says we can't go after the Weirdom anyways on account of the Sarpedons falling to their knees in front of him." (Borderline-disdainfully, as well as discourteously given whose beer it was, this time King Cold was singling out Thrygragos Lazareme.)

"Hell's holy icebergs, youngster, my sister and I can impersonate the Dual Entities as easily as he and Harm can. Come to think of it, anyone here can."

"I still think most of Sedon's inside that vault, oldster," Pyrame added, neatly sidestepping the controversy. (She could have stepped right into it by reminding her eldest brother that it wasn't a matter of them masquerading as anyone. It was a matter of their attributes. Everyman and everyone's ideal of beauty were just naturally godlike.)

"Not our concern," stated smoky Sedona. Composed entirely of particulate matter, she might have been the exception that proved the imitative rule. She was also highly particular about whom she, her father and their tribe should trust. "Did any of you hotheads, or cold-hearts, never think to ask yourselves why the Libertine's lot gave you the go-ahead to ignore my eldest sister's cautions of last New Years?"

"Because we'd have done it anyway?" answered, with a question, the one who did it all the time.

"No, you wouldn't have," snapped said-sister, horn emptied and extended for more. "You're sleeping with him and you still don't get it, do you? You're no vacuous dingbat. You're a wilfully ignorant one. They already have Cabby the Daddy. The Undying Utopian was in fucking Absudyl."

(Lunar Uma epitomized gravity but wasn't always grave. Right now, though, she was clearly having paroxysms of prudery as well as puffery.)

"Fucking Minius," Harmony corrected her similarly firstborn cousin as she refilled her horn with soothing pills.

"*<<Groan>>*," groaned Abe Chaos, finally coming around again.

"Did he really say '*groan*' when he groaned?" Rufous Rudra stopped in mid-swig in order to enquire.

"Hey, I train them well," Lazareme had to answer. He proceeded to drain the ¾ empty bucket of pills Harmony handed him in a couple of gulps. Then he belched, decision made. Not for nothing did he consider beer the incredible thinking fluid. "So, shall we have some more fun with the mortifying Master of Weir?"

"I'm way ahead of you, dad," said Harmony.

========

The revelatory fumes steaming off Titanic Metis's purloined power focus — unless it was confiscated as a spoil of war — showed Morgan Abyss alone in her throne room. She'd just noticed the missing statues and looked so glum, so despondent, she was already borderline-beaten.

'It's supposed to be,' Harmony thought and transmitted out loud ...

========

Preceding Pyrame's triumphant return to Cabalarkon in order to reclaim her prize, its Master and its Mastery, a glowing, quoit-like hole in the air opened up in front of the Weirdom's throne. Out of it appeared the illusion of Datong Harmonia, the Unity of Panharmonium, smiling radiantly.

Words were exchanged. Moments later Morg hellstone-stepped back into the Catacombs of the Thinkers outside the now badly dinted vault wherein she found the Trigregos and Thrygragos Talismans as well as kept the packed ringots and prison pods containing those of theirs she had left. After unlocking the vault, another hole in the air opened up and in short order more than words were exchanged.

Harmony didn't ask for any of the pre-Earth pods with bits and pieces of Sedon inside them. Nor did she ask for any pods containing devils captured prior to the Utopians arriving on the Whole Earth ten years before the Great Flood of Genesis. They weren't theirs, so she didn't want them, and Morg didn't volunteer them. The Master also requested, more so than demanded, some additional compensation for submitting to Silverstar, this besides the devils forbearance when it came to extirpating Utopians.

Harmony didn't need to ask daddy for permission in order to grant her desires. She and her highborn cohorts weren't vampires. They didn't even like vamps and, worshippers being hard enough to come by at the best of times, they especially didn't want any more bloodshed. Seconds thereafter, trussed, gagged and, as she was able to speedily ascertain via her Masters Mace, mind-wiped, into the vault tumbled the missing Sarpedons and Warriors Elite.

Testing fate — her devic half-mother, Wintry Moira, Dame Chance or Fata Fortuna, was in one of the ringots or prison pods about to be given over — she asked the Unity for a further favour. This too Harmony granted, transferring the returnees between-space to the same hospital wherein Quit-It and, as was now apparent, three Quaffs had died (unless Quaff-2 expired before he got that far).

That done, Harmony's spectre watched as Morg reloaded the kibisis she so stupidly had Jordy bring up here. Hers was hardly the only phantasmal sending observing the transferrals. Devils trusted each other because they couldn't break their sworn oaths any more than they could lie or disobey their fathers. But that didn't mean they trusted any non-devils.

As an avowed atheist the Master didn't worship anyone, but she must have recognized Thrygragos Lazareme from Quiff-become-Squirrelly's description of him. Plus, she would have easily identified Pyrame, in her most human guise, the Unities and Lady Lust, because she'd sicked hardening demons on them a few months ago, and Sedona Spellbinder, by her smoking form.

She may or may not have registered that the Thanatoids of Lathakra were, as the saying goes, conspicuous by their absence. However, perhaps due to the fact that they didn't participate in the verbal gloat-session while she sat so depressed in her throne, she couldn't help but wonder if they'd signed onto the Harmony-fronted pact.

Once the bottomless bag had everything in it that Harmony required, she thrust it into the teleportal. Someone yanked it away from her. At which point her wraith vanished and, having left her only relatively recently reanimated, daemonic body behind for Tvasitar, Ghoster or one of the about-to-released Master Devas to take over, Pyrame Silverstar stepped both visibly and spiritually through it. "No more silly buggers," she admonished her former host.

"No more silly buggers," Morg allowed, whereupon she was Pyrame's again current host. Three-eyed now, she said to Lazareme's ghost: "Cabby the daddy?"

"And go through all that constipation again? Not a chance. Him we keep until Sedon tells me differently."

"And if I don't release Sedon?"

"Then you're not his whore anymore. Consider the option our favour to you."

Not liking his offer, but not being able to do much about it right this minute, Pyrame enquired through Morg: "You know what's she thinking?"

"Who?"

"The Master of Weir of course. Who else?"

"What?"

"*So that's how she pulled it off.*' And now she's thinking: '*Well, hey, what she can do I bet I can too.*' And, you know what, I think she could.'"

"Then you better make sure she doesn't, pauper, because I'm in the mood to see how you'd look as an actual silver star; one I'd be tempted to call '*Harridan*'."

The Great God nevertheless recognized an opening salvo when he heard one.

========

Another thing Morg was no doubt thinking was that, irrespective of losing control of her devic half-mother, she was still on a roll.

========

Lunasa, 4825 Year of the Dome – The Laughing Lands

Obviously figuring the deal her dad made with Pyrame (once again occupying the Master of Weir) on Midsummer's Day was as binding as deals made between Master Devas always were, Harmony couldn't be bothered to keep to herself what else ringots did anymore. She reckoned differently she would have found another way to get back the ringots and prison pods containing her siblings and cousins.

There were plenty of those. For example, Pyrame could use hellstones the same as any devil could and, until proven otherwise, she alone was immune to Trinondev prison pods. But Harmony wouldn't have needed a devil to carry anything anywhere anyhow. Psychopomps such as Garudas, who had a normal, human intelligence, hired out.

So did cannibalistic Angelycs, who weren't psychos, of the pomp variety, but could fly and were strong. (Bright as they were, though, their eating habits, and how they preferred to be paid, made most folks wary of employing them.) Plus, there were living bestiaries of blimp-like gasbags and other flying critters, their riders with them, some smarter than others in both cases, available for cartage duties. Vampires even had enormous bats of burden.

Nonetheless, less than six weeks later she may or may not have had occasion to regret her impetuousness. May because she genuinely enjoyed Pyrame Silverstar's company and should have realized that, in some respects like lightning and earthquakes, what can be ring-gotten once can be ring-gotten twice.

Then again, to play her own devil's advocate, it probably never occurred to her that, once they had some, Utopian scientocrats and their still functional, originally extraterrestrial machinery were capable of replicating more. Furthermore, ringots aside, one of Pyrame's first acts upon regaining 'control' of Morg was to reactivate All of Incain in terms of responsiveness to her will.

While that might be interpreted innocently, as a matter of securing a safe and very powerful haven should Morg find a way of getting Pyrame out of her again, it might also be an indicator that pauper priestess and Master were in cahoots. Either that or their joint demon was in total command of them both.

May not because the Thanatoids of Lathakra – and, indeed, the rest of their tribe except for two or maybe three of the least militant Mithradites – balked at making a deal with her father, her, and her fellow Lazaremists to foreswear attacking Cabalarkon. Since such a deal would go a long way to making Harmony's aspirations of Panharmonium a reality, their failure to reach an accord spurred her nastiest personality closer to the psychological surface.

There was much more to it than that of course. For one, it must have seemed to Harmony that – other than Pyrame Silverstar, Beguiling Belialma and, maybe, Geld Neargon – higher born Mithradites would never accept Panharmonium. What with them being the largest devic tribe on the Hidden Headworld, by a factor almost two-to-one when separately compared to either Lazaremists or Byronics, that basically spelt the end to her not-so-diminutive dream of a planetary panacea.

Mithradites thereby effectively declared themselves as unruly as they were when Mithras was still around. And he found his own offspring almost impossible to govern; at least not without the heavy hand of Chrysaor Attis and his legionnaires backing his play. Be that as it may, their steadfast refusal to be reined in by Thrygragos Lazareme made hardly any difference anyways.

The Mithradites' attitude tolled sympathetic bells with the other two tribes. Perhaps counter-intuitively, that automatically included the Lazaremists themselves. In that regard even Lord Order detested laws necessitating enforcement. Stability, everybody born knowing what they had to do, where they fit in a functional society, and how delightfully trouble-free knowing all this would make their lives, was what mattered to him.

The point of no retreat, no surrender, came when Harmony and her father deemed themselves unable to commit to the revised principles of Panharmonium. These were the unfortunately termed '*rules of disengagement*' put forward by Sedona Spellbinder on behalf of her father and their tribe.

Rules amounted to red flags to black-flag Lazaremists. The Unmoving One – a control freak if ever there was one – delegated duties to his descendants, through Sedona, on a near daily basis. Justifiably to their mind therefore, Harmony and her father saw Sedona's revisions as Great Byron attempting to boss them about rather than, if anything, the other way around.

Although, by contrast, Lazareme dictated to his offspring on a near-never basis, he was just as adamant he wouldn't send Cabalarkon back to his eponymous Weirdom so long as anyone, save Sedon, was in charge of the abhorrent Eye-Land. This in turn infuriated more than just Pyrame Silverstar. If only because Chaos was crazy enough to change undying to dead, it infuriated nearly everyone.

In Pyrame's case, she saw having hold of Cabby the Daddy as her pseudo-protectorate's security blanket against devic encroachment, its subjugation and/or extermination. As he'd as good as predicted with his parting shot to her on Midsummer's Day, in the next few weeks Lazareme caught enough earfuls on the subject to catasterize a constellation of pauper priestesses. He had the Unities to help him do it too. She had no one except All of Incain, Morg and her demon, whoever that was, to help her.

The She-Sphinx couldn't atomize anyone any more than she could digest the Great God; this to judge by the last time she tried it, the evening of Thrygragon. Morg and her demon were just as useless. There was always the Moloch Sedon, should she deign to release him. But snakes like Sedon would bite anyone, even their beloved. Cabby the Daddy was his ultimate trump card and Lazareme wasn't about to give him up.

So maybe the Thanatoids didn't bring the disasters of Lunasa Day down upon themselves. Alternatively, maybe it wasn't altogether Morg's fault. Or maybe the Byronics put her up to it in order to dramatically diminish the threat to their subcontinent for another decade at the likely minimum if not, minus the Thanatoids, next door to forever.

Maybe Pyrame did it herself, whereupon she sought to deflect the blame onto her too wilful host-shell and/or her demon. That would explain a lot if she did. Maybe Morg, independently and dominantly, just mistook indicators of a menace imperilling Cabalarkon and overreacted, the same as she arguably did in the lead-up to the Infernal Equinox. Or maybe it had been a Sedonplay all along. That being the case, Harmony should have realized there could only ever be one winner.

In any event, the Unity was so pissed off at the Thanatoids she approached Nemesis-level rage. Sensibly, rather than letting herself go altogether relentless, she instead insisted both Thrygragos Lazareme and Bodiless Byron, through Sedona, put their proverbial feet down (fantasy feet in Byron's case) and expressly forbid any of their children to ever again march alongside the armies of Lathakra.

Great Byron didn't need prompting. The Silverclouds returned to the subcontinent of Aka Godbad, tails between their legs (fantasy tail in Lunar Uma's case). To take their place as devic overseer of Kanin City, Sedona, as always acting at her father's behest, appointed none other than Monk-Eye, Tau Hanuman as Illuminaries had him.

Kanin City was the onetime Weirdom in which he'd acted as the Silverclouds' court jester, driving Lazareme's Librarian positively buggy in the process. He also of bazooka banana fame was correspondingly jubilant at the promotion; Biblio Drek not so much so. (This was especially true after, like everyone else who'd been released, Tvasitar restored his power focus and he acquired another daemonic body, whereupon his father reassigned him to the same ambassadorial post he'd held previously.)

Abe Chaos was slightly more problematic. His pride, not to mention Lord Yajur's constant goading re the alpha-embarrassing events of Midsummer Day, made him loath to let Morgan Abyss get away so comparatively scot-free. Harmony figured he just needed some nursing. He figured dick-dildo but reckoned more than his ego needed stroking. With Lady Lust persistently bouncing in Lazareme's bed, he had a strong notion as to who should do it too.

Ah, the things she did for Panharmonium.

========

The Upper Head's northern lights produced seemingly thousands of eyes staring down at the ground below. Over the course of the six weeks between Midsummer and Lunasa Day, Morgan Abyss, the Master of Weir, scrupulously unnoticed, must have spent hours gazing through a few mobile and truly unreal ones.

A number of starry eyeholes expanded, quoit-like, overtop more than a few designated bull's-eyes and something else – a whole gaggle of some things else – came through them. They weren't flying jalopies. Nor were they restored generational ships. They weren't hovering drones either. But they weren't far off any of the above in terms of the extraterrestrial technology that went into them.

Although the immediate targets were identical, it wasn't the Infernal Equinox all over again. It was much, much worse!

========

The term 'empyrean vessels' was coined multi-millennia pre-Earth. Initially it had nothing to do with Pyrame. Until their source was identified, howsoever-tentatively, few even made the connection. More might have if they knew 'pyramid', from whence her name apparently derived, meant 'in the middle of the fire' but etymology wasn't often studied on the Inner Earth.

(Why would it be when everyone understood everything anybody ever said to anyone beneath the Cathonic Dome? Sedonspeak was the Universal Tongue.)

Empyrean or empyreal – welkin was one of many synonyms – referred to the highest reaches of the heavenly sphere. This, to devils, their fathers and solitary grandfather, was the not-at-all theoretical abode of Celestial God (where the Byronic firstborn much later on Illuminaries named Serathrone Hallow was last seen).

At the same time, also to them, it was the absolutely theoretical paradise where monotheistic fantasists believed their concept of angels, God's holy warriors, dwelt in a state of supreme bliss or sublime happiness. The vessels, called 'vahanas' in some religious bents, chariots of the gods in others, were the Celestials' equivalent of interstellar transport and/or armoured combat vehicles.

A seventh heaven, a dominion of unadulterated fire or light; so monotheist zealots on the Outer Earth propounded as empyreal from their pathetic pulpits. Vessels of both (fire and light) came out of holes in the sky over top of Lathakra's seven widely separated, by then reinforced and reorganized armies. It was Lunasa Day, the first of Hektor, the second month in the Byronic Ternary, on the Inner Earth of Sedon's Head.

Throughout the Northern Hemisphere tradition had Lunasa as the hottest day of the year. Empyrean vessels made that an absolute understatement in four of the seven locations where they erupted as if nuclear fireballs out of the sky's firmament. The resultant non-devilish devastation was so thorough the human and humanoid armies proved but a minuscule portion of the casualties.

Neither was there a ground zero as such. Unstoppable if nebular juggernauts of deadly, radioactive fallout undulated from each impact zone, irremediably wasting the land beneath them. As for the three other sites, not only were there survivors, plenty of them, there was little in the way of a ripple effect; at least there wasn't immediately.

Those who lived to die another day said they first noticed an aureole forming in the sky above them. Starting from a barely perceptible black speck or dot at its dead centre, this aureole expanded from the inside out until it resembled the sun's corona during a complete solar eclipse. Only, instead of the circular moon obscuring the sun, a kind of singularity, a literal black hole, grew huge within it.

There were as many of these ersatz eclipses as there were empyrean vessels. Each seemed composed of, or filled with, oil or some sort of highly flammable petroleum product; either that or daemonic crud like Morg used to coat Grand Elysium before tricking devils into igniting it with their eyefire. The vessels themselves ripped out of these black holes already afire. Rocketing earthward, they detonated, not all upon contact with the ground, thereby combusting the very air itself. Evidently Methandra Thanatos wasn't the only one who specialized in firestorms.

Quite probably not Celestial in origin; more likely bus-sized cosmicars, ones recently salvaged from derelict millennial or generational ships; the scientocrats of Weir must have rendered them only borderline-operable for just this dispensatory purpose. That there were survivors had less to do with the quality of Master Devas at the head of each army than it did with the fact the Thanatoids and their proximate siblings were too occupied saving their bacon to far-scream word of how to defend against the things.

It must never have dawned on the devic leadership of the four armies that had no, or next-to-no, non-devazur survivors that what could explode could also be absorbed.

Heat and Cold (Tantal and Methandra Thanatos); the three fifth born, so-called Earthlings (Yama Nergal, Gibran Nimiki and Shal Ereshkigal); the eighth born Male Apocalyptics (Mars Bellona, Carcinogen the Leper and Nakba Ramazar); their on again, off again mates, the tenth born Female Apocalyptics (Calcutta Famish, Diluvia Ran and Milady Malaise); Pyrame's brood sister in Mithras's Ninth (Cathune Bubastis), whose attribute was Drought, which made her a seventh Apocalyptic; the Medusa (Mater Matare, aka Mother Murder), who styled herself the primary Apocalyptic, that of Death; and the unapologetic Mithras loyalists (Tammuz,

Osiraq and Djinn Domitian): these were just some of those who did most of the absorbing in the case of armies and territories where there were survivors.

In the other four cases, Master Devas mostly from the Great God's teens and twenties in terms of broods simply didn't react in time. Of those too slow or too dense to realize what they had to do, many disappeared, possibly forevermore. While that didn't necessarily mean they died – a goodly number may have taken themselves into the lower levels of what was left of Satanwyck, some of which supposedly contained cross-dimensional wormholes – it also didn't mean they hadn't.

So many empyrean vessels simultaneously detonating on or above a single initially compact area created conditions so near-impossibly-intense even until-then-immortals might expire. Certainly many Mithradite survivors sickened nigh unto just that, death. So did some of the absorptive heroes.

Perhaps ironically a large majority hied themselves to Incain, where All graciously agreed to incarcerate them until they got better. Since the She-Sphinx was once again responsive to Pyrame's will, many reckoned she'd release them within a matter of years, not decades let alone centuries.

The Laughing Lands, and all the pantheistic paradises contained within it, weren't quite receding memories of wondrous realms yet, though.

========

So powerful, not to mention powerfully pissed off, were the Thanatoids of Lathakra they pressed on regardless.

========

Samhain, 4825 Year of the Dome – Henceforth the Ghostlands

Not much more than a month later, in Rudar, the third month of the Byronic Ternary, this one named after Rudra Silvercloud, another hefty dose of empyreal hellfire wiped out the army led by the Earthlings, forcing them to hightail it literally underground, where they probably belonged. As Rudar progressed into Djerridam, the ternary's last month, the army not led by the Thanatoids themselves began to disintegrate.

Portions of it, notably divisions headed by the two remaining, seventh born Reptilians (Klizarod Rex, Saurlord of the Flood Lands, and Chameleon Lizarado, Emperor of the Floodlands, who hated each other almost as much Order did Chaos, and vice versa), as well as the male and female Apocalyptics along with the Medusa, abandoned not just the field but also the entirety of the Upper Head.

Whereas they headed south, into Sedon's Sweat Glands and, south of them, into Sedon's Cheek Lands, the still alive but much-diminished forces of the Ninth – though, with Pyrame in Cabalarkon and the devil child Tralalorn unwilling to leave Apple Isle, only Drought (Cathune Bubastis) was left of them – did a similarly but directionally opposite dot-ditto.

They fled across the Mystic Mountains (Sedon's Crown), back to whence they came, sandy-skinned, cat-faced Cathune's nominal protectorate: Sisert (Sedon's Bald Spot or Cranium), a largely uninhabited, near-arctic region that was actually a frozen desert at the top of the Hidden Headworld.

Infuriated beyond rationality by the destruction and/or defection of two of their remaining armies; in all likelihood desperately ill as a result of never-ending bombardment from the remotely controlled vessels; the Thanatoids single-mindedly led their last army down from re-conquered Mythland towards the Weirdom of Cabalarkon.

Pyrame herself long-distance pleaded with them to pass it by. Monomaniacal to the end, they refused, blaming the empyrean vessels on her, her host, their demon and the idiots of Weir. Frantic, Pyrame went to Harmony at her mobile High Seat in Sedon's Hairband. There she begged her to intercede with her father and return Cabalarkon, the still undying Utopian, to his rightful as well as prophylactic resting place beneath his, and now her, Weirdom's Citadel of the Thinkers.

Perhaps figuring it the same way the Thanatoids and the remaining Mithradites, Lady Lust among them, did – namely that she, the Pauper Priestess, was behind the still creeping ruination of the Upper Head – Harmony refused to help her. A direct appeal to the Lazaremists' father got no response mostly because he hid himself so well even the ever-resourceful Perpetual Presence couldn't find him.

Going to Admiral Chaos was pointless because of what Morg did to him on Midsummer's Day. For his part, Lord Order declared himself happy the Mithradites and the Utopians were seemingly on a cataclysmic collision course. The Headworld would be a better – read orderly – place without either of them. Now if Pyrame could do something about Abe and Harmony, hey, he was listening. She couldn't; he didn't.

The Lathakrans kept coming. Either Cabalarkon ran out of empyrean vessels or the Weirdom was never the source of them in the first place. And if the Utopians weren't behind it then who were? The Byronics? Were the Dual Entities back, and if so who was humanizing the Mnemosyne Machine, All's maker and the reason Pyrame was exempt from prison-podding? No matter. The Thanatoids and their remaining forces faced no more impediments.

Pyrame, if it was she and not either Morg or their demon, nor anyone else, hadn't given up the fight; she'd given up on her elders. She released the three Mithras loyalists from her thrall, All of Incain. Returning to the Upper Head, she set them blocking the path of their firstborn siblings at what was virtually the northern Gates of Cabalarkon (not that the Weirdom had gates as such – the northernmost gap in the Hills of the Sleepers then).

King Cold told the masochistic Djinn Domitian to go to hell. Dutiful sort that the trumpeter always was when it was still the Age of Mithras, he obliged his eldest brother and did just that, whereupon he promptly vanished from the annals of devazurs upon the Whole Earth. Tantal probably told Tammuz and Osiraq to do a fucking dick-dildo; certainly Methandra wouldn't have.

And maybe they tried. Who could say for sure? No one yet, that answers that.

========

The horrible 4825-day the Atomic Twins, aka Mid-Spring and Mid-Autumn, blew themselves up so idiotically came at the end of Djerridam (named after Djerrid Ruin, Byron's Bowman, also his Zodiacal Green Man, and the last month of the Byronic Ternary). Like so many of the main events in this chronology – Yule, Imbolc, Ostara, Beltane, Midsummer and Lunasa – it was a significant date in calendars on both sides of the Dome.

Some said Samhain, aka All Hallows Eve or Halloween beyond the Dome, marked the time of year when the boundaries between the world of the living and the world of the dead become thinner, at times even fading away completely, allowing spirits and other supernatural entities to pass between the worlds to socialize with humans.

While such quaintly superstitious notions hardly applied to the Otherworld that was the Hidden Headworld – particularly in Iraxas, wherein living Iraches served their Vetalazur-animated ancestors tea and scones on a daily basis – Samhain 4825 definitely marked the end of the empire of Lathakra as well as its two main Mithradite inceptors and movers, Tantal and Methandra Thanatos.

It also marked the day that virtually everything that still moved in the Upper Head became charter members of Death's Angels, the rain-allergic Ambulatory Dead who follow Yama Nergal, the Mithradites' Grim Reaper, and feed on just about anything they can find, radioactive or otherwise.

How the torchbearers came by the sheer, if not utterly unprecedented, magnitude of their explosive might have had everything to do with how they thwarted the Master's last gasp, kill-everything efforts to destroy the regrouped and refitted armies of Lathakra at the beginning of Hektor. Retrospective reconstructions of Samhain's big bang indicated that what could be absorbed howsoever many times could not be kept bodily bottled-up indefinitely.

After the Infernal Equinox, the Thanatoids could have rebuilt and/or marshalled their armies almost anywhere on the Inner Earth save the Subcontinent of Aka Godbad, Yajur's occipital regions or the Weirdom of Cabalarkon. That they chose to muster in the Upper Head could have been down to wanting more than just allegiance from all the Mithradite protectorates in the Laughing Lands of pantheistic paradises. It could be they wanted to inflict upon them the humiliation of irrefutable capitulation.

Or perhaps they just wanted to march into Mythland full force, for purposes purely pretentious. Regardless of whether either/or was the reality; regardless of whether the Byronics put her up to it, which was another theory; once again, Master Morg presumably took their actions as a prelude for aggression against not just her realm but as the start of a potential genocide aimed at Utopians throughout the Whole Earth.

As for why Tammuz and Osiraq turned on their elders at the Gates of Cabalarkon, well, maybe they didn't. Maybe they just couldn't contain themselves anymore.

Of course it wasn't just the final remnant of the seven armies loyal to the Thanatoids of Lathakra that got wiped out. So did the balance of the Upper Head, at least it did in terms of habitable territory for most living beings. And for all anyone at the time purported to know, that included the Weirdom of Cabalarkon. Hence why what to this day some considered Morg's legacy were thereafter called the Ghostlands.

This day being two-thirds of a millennium later!

========

5456 Year of the Dome – The Weirdom of Kanin City

"Now pass me another pilsner and let's talk about tomorrow."

Zalman Somata, the Master of the Weirdom of Kanin City, obliged. His wife, Melina born Tethys, was reluctant to let his months of tale-telling end.

"Are you implying Harmony was behind what happened to the Thanatoids, Jordy?"

"Now that you'd have to ask to her. Me, I need Nemesis's attentions like I need a third eye instead of this scar."

****

Contagion Collectors

- Years of the Dome 5456 to 5476 -

Jim McPherson

A *PHANTACEA* **Mythos** Mini-Novel
published by James H McPherson

ISBN 978-0-9781342-6-6

Two-1: Quotidian Quidnunc

Up to 5456 YD – The Mastery of Marutia

"In the year of 1284, on the day of Saints John and Paul, the 26th of June, 130 children born in Hamelin were seduced by a piper, dressed in all kinds of colours, and lost at the calvary near the koppen."

These words, translated into the Universal Tongue spoken throughout the Hidden Continent of Sedon's Head, are recorded in a localized, Outer Earth language on the walls of the so-called 'Rattenfängerhaus', or House of the Piper, in the German town of Hamelin. The Legendarian knew this because he did the translation.

========

A decade or two after the events thus recorded, bereaved locals paid an itinerant, yet highly talented craftsman to prepare a stained-glass window commemorating the tragedy in the town's Market Church. (Obviously having learned their lesson, they paid him properly too, without quibbling.) The artist scratched his name into the bottom right hand corner of the window once he finished it. The name he scratched into it? Jordan Q Tethys of course.

Tethys's window depicted the piper dressed in multicoloured clothes leading a crowd of kids dressed in white towards the dark, vaguely skull-shaped entrance to a cave within a nearby hill. He reckoned that, even though it was shaped more like a Tholos or beehive than a human head, the word *Koppen*, meaning just that, head, must refer to that hill whereas the word *Calvary*, place of the skull, probably referred to the cave's mouth. Hamelin's townspeople clearly had an even more vivid imagination than he did.

Although it was now twenty years shy of two centuries after the events he depicted in stained glass, chances were the hill, and the cave within it, still existed. While, at a stretch, the word Koppen might refer to the Head, capitalized, by the time he visited Hamelin it definitely didn't contain a link to the Hidden Headworld. That it had in 1284 (5284 on the Head) was pretty much a given, he reckoned.

He reckoned as much because he was almost as certain the Pied Piper had a name he never gave to the townspeople. That name wasn't Tethys. It was Tomcat Tattletail.

========

Star Sedon disappeared from the night's sky on the 25ᵗʰ of Tantalar, 4824 Year of the Dome. It had long been back upstairs some 30-plus years in excess of six centuries later.

========

Jordan Q Tethys was a half-black who looked all-black. These days that might mean he had Utopian relatives. Just as likely it might not. In contrast to his ever-wayward father, who wasn't the black forbearer, he did not have a scar in the lower part of his forehead. Nor did his middle initial stand for *'Quill'*. If the woman who was his black forbearer could be believed, it stood for *'Quidnunc'*.

'That's your father's idea of a joke,' she often told him while he was growing up in southwestern Marutia, Sedon's Cheek Land.

A quidnunc was a busybody. Then again, in Marutia a jordan, small case, was a chamber pot. While it might be argued that one was no better than the other, there were hundreds of Jordans, upper and lower case, in Sedon's Cheek. By comparison, as far as he'd heard anyhow, he was the only Quidnunc, capitalized. Since neither name appealed to him very much, he came to prefer Quid.

Even though he was named after him, his mother didn't approve of his father. For his part, young Quid couldn't recall ever meeting him. He did learn, once he became a star cadet in the Marutian military and was allowed to go to bars – though, at the risk of homelessness, never to drink alcohol – that joining the army in general, and not drinking beer in particular, were two of the last things his father would have done.

Those who knew Jordan *'Quill'* Tethys held that he'd never have done either/or unless he'd first committed suicide, been resurrected as a Born Again zombie, and then conscripted into one of the armies of the Inglorious Dead's booze-free divisions. Which did exist, they further assured him straight-faced.

(As did Fata Fortuna, the highborn Lazaremist who'd possessed his birthmother when she conceived him – though the decidedly naughty nanny, aka Lady Luck, Dame Chance or sometimes *'Damn Her 3-Eyes Anyhow'*, was more of a straight-laced sort, albeit only when it came to her bodice. Quid knew this because, while he was growing up, she popped physically by to visit he and his mother once in a while, ostensibly just to see how he was doing in these pox-stricken times.)

His birthmother's unbending antipathy to his fertilizing father explained why she brought him up as an abstemious teetotaller. It further explained why she insisted he become a soldier. That he also became a rakish, thoroughgoing sexual predator, what less charitably inclined Marutian progressives condemned as a throwback to the age of manly barbarism, well, nature was stronger than nurture. It certainly was when it came to the slew of incurable illnesses then plaguing Sedon's Cheek like a lifelong outbreak of far worse-than-unsightly pimples. It was all the more so, in some respects oppositely so, when it came to penile swords.

Despite his paternal heritage, he took to the blade like a sculptor to a chisel or a wizard to a wand. In a way, that was understandable. The Utopian Mastery of Marutia had been at peace within itself for so many centuries that fighting-and-dying soldiering was less a thing of the past than approaching the stage of becoming an oxymoron. It being the Age of Panharmonium, there were more prospects of fighting and dying in a Kanin City playground than on a Marutian battlefield.

Sure, many pockets of inviolate devic protectorates endured within, and on the boundaries of, the Cheeks proper. Since disputatious Mithradite Master Devas controlled most of them, they remained dangerous, even tumultuous territories both inwardly and outwardly.

However, few true Utopians dared venture into devic protectorates because fewer survived long enough to venture out of them. Unless as members of a large battalion, they especially didn't venture into them armed with eye-staves. They did so singly or in small groups, odds were even or poorer they'd ever be seen again.

Devils hadn't considered true Utopians lesser beings since the time of the mass murderous Death's Head Hellion. As a result, their more overenthusiastic supporters considered them sport to be hunted down and shot. If they weren't shot dead right away, well, sport could be had in many a mostly unmentionable manner. Typically, though, release came in the form of death and not as a result of ransom or escape.

Rather, it had. Other than in terms of flashing steel, Quidnunc was no bright light. But even he must have realized that by the 55th Century of the Dome the only purebloods left beneath the Dome lived far to the north of Marutia, in the next-to-unreachable Weirdom of Cabalarkon, Sedon's Devic Eye-Land – next-to-unreachable since the waning months of Morgan Abyss's hellacious Mastery, as it happened.

No matter how dilute their bloodline had become, Utopians of Marutia, chiefly those in its armed services, nonetheless retained one maxim above any other: *'You lose your edge, you risk losing your life on the edges.'* When it came to staying out of devic protectorates, Quid was no different than his fellow soldiers. Where he was different, by a considerable measure, was in the practise yard and showground.

He was such a splendid swordsman that, in his teens, he emerged victorious in verging on countless fencing contests throughout the Cheek's hinterlands. He won so many tournaments that many neutrals, and more than few of his adversaries, sour-griped he had to be devil-possessed as well as at least a quarter devil-conceived.

More specifically, they maintained Unholy Abaddon, the Unity of Chaos, who had a well-deserved reputation for upsetting the status quo purely for the sake of disruption, possessed him. Which, while possible, wasn't very probable since Abe Chaos claimed he never intentionally possessed anyone. And devils couldn't lie.

Be that as it may, in due course Quid found himself in Kanin City, just below the Gregarian Fields (to not just devils aka Sedon's Mole). There, in the Mastery's megalithic as well as antediluvian capital, the lad challenged for possibly the supreme accolade available during the cyclopean city's annual Midsummer Games: namely, the Five Blades Championship of Weir.

Shockingly, Quid won that too, the Utopians' highest honour for individual swordsmanship. Doubly shockingly, at 21 he was the youngest recorded winner ever. Trebly shockingly, he won it with Abe Chaos, flanked by his two fellow Unities of Lazareme, Order and Harmony, watching his every bout. Significantly, despite what their frothing-at-the-mouth flock of fanatical followers may believe, even first-born devils can't be in two places at once.

Only the mighty Moloch could do that, and then only debatably. It could be his Sedon Sphere – aka Cathonia, the Cathonic Zone or Dome – did not need to retain any measure of his presence in order to remain in place whenever he ventured downstairs, on either side of it. Which he occasionally did for purposes courtly, procreative and/or much more devilishly sinister.

As everyone beneath it knew, Sedon raised Cathonia out of his own essence to prevent the Genesea – or Great Flood of Genesis – washing over the then archipelago of Pacifica, thusly referred to, accurately or inaccurately, as the Places of Peace during the Golden Age of Humankind and its Edenite precursor. Give or take howsoever-many days, weeks or months the Dome had, for the most part, kept the Outer Earth separate from the Inner Earth throughout the intervening 5,456 years.

Star Sedon had vanished from the night's sky many times during the course of its multi-millennial existence. Although only devils and a couple of recurring deviants had memories that went back to 4824/5 YD, at least one of his absences lasted many moons. Nevertheless, no one who persisted in, on, below or above his Hidden Headworld ever had to build an ark, sprout gills or learn to swim underwater against his or her will.

In this regard, many living beyond the Dome came to believe Sedon – albeit as Satan, hellfire's capitalized Devil – shunned water. In their faiths he did so because he feared liquid extinguishment, hence both regular baptism and Holy Water. Suchlike twaddle was of course understandable. In the absence of visible gods to physically hold their hands, Outer Earthlings hatched oceans of exceptionally nonsensical notions.

Inner Earthlings sometimes did too. One of the most enduring was that Piscines, who generally worshipped the Byronic Zodiacal known as Pyçonja Volant, hatched out of eggs laid by their mothers in Akadan, the Head's interior ocean. The truth of that was Piscines hatched out of eggs laid by their mothers in any of the Head's four oceans.

Then again, in a manner of speaking anyhow, each and every animal, including humans, did as well. And they did it anywhere they could. It was called gestation.

========

Quid Tethys also didn't win the Five Blades Championship of Weir purely by luck. Devic half-mom Fata Fortuna was another god-devil visibly in attendance.

========

Azky 21, 5456 YD – The Weirdom of Kanin City

With skin nearly as black as midnight on a cloud-covered, moonless night, Zalman Somata was the unassailable Master of Marutia in 5456 YD. In deference to the over 5,000 years of originally extraterrestrial Utopians who'd preceded him as Masters of the Weirdom of Kanin City, he continued to proclaim himself Kanin's Master of Weir.

Amongst themselves, his adoring, non-devic public referred to him as Zal. His popularity only partially explained why his position remained so incontrovertible. While they may not adore him, nor even like him, Master Devas from any of the three tribes knew better than to mess with him. You messed with Zalman Somata; you chanced messing with his patrons. You did that, you're a devil, and you might be up top with Grandfather Sedon, shining down on Marutia before you could say sorry.

Quidnunc stood proudly as the Master came to pin the Five Blades' medal on his chest. Zal had a big grin on his face. So did Zal's patrons: the same three firstborn Lazaremists who'd watched his every bout. So too did Zal's very pregnant wife, whose first name was Melina but whose maiden name just happened to be Tethys. And, because Sed was hardly the only one back in relative action on the 21st of Azky, 5456 YD, so did the Somatas' court chronicler.

That would be none other than Quidnunc's conceptive father, Jordan *'Quill'* Tethys.

========

From the looks of her, Zal's Mel may be something of a regenerative mutant. But she couldn't possibly be a pureblood Utopian. For one thing, she was no inbred imbecile like the majority of Cabalarkon's purebloods. For another, her gracefully aging parents lived with her in Kanin City at the Masters Palace.

While they could trace their ancestry back much more than a thousand years, to the borderline-legendary pair of George Masterson and Ute also born Tethys, they weren't purebloods either. Indeed, Mel's Daddy Tethys was more white-skinned than black-skinned whereas Mommy Tethys was the reverse, exactly the opposite to the usual state of affairs in most Weirdoms, Kanin's included.

Finally, she wouldn't have been allowed to marry Zalman if she was a pureblood for the lone qualifying reason that devil-gods – third generational Master Devas – could not possess purebloods. You didn't need to be a tale-telling court chronicler like Quill Tethys, an Illuminary of Weir like both Zal and Mel, or even a deliberately kept barely educated, howsoever-superior swordsman like Quidnunc Tethys, to know that was the secret behind the roughly 600-year success story of the Mastery of Marutia.

Its Masters, to a one, were deviants. The fact of the matter was one of the three immortal devils advancing towards Quidnunc behind the current Master was Zal's half-father. Like so many of their fellow Lazaremists Abe Chaos was a complete anarchist. Unlike most of them, though, he never possessed anyone. Consequently Zal's half-father had to be Order.

He and his immediate siblings were often misidentified with the Outer Earth's Hindu Trimurti: the post-Vedic, Indian Lords delineated Brahma the Creator, Vishnu the Preserver and Shiva the Destroyer. Be that as it may, Order was the only one of the three Unities who, on a daily basis, made a point of looking as if he was from the Indian subcontinent. As therefore per usual brown-skinned, with shockingly electric, sparking hair, antique Illuminaries named him Lord Yajur.

They called him thus after the vajra thunderbolts he generated, Vishnu-like, from his Tvasitar Talisman, his Lightning Blade, when it was unsheathed (which it wasn't), and he'd mentally triggered it (which he hadn't). It, in its sheath, was strapped to Yajur's back. Although his faux-feathery drawing tool, Rumour of Lazareme's Tvasitar Talisman (which Tethys sometimes referred to, faux-facetiously, as his power pen), was many times mightier than most swords, Yajur's Lightning Blade was, approximately, inconceivably mightier than Quill's quill.

So too was Unholy Abaddon's Chaos Blade. It was sheathed as well; in what most people erroneously thought was his power focus, his Shiva-like trident. Although devils could vanish their power foci as easily as they could transmute them, he held his, with his left hand, in full view of everybody attending the medals ceremony.

Other than his left-handedness and refusal to possess anyone, Abe Chaos was normally consistent solely in terms of inconsistency. He'd go to sleep as a whatever. He'd stick with howsoever or whomsoever he awakened as until he changed his mind, which he sometimes did on an hourly basis, if not less.

This hour dressed in a cobalt-coloured robe, he affected the glamour of a clean-shaven, humanoid demon, albeit one without a serpentine tail or leathern wings. Sporting splotchy, blood red skin, he had jet black hair flowing down his back to his waist and eight unlit, glisteningly silvery, trident-like prong spikes haloing his face and head.

By contrast, their triplet sister, the Unity of Harmony as well as Panharmonium, had much in common with their father. Somehow or other, whoever was looking at that Great God perceived him as his or her ideal of godhood; hence why even devils often referred to Lackland Lazareme as Thrygragos Everyman. While in her case every man and every woman, of any sentient species, saw her exactly as she wanted them to see her, they invariably considered her incomparably gorgeous.

Her universally admired attractiveness combined with an overstated capacity for compassion – overstated due to her seldom seen and therefore thought-fabulous, as well as ill-natured, Nemesis persona – helped to make the Unity the most popular devil-goddess of the time, if not necessarily all-time. Trimurti-worshippers said much the same about Brahma the Creator of course. However, as good-looking as he reputedly was good-hearted, Lord Brahma was, resolutely, never Lady Brahma.

Today Datong Harmonia, the name uninspired Illuminaries of yore accorded her, appeared entirely human. Which is to say as entirely human as a manifestation of unrivalled womanhood with three eyes could appear. With long, richly dark and crinkly hair as well as butterscotch skin, she affected a similar look to Lord Yajur's in that she might pass for a native of the Outer Earth's Indian subcontinent.

Rather, put in terms appreciable by most of the non-devils there, she could pass as a native of the Inner Earth's occipital region of Ophir-Moorset. In addition to open-toed sandals, scales-of-justice earrings, bracelets, anklets and a bellybutton bauble shaped like an almond, she even wore a midriff-baring sari with a green top and yellow wrap.

About her neck was her Tvasitar Talisman, presumably the same golden torc that inspired the Outer Earth's possibly not altogether baseless myth of a malignant Necklace of Harmony. Because everything about her glimmered with the telltale glows of Brainrock-Gypsium, there were those who claimed her clothing and, indeed, her entire body-beautiful depended from her power focus. That may be as well, because very few devils were more of a consistently possessive Spirit Being than her.

Perhaps she did it so much in order to make up for her conscientiously inconsistent brood brother's refusal to possess anyone. Then again, unlike every other known Master Deva, most likely including her immediate siblings, perhaps a debrained demon didn't individually solidify her. Perhaps her body was all-devic, like that of a Great God or Sedon Himself.

She, the as yet only potentially half-birthmother of his twins-to-be, the very same devil who'd been occupying Missus Master when they were conceived, tapped Zal on the shoulder. She wanted to pin the medallion of swordsmanship excellence on Quidnunc Tethys herself. With a smile that was as bright as the sun and far brighter than the moon, men refused her only at risk to their sanity. Zalman Somata was exceptionally sane, if more than just seemingly shocked by her request.

Harmony couldn't help herself laughing as she did so. "And to think, young Jordy, your forefathers avoided the military like death itself."

========

That Harmony didn't just pin the Weirdom's medallion of swordsmanship excellence on Jordan 'Quidnunc' Tethys's chest-covering; that she actually poked it into said mightily masculine chest; that too could be disputed. What could not be disputed was that, milliseconds thereafter, the masterful, much honoured and well-laid, young swordsman clutched his chest more so than his medal, collapsed in a heap, jerked a few times, and promptly expired.

Not so certain was which one of the Terrible Twins, Janna or Sraddha, chose that precise moment to begin a-birthing.

========

Simultaneously, if nowhere near so heart-attack-abruptly, Melina born Tethys screamed then went down herself, albeit in the throes of parturition. Wasting nary a second's concern on freshly falling Quidnunc, Harmony flew quite literally inside of Zal's Mel. Her immediate siblings, Chaos and Order, spared just as much of nothing on the stricken swordsman. Instead, they exchanged hate-laden glares at each other. The singular slurp of a collective sucking-in-of-breath suddenly superseded the inane nattering of the awards ceremony onlookers.

What had, effectively, been the Age of Panharmonium for so many centuries began as an almost afterthought-addendum to what was still nominally the Age of Lazareme. Third generational devils were genetically as incapable of disobeying their fathers as their fathers were of disobeying the Moloch Sedon. However, the three Unities' father, besides spending most of his time asleep on the Isle of the Undying One, was a notoriously laissez-faire libertine.

Fortunately for mortals, Thrygragos Everyman was the live-and-let-live kind of Great God. The two male Unities had, unfortunately, earned their reputations as very much the unkind, live-and-let-die sort. Presumably painful, premature circumstances having forced Harmony to occupy Mistress Melina and thereby help her out in the birth-giving department, the assembled gawkers responded with a terrified hush less of alarm for the well-being of the Mastery's High Illuminary, let alone the fate of today's just-dropped-dead hero of the Championship, as for their own hide.

Given the two male Unities' allegedly opposite attributes, everyone understood Unholy Abaddon reviled Lord Yajur beyond any extremes of conventional irrationality. The feeling was mutual. Even the cousinly hatreds wrought by interdenominational schisms, such as those tearing apart so many of the previously superbly organized, patriarchal religions of the day, and not just those practised principally on the Outer Earth, paled by comparison.

With or without the Moloch Sedon's tacit approval, if Harmony much more so than their father hadn't been around to balance off her brood brothers, her Age – and by extension Lazareme's with it – never would have flourished as fruitfully as it had to date. In truth, her two immediate brothers were so surpassingly powerful many feared not even Sedon had the clout required to cathonitize them should their rage reach the point where they went at each other unrestrained.

That happened, the Hidden Headworld itself might be terminally endangered. That apprehended, the mere fact they were seen together in Kanin City, let alone seen smiling amidst the same company, was an occurrence noteworthy for its close-to-unprecedented matchlessness. It must have struck the crowd gathered as a pure wonderment they could look at each other without drawing weapons and spilling blood.

Yet, significantly, not to mention retrospectively suspiciously, as if the day's startling events had been prearranged, ever so callously, to the detriment of Quidnunc much more so than anyone else, heads didn't instantly fly off shoulders. Not only that, Harmony being otherwise occupied, they did it again. Then they smiled at each other.

As if in unspoken, telepathic concord, Chaos went to assist Quill Tethys and his lower-born, variously named Lazaremist of a sister, Dame Chance – Quill's, as well as Quid's, devic half-mother – with their poison-pricked son, who had sadly ceased convulsing. Hesitating no longer, Order did a ditto with Zal and Mel, their immediate sister still inside the latter, adding her shrieks to the Master's beloved.

The collective whoosh of relief must have seemed, if not necessarily sounded, cyclonic.

========

Quidnunc Tethys died on the 22ⁿᵈ of Azky, Year of the Dome 5456.

========

"It's about time you came to, Quill," said the Jordan sitting beside the bed in Kanin City's ancient, yet kept sparkling clean, hospital.

"A Quit-Quill," marvelled the Jordan lying in bed. A young, extremely fit-looking fellow, he had a scar – which he never had before – in the lower part of his forehead, about where his eyebrows would have met if they'd kept growing. No one would have noticed that he'd just had a heart attack. Then again, he hadn't, had he. Quidnunc had, hadn't he.

"Congratulations," he said to the other Jordan, the one in the chair. "Um, … grandson, wasn't it?"

"Grandson it was, granddad, though my notes indicate we aren't that rare." Bodily nearing sixty, but looking older, the speaker was so flushed, podgy and thoroughly out of shape a casual observer might have wondered why he wasn't in the bed instead of the very much former, oft-times-champion swordsman.

"Notes? Oh, right. I've all your memories."

"Only those of your pre-me incarnations. I can recall most of mine, and that includes pre- and post-you. Still a bit fuzzy, I see."

"I usually am. Quidnunc isn't as strong as you were, though. I seem to remember you fought me tooth and mental nail after you died."

"I fell off a horse. I was only fading away when you revivified me. Assuming for the sake of argument you didn't have the heart attack you looked like you had, that was awfully fast acting venom Harmony jabbed into you. It wouldn't surprise me to find out an Athenan War Witch or a Hecate Hellion concocted it.

"Hell's Teeth, maybe Mel did it herself. She's a highly skilled witch and, believe me, until today she hasn't had any kids, let alone a daughter she can trade to the life-loving Anthean Sisterhood for any of their tiptop, though usually non-lethal, training. Of course that doesn't mean she hasn't been trained by any other craft, even one of the killer Sisterhoods."

"Got your facts wrong there, descendent. Neither Zal nor Mel jabbed anything into Quidnunc pre-me. Murder isn't like us. It isn't even like Tethyses who don't become me. Were you that desperate to become a Quit-Quill? Is Harmony that confident her Grandfather Sedon won't cathonitize her?"

"You're not a lesser being so devils don't count killing you as murder."

"Wrong again. It wasn't me she killed. Quidnunc was just an ordinary Joe, even if he was a Jordy, Jordy. Or should I call you Jordy?"

"Tell you what, since we're both Jordan Q Tethyses, maybe we better stick with the q-names."

"That'd make me Quill and you Quit-Quill. Funnily enough, Quidnunc's mother always said your middle name should have been *'Quitter'* not *'Quill'*. Where is it by the way?"

"Call me Squab."

"That isn't a q-name."

"It's got a *'q'* in it so that's good enough."

"Why Squab?"

"Hey, if it walks like a duck and talks like a duck then it's a duck. Me, I'm short and fat so I'm a squab."

"Quibble, that was it, your original q-name – Jordan *'Quibble'* Tethys. Got an answer?"

"As to whether you had a natural heart attack or an induced one? I'm sure Harmony would insist the excitement just got the better of ex-him, now-you. Tragic, really, especially for one so young. Plus, she'd also insist you were only dying, not dead, when Quill took you over, so technically she didn't kill anyone. Patience has never been one of his – your – stacks of knacks so, if someone has to be punished, maybe it's you?"

"Not much of a flagellant either, am I."

"No. Besides, I left my scourge at home. I brought your cap, though."

Sitting up and stretching out, the Quill once Quidnunc reached out to take it with his right hand. It had six fingers. "Oh, there it is."

"Guess that's the answer you're looking for then."

With his five-fingered left hand, ex-Quidnunc pulled out the extra finger of his right hand – thereby rendering himself no longer a polydactyl poltroon, as he'd have had it should he be tale-telling and fay-saying simultaneously, which he usually did. It instantly transformed into his faux-feathery Brainrock quill, what along with the scar tissue in his forehead automatically transferred to him from one lifetime to the next.

As if a family heirloom being rightfully passed on, which in a way it was, the latest Legendarian accepted his predecessor's peaked tweed cap. "I was afraid you were trying to pull a fast one, Squab," he said, about to stick Rumour's power focus into a well worn hole in the cap beside the real feathers of a variety of plucked bird-ies, including that of a Garuda, who were, technically, avian-human birdmen. "You recall the story about the Steg who killed a bunch of Quill Tethyses trying to make it her own?"

"Can't say I do but, speaking of stories, you want these? I'm afraid I've already forgotten how to read them." He was referring to the dozens of tee-tee tails attached to his shaved-bald pate by their own ichors.

"Might as well, though I've still got a full head of hair."

"Splotch them in then."

"I will."

So long as you had the requisite willpower – they being primarily composed of Brainrock-Gypsium – you too could secrete stuff between-space within devic power foci. Most witches, in most sisterhoods, could do a ditto with their bottomless bags, called kibises, or even via their similarly ensorcelled stepping-stones.

Touching tip to tail, Quid-Quill proceeded to vanish the tee-tee tails one by one into the Weird. It doing so instantly reminded Quit-Quill-Squab of a hungry kid slurping noodles down his throat. He couldn't help but be figuratively bowled over at the ease with which a physical youngster, one barely into his twenties, was picking up on the Legendarian's bags of bric-a-brac bents and idiosyncrasies.

It'd certainly take some getting used to not being able to do anything like that anymore. He just hoped he could still remember how to actually draw something with an ordinary quill and non-Brainrock ink.

"Death came calling," said Quit-Quill, as if by way of conversation.

"And I arrived," said Quill, thinking an explanation was belatedly forthcoming.

"I didn't mean Quidnunc. I meant Death came calling for Mistress Mel's twins."

"Twins, eh? Wasn't that a bit premature? Sure, I'll grant you stillborn births and infant mortality are shamefully commonplace these days, but her twins have to be deviants. They'll be tougher stuff. We wouldn't be here if deviants were pansies."

"Actually Mel was spot on her time. But I take your point and I guess, now that I think about it, so did he. Deviants do tend to live much longer than your everyday average sentient being. Plus, both Zal and Mel still have some U-type blood inside them. Even nowadays, Utopian hybrids consistently outlive humans two or three years to one."

"From the looks of her Mel has a lot more than just some Utopian inside her."

"I'm with you on that, and I'm not the only one. Her twins were proper Utopians. The boy's more black than white and the girl's the other way around, though I grant you it's still too early to tell how starkly black and how starkly white they'll turn out to be. Allow me to rephrase: Death came calling for them later. In other words, he served notice they belong to his tribe and not to the Lazaremists. He wasn't alone either. The other two Nergalids were with him."

"Ah, that Death. I didn't think the Thanatoids would be awake so soon. And I'd forgotten how close it's coming to the half-millennial date of transference. What happened?"

"What do you think happened? The Unities drove them away. Even if the Thanatoids of Lathakra were awake and fighting alongside them, thirty Mithradites couldn't handle the three of them acting together. Besides, it's 44-years till the Lazaremists have to turn over Kanin City's half-Mastery to Mithradites."

"That's 14 more than I'll be 30-Years."

"I'd give up the sword if you hope to make it that far."

"I'll do that, too. Fact is I think I'll have a beer. In a manner of speaking, it'll be Quidnunc's first."

"Splotch out two, will you, Quill? It's too early to start working on becoming a Squib."

========

Thus began a beautiful, if perverse, as in reverse, relationship.
****

www.ingramcontent.com/pod-product-compliance
Lightning Source LLC
Chambersburg PA
CBHW051831170626
46807CB00003B/1123